DEATH
AND
DONUTS

DEATH
AND
DONUTS

SHADOW TRADE:
THE RUIN OF RELICS

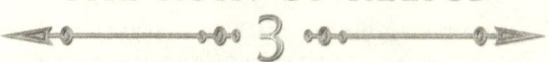 3

MELISSA NICOLE

Shattered Glass
PUBLISHING

To all the questionable choices we make in life...
like donuts.

CHAPTER ONE

My phone buzzed on the counter beside me. I set aside my rolling pin and wiped my hands to check it.

Cross: Do you have time to meet at the property today before your shift?

"Which of your boy toys is it this time?" Vena called from the living room.

"It's Cross. He wants to know if we can come over."

I heard her pop up from the couch.

"Does that mean he closed the deal on the club?" she asked.

"Probably," I said.

In the weeks since Anchor's rescue, Vena had been using Cross' business as a distraction from her non-existent sex life. After Cross got his identification papers, Vena had been right there to help him start a bank account and set his password–as if he had no clue what she was up to. When it had come time to tour the club formerly known as Juicy as a potential property to purchase, she'd volunteered us to go with him. If her involvement kept her happy and distracted from Anchor's absence, I was fine with it.

She appeared in the kitchen and leaned her athletic body against the counter. Her long brown hair swayed to the side as she moved. I always envied her trim body but loved baking and desserts more than running. Thelma and Louise, as Vena likes to call my girls, weren't made for cardio.

"What do you mean, probably?" She gazed at me with her dark blue eyes. "Don't you talk to him every night?"

"We do talk. I just don't pump him for information like you do."

She snorted. "How else will we know if he's spending our money wisely unless we pump him?" She wriggled her eyebrows at the innuendo.

"You're lucky he puts up with you."

Her expression fell a little. "Like Anchor, right?" she mumbled.

"Hey, you know he's crazy about you. Didn't he just take you out for a treasure hunt last week?"

"Last week. How many times has he come over *this* week?"

"They're still cleaning up the vampire issue," I said. "You know he's out searching with everyone else now."

"Exactly. He's constantly gone. Why is Doc on our couch at night instead of Anchor?"

"Probably because you kept trying to molest Anchor in his sleep."

"I was cuddling!"

"He was fighting to keep your hands out of his pants."

"That was for research. I needed to check what his unimpressively loose jeans were hiding." Her gaze grew wistful. "His merry mama maker is impressive as hell, Everly. I grazed it. It was hot and hard and–"

"This is why he's keeping his distance, Vena. You've only got one thing on your mind lately."

"Can you blame me? I thought we'd have sex once we found him, Ev. Happy reunion sex. Instead, I've been denied his fun funnel. So, yeah, I'm a little upset about it. But if I can just get my mouth on his peace pipe, I know we'll both feel a lot better."

My phone buzzed again.

Tank: Can you please remind her that I can hear everything?
Me: That's why she's saying it.

Vena smirked at me. "Tank whining again?"

I nodded, and she turned to shout to our guard sitting outside, "Tell Anchor to stop running then!"

"Let's go visit Cross," I said, taking pity on Tank. "Text him that we're on our way."

After putting away the sheet of pastry I'd been laminating, we piled into my aging compact car and drove to the old vampire lair.

"It's a little ironic that the werewolves wrecked Juicy to chase out the vampires, but now a vampire is moving back in, don't you think?" Vena commented. "Has Cross told you what he wants to do with the building?"

"No. Hopefully, not a seedy club, though. I never want to step into one of those again." I shivered at the memory of being trapped in a storage closet filled with syringes and tubes. If Cross hadn't shown up when he had, Vena and I might have died.

Vena saw my shiver. "Hey, with Cross' fat bank account and his love of posh things, there's no way his business would be seedy. He'll gut the place, and it'll be like Juicy never existed."

As I pulled into the parking lot of the three-story brick building, I saw Vena's guess hadn't been wrong. The For Sale sign was now marked as Sold, and remnants of the old club filled the two dumpsters near the door.

Cross walked out of the building with a red leather chair. His pec-hugging t-shirt stretched over his broad shoulders. The ripped jeans he wore molded to his backside as he leaned forward and chucked the chair into the dumpster as if it weighed nothing.

His typically styled-to-perfection auburn brown hair was mussed–but in a really sexy way that stripped away some of his flawlessness and made him more…touchable.

Vena let out a low whistle. "He dirties up nicely."

I shushed her as I parked.

Cross looked over at us and waited as we got out of the car and walked the short distance to him.

He leaned in to kiss my forehead. "I'd hug you, but apparently, I'm nicely dirty."

"It was a compliment," Vena said. "Looks like you've done a lot of work already. When did you sign the papers?"

"Yesterday. I'm tearing out everything. In another day or two, the only thing that will look the same is the brick, but even that will get cleaned."

We followed him inside, and I had trouble remembering what the club had been like before. The stage, lounge, and stripper poles were already gone, leaving an open, dust-filled space with holes in the ceiling and drywall—a space that had potential—but no one else was in it.

"Cross, who is helping you?" I asked.

"No one. I'm doing it myself."

"I bet taking a crowbar to things makes for excellent therapy," Vena said.

"Who said I used a crowbar?" Cross shrugged lightly. "Werewolves aren't the only ones with enhanced strength."

He caught me looking at his chest, and the way he smiled made my heart skip a beat.

"Let me show you around." He led the way around the first floor, pointing out the windows that were still blocked and the storage walls that still needed to be removed before guiding us over to a staircase in the back.

"What's up there?" Vena asked. "We only saw the first floor last time we were here."

I wondered the same. The place had more space than I'd imagined.

"Right now, there's nothing up there," he said. "I've removed everything, but it looked like it had served as a sex den."

"Sex den? I thought vampires were more into blood than sex," I said.

Cross' gaze met and held mine for several beats. A blush crept up my neck, which brought back his slow smile, making my heart skip another beat. Was he purposely teasing me?

"Do I need a hazmat suit to go up?" Vena asked even as she started up the stairs. "I don't want an STI. I need to be ready to go when Anchor decides to un-cock block me."

Distracted by her ridiculousness, he looked away from me.

"I wouldn't bring Everly to a place that could harm her health."

"But you would with me? Wait, is that why I'm going up before Ev?"

"No, it's because your curiosity overrides your common sense," I said.

"You're not wrong," she said as I followed her up.

At the top of the stairs, I had a clear view of Cross' efforts on the second floor. Ducts and wires were fully visible in the exposed ceiling and walls. Yet, despite the demolition he'd done, the space was free of debris and flooded with natural light from the large, arched windows.

The vampires who'd previously used the space must have blocked off the sunlight when they were here, or they would have died. Only Cross had a ruby ring that allowed him to walk in the sun.

He led us to a folding table in the middle of the room. Blueprints lay open on the surface.

Vena leaned over the top one, studying it. Shaking my head at her, I glanced at Cross.

"If you leave stuff out, she'll look at it. She's nosey like that."

"The blueprints are why I invited you. I would like your feedback on the design plans."

I joined Vena and stared at the first floor's proposed layout.

A beautiful glass arctic entry would keep the interior toasty during the colder winter months and cool during the summer. Once inside, guests would see a long display counter for coffee and bakery orders. Behind that, in the center of the large, open space, double doors would give access to a large industrial kitchen. Bookshelves lined the perimeter of the building's first floor, and over two dozen tables took up the horseshoe-shaped space between shelves and the kitchen. The plans even had bathrooms at the back of the building.

The well-thought-out layout made a cute and functional bakery and bookstore.

"This is amazing, Cross," I said.

When I looked up, I caught him studying my face.

"Amazing enough to return to, day after day?" he asked.

"I'm not sure I follow."

"Please. Sit. Allow me to explain."

He pulled out one of the three chairs for me. Vena quickly took a seat, and while her expression bordered on giddy, I felt a bit more wary as I sat.

"I would like to establish a partnership," Cross said.

Vena snorted softly under her breath.

"With both of you," he clarified.

"Whoa. You're hot and rich, Cross, which is tempting, but I'm holding out for Anchor. He's close to breaking. Maybe after I've sailed on his banana boat for a while, I'll check out your schooner."

I slowly turned my head to stare at her. No words were needed. She immediately did the zipping her mouth motion and folded her hands in her lap.

"Please excuse Vena," I said, focusing on Cross. "I think Miles tested malfunctioning charms on her as a baby."

Cross' lips twitched like he wanted to smile.

"I've grown used to Vena's erratic behavior and know when to ignore her. Don't distress yourself on her behalf.

"The partnership I'm suggesting is strictly business. You wish to run your own bakery but lack the capital. I have the capital and the space but lack the skill."

"You want to run a bakery?" I asked, doubt lacing my words.

"Yes and no. I'm thinking of something more than a simple bakery. The key to making this place stand out will be to keep everything—the books and the food—centered around *all* the races.

"The fae adore their exotic food restaurants, which are in high demand but too overpriced for most people. The werewolves like whatever humans like. And while we both know what vampires like, they're not welcome anywhere. The rest of the creatures prefer to stay in the Shadow Trade markets where they put themselves on exhibit so humans see them as beneficial and less threatening."

I studied Cross' face. He didn't look angry. He didn't look anything other than his usual self. Yet his words conveyed a resentment his tone didn't.

"Are you all right?" I asked. "Have the vampires tried anything lately? Or are Shepard's people being—"

Without seeing Cross move, he was suddenly leaning close enough to cup my cheek. "That you worry about me endears you more to me."

"Hey, I'm worried too," Vena said. "Like, how much is all this renovation going to cost you? And who exactly are your target clientele when just about everyone in the city doesn't like you? I don't want you throwing your hard-earned cash at a sinking ship."

I loved my friend, but sometimes, she was a little too money-focused. I quietly kicked her under the table.

Cross leaned back in his chair and regarded Vena.

"The investment will quickly repay itself if we create something that can't be found elsewhere—a place where an everyday human will be welcome yet not solely catered to. A place for otherworlders to come and relax and enjoy tasty sweets."

"We?" I echoed, having not missed that little inclusion.

"Yes. We. I want the three of us to own the business equally and split the profits. I would run everything behind the scenes—all the administrative bookwork, accounts, and connections.

"Everly, you would have full control over the kitchen to create food options for all races. Vena, you can curate the book selection to your heart's content as long as it's not only about treasure hunting. We want everyone to feel welcome."

I hurt for Cross, understanding that he wanted to give what he hadn't received. None of the other races wanted anything to do with him, not even his own race. He was truly alone, except for Vena and me, which was why I wanted to agree to his proposal. I wanted to show him and the world that I believed in him as much as he believed in me.

However, Vena and I still had a year left of college and our jobs at Blur. While I'd always known I'd leave Blur at some point after college, I wasn't yet ready—not when there were so many financial uncertainties.

Cross noticed my hesitation.

"Don't feel burdened to accept."

"I don't feel burdened," I said. "I love the concept and would be excited to be a part of it, but I need to be honest with you as well. Vena and I have a year left of college, and I'm not ready to quit Blur. It's paid for my school so far."

"I would never ask you to give up anything," he said, taking my hand and running his thumb over my skin soothingly. "I want this to enhance your life, not take away from it.

"What if, for now, you're the creative mastermind in the bakery and I hire someone to assist you? We'll need employees anyway. You can use them in whatever capacity you need, which will free up your time to focus on school and Blur."

I considered the idea, not hating it. I didn't see a downside if I could still work at Blur. Having a fully equipped kitchen to test recipes in was a dream come true.

"Then, I accept," I said.

"Do I get that sweet deal too?" Vena asked.

"Of course," Cross said. "I want this place to be a haven for both of you. Which is why..." He released my hand and pulled away the top blueprint of the first floor to reveal the second floor's generous, private living space.

Vena gasped, pulling the paper toward her. "This will be gorgeous."

The master suite took up almost a third of the floor space with another third dedicated to the open-concept kitchen and living area.

"Three bedrooms?" Vena looked up at Cross.

"So you have a place to stay whenever you need it, especially if you find yourself in danger again. You will both have access to the second floor. It will be yours to use however you want."

"But only for safety?" Vena questioned.

"However you want," Cross reiterated. "If that means spending the night when you've worked a long shift, it can be used for that. Or if you want to live with me rent-free to help save for school, you can move in as soon as it's finished. No strings attached."

His generosity was sweet, but we couldn't—

"Sold!" Vena shouted.

"No, it's not," I said. "I appreciate you thinking about us, Cross. I really do. But moving on top of all the other changes we're making is more risk than Vena and I are willing to take on right now."

Vena gave me a "what are you talking about" look while Cross nodded.

"I understand. For now, accepting a partnership is enough. I only need you to think about what you'd like in your kitchen. I'd like you to come up with a few recipes to start, too. The rest can wait until you're ready."

Vena sighed. "Fine. But since this place is inclusive, we could use it to gather information, especially if we incorporate some blood-infused treats to tempt a few vampires to talk."

I was about to shoot down that idea, but Cross agreed. "It wasn't the goal when I came up with this business plan, but I had thought of the same thing."

"Wait. Are we actually on the same page?" Vena asked him.

"I think, for once, we are."

"I'm not," I said. "Do you know what happens to me when Vena gathers information?" I started counting past events on my fingers. "I fall into a cave. I get locked in a supply closet. I get–"

Vena covered my mouth and shot me a guilty look.

"It will be a simple gathering of information to aid Shepard in flushing out unsavory vampires in D.C.," Cross said. "Won't it, Vena?"

"Of course. I promise I will only bribe people with tasty treats."

"No bribing," I said, ducking away from her hand. "You will leave all information gathering to Cross, or those spare bedrooms can go to a troll."

"They'd never smell the same after."

"Exactly."

She sighed. "Fine. Cross can have all the fun."

"You'll get to have fun too," I said. "Just think about all the books you get to buy."

As she began listing the collections she wanted to bring in, I considered what foods we would need to offer and had an uh-oh thought.

"Cross, if I make blood-infused treats, won't that create a donor link between the vampire and the human?"

CHAPTER TWO

VENA STOPPED RAMBLING ABOUT HER BOOKS AND LOOKED AT Cross expectantly.

"I vow no bonds will be created because of the treats we offer," Cross said. "Links only occur when consuming blood from its source. Infused confectionery won't cause any problems.

"Which is one reason I wish to offer them. Juicy was a known feeding den—a place to secure a meal without having a bonded feeder. While I believe my kind went about it in the wrong way, the concept itself wasn't wrong. I would like to show my kind they were close to finding a way to coexist with other species."

I nodded, agreeing with him until I had another thought. Each time I'd cut myself before while baking had been accidental. The idea of purposely cutting myself made me cringe.

"I like the concept of having something appealing for every race, but I'm not okay with bleeding into all my creations on purpose."

"Not your blood, Everly," Cross said. "I would prefer any treats that taste like you would be mine alone. I will find a volunteer donor to provide what you'll need."

"Okay. Just one more question."

"You can ask as many as you'd like."

Vena snorted, and we both ignored her.

"How much blood should I use in these recipes?"

"Drops at most. Nothing that will change how you bake."

Relieved, I focused on Cross' explanation of the bakery's kitchen, the necessary appliances, how large the freezer and refrigeration spaces would be, the dimensions of the storage room… and other things I'd never considered before.

"I'll need to do some research and figure out what baked goods I want to offer."

"You have time. If you approve of the second and third floors, I'll focus the work there first."

"There's a third floor?" Vena asked, flipping the papers back.

We both looked at the rooftop design, which included a heated space with windows leading to a deck area with cushioned seating and a gas fireplace.

"This place is epic," Vena said.

After seeing that, I knew she would push hard to move in, so I flipped back to the second floor for another look. Living above the bakery would save a lot of time, but it would also come with a list of problems Vena wasn't considering.

"Do you want to add anything to the private kitchen?" Cross asked, watching me.

"No, it looks good," I said.

"Bigger than ours at home," Vena said, nudging me as if I didn't have eyes or a brain to notice the same thing.

"It is," I said. "The whole place looks amazing, Cross. And I can't think of anything to change or add."

I stood. "We really should get back so we can get ready for work. Should Vena send you a list of book suggestions, or do you want her to bargain hunt for you? I recommend giving her a budget and telling her to fill the shelves within that budget—and make it low. She loves a challenge."

"Hey," Vena said with a scowl. She didn't contradict me,

though. Baking was in my blood, and bargaining was in hers. However, she loved money and would have bargained for the books and kept the change if there was any wiggle room.

Cross stood as well. "Send me a list, and I will set the budget and transfer the funds."

She perked up a little and followed us down the stairs without complaint.

"What kind of access and safety are you going to have once this is all finished?" she asked. "I mean, you're doing something that some people aren't going to like. At least, not at first."

"Very true. I'll ensure it's the safest place for you both. Day or night."

Vena nodded with a side glance at me. Was she already up to something that would lead us into trouble? I really hoped not.

After saying goodbye, we drove back to the house. Neither of us talked much; we were both lost in our thoughts.

As soon as we were home, I went to my notebook and started flipping through the recipes I'd perfected. Most of them catered to humans, which meant werewolves would like them. But what about the other races?

I texted Miles.

Me: Are you up for some idle research?
Miles: Sure. What do you need?
Me: A list of favorite foods by creature.
Miles: On it. When do you need it by?
Me: Tomorrow?
Miles: You need to work on your definition of idle.
Me: I ate that dick cake. You owe me.
Miles: Tomorrow it is.

I shuddered as I remembered the rolled sheep's scrotum he'd hidden in an innocent piece of cake. Why would anyone use scrotum leather to make a map? And why had he picked cake to hide it in? For safe keeping, obviously, but I still found it unreasonable.

Both he and Vena owed me for the trauma I endured at the beginning of this summer. Although, to be fair, Miles' suffering had been worse with his kidnapping and vampire thrall. But still…dick cake!

"Why do you look like you're going to heave your cookies all over the floor?" Vena asked.

"I asked Miles to send me a list of favorite foods by creature. For a fast turnaround time, I reminded him I ate dick cake."

She snorted a laugh. "I remember the horror on your face when you told me."

When I narrowed my eyes at her, her laughter died. "It was a horrible thing my brother did." She added, "He's a monster."

I rolled my eyes at her.

"I'm surprised he agreed to a fast turnaround, though," Vena said. "He talked Mom and Dad into taking him with them to Dwarf Mountain for their negotiations. I bet he has a list of questions he plans on asking."

"Is that today? Should I tell him I can wait? It's not like I need this information right now."

She shrugged. "It will keep him busy if he finds downtime. And he'll be in the perfect place to learn more about dwarven foods."

Nodding, I refocused on my notebook. I had a decent start, but I'd need to refine my list once I got the information from Miles.

"We're going to be late if you fall down that rabbit hole," Vena said, moving toward her room.

Knowing she was right, I closed my notebook and went to my room.

"Once Cross opens his place," Vena said from her room, "we'll be able to quit Blur. We might even be able to quit sooner. It'll take a lot of work to get the books shelved and the kitchen stocked and ready."

"Did you not listen to a thing I said to Cross?" I asked.

She hopped from her room, one leg in her slim black pants and the other out. "I heard you make excuses, Ev. But this is our chance to do something we've planned on doing since we decided on our college degrees. Cross just handed us our dream. Even Shepard would understand why you would choose Cross' plan over Blur."

She pulled up her pants and slung an arm around my shoulders. "Life is about taking chances when they become available. This is our chance."

"I never said I wasn't in, Vena. I'm just not going to quit Blur. Not yet. Do you really want to leave Anchor defenseless against all those women and men who look like they want to eat him?"

"You found my weak spot," she said with a frown that turned into a smirk. "Which is why I'm going to claim him as my own. Is there a wolf mating ritual that I need to do? Like, do I howl while riding him outside under a full moon? I heard something about biting. Do I bite him, or does he bite me? And I'm very curious about this knotting thing they discussed on *The Other House*."

"Get dressed and drop your hormones down ten notches before Tank needs therapy. All I'm saying about the business plan is that we should take it one day at a time and see what happens. We don't even know if the other races will allow a vampire to run a business. Until we know, we have to work to pay bills."

It was safer to stay the course we'd already set. At least for now. However, Vena hated delayed gratification. It was torture for her. So, I wasn't surprised that she wanted to jump into Cross' business idea with both feet.

I steered her to her bedroom with a stern order to finish getting ready and went to do the same. After changing into a white button-down shirt, black tie, and black pencil skirt, I pulled my blonde hair into a ponytail and twisted it around my finger to adjust its natural wavy curl.

On our way to Blur, Vena attempted to launch into another long list of pros for Cross' bakery and bookshop endeavor, but I sidetracked her.

"How do your parents feel about the upcoming meeting? Do they think the dwarves will buy the map they found during their last dig?"

"Mom seemed pretty optimistic. Having dinner with the royal family is a good sign."

"You don't think so?"

She shrugged and looked out her window.

"What's going on in that deviant brain of yours?" I asked.

"Nothing."

"You sit on a throne of lies. The Vena that I know should have been begging to go along too. I mean, gloomy spaces filled with treasure are your thing."

"They are. But Mom and Dad could only bring one guest, and I think Miles earned it, don't you? Besides, I promised Shepard I wouldn't leave him high and dry, especially when Sierra isn't quite back up to working yet."

"Wow. That's very responsible of you, Vena."

She flashed me a smug smile.

"An extremely responsible person would also know it's smarter not to quit a stable job with a steady income to chase a job with no guarantees," I added.

Her humor turned into suspicion. "Are you talking about hunting or the amazing opportunity Cross laid at our feet earlier?"

"Cross' offer, actually."

"Why are you so against it?"

"I'm not. I'm being careful. At Blur, I know what I can financially count on from my wages and tips. With the new place, who knows how long it'll be before it takes off? We're splitting profits,

Vena. How much capital do you think Cross needs to invest? How long before that investment is paid back and we're profiting? It could be months, if not more than a year. That's why there are business loans, right?"

"I don't like 'smart and safe' Everly. I like 'wild and fun and goes to clubs' Everly," Vena muttered.

"Pfft. You love all my sides, just like I love all of yours. And speaking of sides, have you noticed that Anchor and Cross are never in our house at the same time? They always wait for the other to leave. You know that means it won't be possible for us to live with Cross to save money on rent so you can quit Blur sooner."

She shot me a dark look. "Did you pick up a mind-reading charm?"

"You know there's no such thing. I just know how your crazy works."

I pulled into the employee parking lot and waved at Boulder, who was watching the back door.

"Besides, I know you've grown to love slinging cocktails here. Not as much as hunting, obviously, but I think you'd miss working here if you walked away."

She rolled her eyes before getting out. It was her way of admitting I was right without saying it. Grinning, I followed her to the door.

"Are you thinking of quitting, Vena?" Boulder asked with a hint of worry in his gaze.

"Yeah, Vena. Are you?" I asked mischievously.

"You're both terrible people," she said, grabbing the door and opening it.

I grinned at Boulder to let him know everything was fine and hurried after her.

"Can you imagine what your days would look like? No Anchor eye candy for eight hours, followed by snuggle time."

She scoffed. "What snuggle time? He hasn't spent the night in over a week."

"Oh-oh, someone needs a hug," I said with a grin.

"No, someone needs an orgasm from something that doesn't vibrate."

I cringed and held up my hands.

"You win. I'm shutting up."

"Too late for that," Vena said with a glance over my shoulder.

I followed her gaze and saw Anchor standing there. His expression was hard to read. Even though he was a six foot three tower of chiseled muscle and a bouncer for the VIP section, when Vena was around, he looked nervous or unsure, which was Vena's catnip. Right now, he looked a little tense and ready to pounce.

"Are you thinking of quitting, Vena?" he asked.

"Yes, I am. Why is that such a problem? I'm a grown woman and able to make my own decisions."

"Is it because of me?"

She opened her mouth, and I clapped my hand over it.

"Sexually frustrated Vena has nothing nice to say right now. But I promise it's not because of you. In fact, she was just asking how she could—"

Her hand was then on my mouth, and I was gently pinned face-first into the locker a second later. I licked her palm.

"Gross, Everly," she said, pulling it away.

"I thought you liked fun, spontaneous me," I said, turning to smirk at her.

"I changed my mind. Go back to the boring version of you, who doesn't say things she shouldn't, and let me be the crazy one with no filter."

I saluted her and grabbed my apron. "I'll see you in the meeting room."

Gunther glanced at me as I walked through the kitchen, and I gave a friendly wave to let him know everything was fine.

"Sounds like Vena's upset," Buzz said when I walked out into the main bar.

"Since I left her or before?" I asked.

"Before. I don't hear any talking now."

"She's not upset, and she won't quit Blur. She just likes talking about the possibilities, and sometimes I like poking the bear."

"You knew Anchor would hear," Buzz said with understanding.

"I did," I acknowledged. "And just in case he's too distracted to hear this, let him know she's close to dragging him down the aisle. I think the treasure hunt he arranged for her last week tipped the scales. She knows it's hard to find someone willing to support another person's dreams, especially hers."

With a wave, I left him and walked upstairs.

Vena and I liked coming in a little earlier than the other wait-staff. It gave us time to ask questions about the ongoing vampire problem without being overheard.

Since she was occupied, I went to Shepard's office alone. His door was open, and he was waiting for me in front of his desk. His white button-down shirt pulled tight against his muscles, and his dark blonde hair grazed against the stiff collar.

His light grey gaze held mine as he watched me enter.

"I'll give you the update I know you want if you answer a question for me," he said. "What are your dreams, Everly? Is opening a bakery everything you want, or is there more?"

CHAPTER THREE

I PAUSED, WONDERING WHY SHEPARD WAS ASKING ME ABOUT MY dreams, then continued forward.

"Opening a bakery with Vena has been a goal of mine for years, but owning a place and doing the work I love isn't everything. I'd like to think life is a balance."

He nodded. "I'd like to think so as well."

I grinned at him. He was the worst offender of having a work-life balance.

"You're not doing a good job of it."

He frowned, drawing my eyes to his kissable lips.

"What do you mean?"

"Unless I'm missing something, your life currently consists of running Blur and hunting vampires."

"I've been busier than usual lately," he admitted. "Which is why I'm asking in a roundabout way if you've thought about everything that goes into opening a business. It's hard work and a lot of hours."

"Is this about Cross' new place?" I asked, finally understanding where this conversation was coming from.

He scrubbed a hand along his jaw. "I just want you to think about every aspect of owning a business before you leap into something."

"I *am* thinking about things, and I'm not leaping. And the business wouldn't just be run by me. I'd have two co-owners helping it thrive. I'll only be responsible for the recipes for now."

I folded my arms, unintentionally drawing his gaze to my generous chest. While I hadn't done it on purpose, I couldn't deny the way my pulse skipped a beat at his attention.

"If you're worried that I'll quit Blur, stop. I'm not going anywhere. I like my job here. The hours and pay are dependable."

His shoulders relaxed slightly. "Good. I want you to achieve your dreams, Everly. Truly. Actually, I was hoping you could come up with recipes for Blur. You could make a name for yourself here before you expand."

"Griz is the head chef. He comes up with the recipes." I'd met enough chefs to know they were territorial about their kitchens.

"Yes, but his focus is on savory appetizers and tapas. We've never had sweet options, and I'd like that to change. But let's table this discussion for now. I need to give out assignments before we open." He moved toward me as if to escort me out of the office.

"Not so fast. You never gave me the update you promised. People are still going missing. I heard another person disappeared recently."

He placed a soothing hand on my arm. I soaked up its warmth but refused to step aside until I got an update. Both Shepard and Cross didn't like to include me on the vampire hunt, and honestly, I was okay with not knowing everything. But that didn't mean I wanted to live in D.C., oblivious to what the vampires were up to after that huge fight between vampires and werewolves a few weeks ago.

While the vampires had taken a considerable hit to their numbers that day, including Adriel, the vampire Miles and Sierra had known as Master, many vampires were still alive, including Adriel's lover, Vivian, who he'd affectionately called Pet. I didn't even want to think about what level of grudge Vivian and his followers were carrying now.

"We're still working on it," Shepard said when he realized I wouldn't be placated. "I'm looking into the most recent disappearance to see if it's vampire-related. Cross is…working on his end as well to assist us."

I smiled at him. "By the way, thank you for helping Cross get set up with papers and facilitating his purchase of the former Juicy building."

"I did it because he's the lesser of two evils and because you asked."

My smile widened, and Shepard leaned in.

"I'd do just about anything for you, Everly."

Someone cleared his throat behind us. "Everyone is assembled," Anchor said. "I'll just…" I listened to his footsteps retreat as Shepard closed the distance between us and kissed my forehead.

"I meant what I said, Everly. Anything." He took my arm and escorted me out of his office to release me just outside the employee room so I could enter first.

Vena gestured for me to join her as the rest of the assembled staff continued to converse.

"Why is your hair a mess?" I asked, reaching up to smooth her silky dark hair back into place. "And your tie is crooked…" Realization hit me, and I lowered my voice to scold her. "Seriously, Vena, here?"

Her cat-like grin made me cringe.

"People can hear and smell things here."

She snorted, which earned her a raised brow from Shepard as he went over assignments for the night.

"Never mind that," she whispered. "Did you see the group text from Miles?"

Shepard had a rule about not using phones on the floor, but

since I wasn't technically on the floor yet, I pulled mine out of my pocket and peeked while everyone started filing out of the room.

Miles' text to Vena and me had photos of a library filled with books and a long hallway with intricately carved stone walls. I wasn't an otherworlder nerd like Vena and Miles, but even I was impressed with the history shown in those two pictures.

Vena had already sent a response asking if any of the books were for sale. Each one looked old and was labeled in dwarvish. She was obviously already searching for literature for Cross' new business. *Our* business, technically.

"Problem?" Shepard asked, startling me.

I glanced up and saw that Vena had slipped out of the room without me. Probably to chase down Anchor again.

"Not a problem," I said, facing Shepard. "Just got a little lost in thought."

Worry seeped into Shepard's gaze as it lifted from my phone to me.

"Is Miles in trouble? That hall looks familiar."

I chuckled and shook my head. "I understand why trouble was your first thought, considering everything that's happened recently. But I promise you don't need to add us to your list again. Miles is with his parents, meeting with dwarven royalty tonight to discuss a map they found a few weeks back. Actually, it's the one they mentioned the night you met them. Miles is just geeking out over all the cool stuff he's seeing for the first time."

"Why's Vena interested in books?"

"Vena is part of Cross' business plan, too. He wants a business that will appeal to all species. Sweets from me and books curated by Vena."

Shepard's gaze locked with mine.

"You know he wants more than that, though, right?"

"Are you still worried he's going to turn us into blood slaves? I thought he'd proven himself to you already. He's been working with you for weeks, Shepard. Establishing contacts. Helping find nests."

"Did he tell you he's not revealing his contacts? That he's setting up his own network and protecting some of his kind?"

"No, but we talked about creating treats with human blood in them, and I'm smart enough to figure out that means he wants to be on good terms with some of his kind." I reached out and clasped Shepard's forearm. "I believe vampires are like humans. They aren't all good or bad but a mix of both and capable of either. It's their choice who they want to be. Just like it's your choice to kill the innocent ones with the bad ones."

"Innocent?" Shepard scoffed.

"Do you think every vampire asked to be turned? I don't. But now I know how you'd see me or Vena if either of us is attacked and survives the process."

I gave him a sad pat and turned away. He caught my arm and spun me around. Hands framing my face, he looked down at me with an intensity that stole my breath.

"For you, I'd break every rule we have, Everly. Don't you know that yet?"

His mouth crashed down onto mine. It'd been weeks since he kissed me, and I hadn't realized how much I'd craved it. The first touch of his tongue almost brought me to my knees, and his hungry urgency had me responding in kind.

My hands gripped his wrists, holding on for dear life as I lost all sense of time and space. There was only Shepard and his warm, insistent lips.

When he finally pulled back, I was panting and dazed. Gold flashed in his eyes as he stared down at me.

"You need to have the strength for both of us right now and walk away," he said, his voice gravelly.

I nodded and robotically turned and left the room. It wasn't until I reached the stairs that I realized what he'd meant, and my eyes rounded. Had he really been that close to—

Glancing over my shoulder, I saw him standing in the hallway, watching me. The way he gripped the doorframe confirmed what I'd suspected.

Shepard wanted me like a vampire wanted blood.

Facing forward, I hurried downstairs, glad that he'd given the VIP section to Adrian.

Vena's sharp gaze missed nothing. She took her phone out and frantically typed as I went to my assigned section beside hers.

Vena: You look recently bent over. Not fair! Tell me how you did it. You flashed the girls, didn't you?! Curse fate for giving me running-sized boobs!
Me: I was not bent over. Focus. Doors are opening.
Vena: Fingered? I'd take that too.

I dropped my phone, accidentally kicking it under a table. Vena cackled like a madwoman.

"I'll get that for you, Ev," Anchor said from behind me.

He stooped and picked up my phone for me. His sheepish expression when he handed it back had me patting his arm in shared misery.

"She sure knows how to test a person, doesn't she?" I said.

He nodded.

"Hang in there. You'll have her in a tiara and holding a bouquet in no time."

He flashed me a grin as my phone vibrated.

Vena: Stop flirting with my man. You have two of your own.

Anchor chuckled and returned to his place at the bottom of the VIP stairs.

Music came on, and I pocketed my phone as I greeted the first group of patrons to claim a table in my section.

"Everly," a familiar dwarf said as he and his companions settled at one of my tables. "You look lovely, as always."

Brott and his friends were regulars and fond of Blur's lamb skewers with an herb dipping sauce and one of the signature drinks, Effervescence.

"Thank you," I said. "Can I get you your regular order, or would you like to try something new? Chef Griz has a delicious goat cheese and roasted tomato tartlet tonight."

"Let's do our regular order and add the tartlet as well," he said.

I placed the order on my handheld POS and excused myself to welcome the new customers who sat down in my section. By the time I was about to check on the order for the dwarves, they were flagging me down.

"Is everything okay?" I asked. "I was just going to get your order."

Brott shook his head. "I'm sorry, *Vezrama*. We have to go." He handed me a fistful of cash that was much more than the cost of the drinks and food. "Keep the food for yourself."

"I can box it up," I said. "It will only take a moment."

"A moment is more than we have, I'm afraid. We must go, *Vezrama*."

They moved quicker than I'd ever seen them move and were gone before I could say goodbye. I headed to the main bar at the back of the room to cancel the order, but it was already ready.

Shepard was behind the bar with Buzz, so I called him over.

"Brott and his friends had to leave. They paid me for their food and drinks. Can I give them to another table so they aren't wasted?"

He nodded, but his brow furrowed. "They weren't the only dwarves to leave suddenly."

Vena popped up next to me with a wad of cash. "My table just left after ordering, but they paid cash before anything was ready. Can I keep it?"

"Were they dwarves?" I asked.

She nodded.

"So, can I keep it?" Vena asked.

"You can keep the difference in the cost of their order," I said. "And Shepard agreed to give the food and drinks to another table in your section."

"Excellent," she said. "My tables will love me and tip me well."

As she grabbed her order and practically skipped away, I looked at Shepard.

"Do you think there is an issue with the dwarves?" I asked.

"Doubtful. They are one of the most stable creatures."

He was frowning, though, so I quickly pulled out my phone and sent Miles a private text.

Me: Just checking in to see if everything is okay. The dwarves left Blur suddenly.

"I'm sure everything is fine, Everly," Shepard said.

"You're probably right, but let me know if you hear why they left."

I hurried away with the order to split it between two other tables and spent the rest of the night running back and forth between customers and the bar. No other dwarves came in, and it wasn't just me who noticed.

The wolves at Blur seemed to grow anxious with every passing hour.

Something was wrong.

It wasn't until the end of our shift that Vena nearly bowled me over with her phone in her hand.

"Did you see the group text from Miles?"

"No." I pulled out my phone from my apron pocket.

**Miles: The Dwarf Mountain is on lockdown because the
prince died. Be in touch soon.**

"Uh, that can't be good," I said, looking up at her.

"No kidding. I tried calling Mom and Dad, but they didn't
pick up."

"And they likely won't," Shepard said, approaching us. "We'll
talk before you leave."

Counting out tips was painful because Vena had the patience
of a gnat. Her fidgeting kept drawing attention.

"Anchor," I said under my breath, hoping he'd hear me from
the kitchen. "You're going to need to distract Vena."

"Vena, can you check the ladies' room for me?" Anchor called,
coming out of the kitchen. "Someone mentioned a clog."

Buzz made a choked noise as Vena bounded off her stool.

"He could have gone with anything, and he went with a
clogged toilet?" Buzz said softly.

Shepard elbowed him and said goodnight to Pam and Adrian.
As soon as it was just the wolves and me at the bar, Shepard set
aside the glass he'd been drying.

"The prince was young. Late twenties, maybe. It's unlikely he
died from natural causes."

"What does that have to do with Vena's parents not answering
their phones?" I asked.

"As guests, Vena's family won't have anything to worry about.
However, due to the investigation that likely needs to take place
regarding the prince's death, the dwarves are probably limiting
outside communication for now."

"If the mountain is under lockdown, why did all the dwarves
leave like they did?" I asked.

"To return home and mourn their prince. We probably won't
see our regulars again for a while."

"And Vena's family?"

"They will remain the king's guests until he has answers. But don't worry. He'll want answers quickly. Worst-case scenario, they'll be home by Monday. Until then, it's business as usual for the rest of the world."

That was easy for him to say. He didn't live with Vena. The likelihood of her being okay with her family locked away in a mountain was low.

CHAPTER FOUR

A LIGHT BREEZE ON MY ARM WOKE ME. I OPENED MY EYES, expecting to be greeted by familiar amber ones. However, I was alone. Again.

My gaze drifted to my window screen–the one Cross had thoughtfully repaired after he'd busted through it to escape whichever of Shepard's men had been guarding us at the time. Was it the steadfast presence of werewolves keeping him away? I doubted it. He and the werewolves had made peace since then. Sort of. It was more of a grudging tolerance.

While Cross' morning absences were slightly disappointing, I was also relieved. Especially after the kiss Shepard had laid on me last night. Why was I even thinking of another guy after kissing Shepard like that? Didn't I have more important things to do?

Shaking my head at myself, I got out of bed. I had potential recipes I wanted Cross to try today.

After dressing, I started a simple bismark dough and another batch of the bonbons he'd liked. While he'd said sweet treats, I wasn't sure what a vampire's sweet threshold was. Did they vary like humans, or was there a general preference?

I sent Cross a text to find out.

Me: Do vampire sweet preferences vary like humans?
Cross: I would imagine so. It's not something I've ever
discussed with others. Why do you ask?
Me: I'm making something for you to try if you have
time this afternoon.
Cross: For you? Always.
Me: Okay. Don't come running when you sense me
bleeding.
Cross: Ensure the injury is small, and I will try to
restrain myself.

Vena shuffled out of her bedroom just after I finished frying the bismarks.

"Something smells good, wifey," she said, leaning on the counter. "What are you feeding me?"

"Nothing," I said with a fake glare. "You kept me up last night."

Anchor had taken his role as a distraction very seriously. Poor guy.

She made a face. "You can't be mad. The rule is no sex while you're home, and we didn't have sex."

"But you would have if he'd given in to your begging."

"You heard that?"

"I think China heard you. 'Please, Anchor. You won't need to do any work. Just lie back and let me pounce. I promise it'll be good for both of us.'"

"Eh. The walls are thinner than I thought. Did you hear his answer?"

"No. Thankfully."

"Cause there wasn't one. His mouth was full."

I threw a hot bismark at her. She caught it with a grin and bit into it.

"Aw! There's no filling."

"I think that's what you said last night." I smirked. "It needs to cool before I fill it."

She snorted. "I wish Anchor would have given me his filling. But seriously, what's supposed to go in this? It's too plain."

"The filling's in the fridge, but it's not for you. I bled in it."

"Not playing favorites, I see. I guess it's fair that Cross gets a taste since Shepard had one last night."

After her impromptu make-out session with Anchor in the women's bathroom, she hadn't brought up my post-meeting "just been kissed" look. I should have known she wouldn't let it drop.

"I don't know what you're talking about."

She laughed. "Either you talk, or I do. Your choice."

Since I knew what she'd start sharing, I gave in quickly.

"Shepard kissed me. That's it. There was no begging involved, unlike some people."

"That's just because you don't know how to have your cake and eat it too. I'm telling you, be the human cream in their other-world cookie sandwich. No one will walk away mad."

"You're banished from the kitchen until it's time to check in with Cross. And if you mention anything inappropriate about my sex life while there, I won't cook for you for a month."

She immediately sobered. "Yes, ma'am."

When it came to food and sex, Vena had a one-track mind. Unfortunately, the latter got her in trouble more often than not.

"Go," I said. "Once these are done, we can leave."

"Save me another bismark, but give it a little sugar coating this time, mama."

"I will chuck it at you again if you don't go away."

She laughed. "You know I'm great at catching. I'm kind of great at everything. Just ask Anchor."

I lobbed another bismark at her, which she caught and sank her teeth into. With a grin, she skittered off to her room.

Anchor was going to be so screwed when he took her off my hands. The thought made me a little sad. Vena and I had been living together for three years now. Before that, we'd slept over at each other's homes non-stop. Vena had never *not* been at my side. What would I do when that day came?

It was later than I had expected by the time I finished the bismarks and bonbons.

"It's nearly lunchtime," Vena said as I placed the plastic containers in the backseat. "I bet we can get Cross to spring for a meal."

"You always want him to buy you food."

"It's not like he needs the food money. And those bismarks were a letdown."

"My bismarks are not a letdown. They're big and have an amazing texture."

"That's what she said," she said with a snicker. "I just meant they were plain, and now I need something to appease my palate. Anchor already said no when I texted him an offer."

"Get in the car," I told her. "You are so over the top right now. Anchor needs to run away to the L.A. pack so they can safely lock him up again."

"Ew. Don't mention that pack to me."

"Then give your hormones a rest. Remember, wolves mate for life. Life, Vena. You've got about sixty more years to live."

"I think eighty."

"Fine. Eighty years. That's a long life to be with one man. And if you decide you don't want Anchor, you might be able to skip away, but he can't."

She frowned at me. "All I said was I was hungry."

"And are you still?" I asked smugly. "Why don't you focus on that book list you need to give Cross to get your spending money instead of Anchor's pocket prize?"

She was quiet on the way to Cross' place as she played on her phone.

I felt a smidge of guilt for reminding her about a werewolf's life commitment. I knew she had deep feelings for Anchor and wouldn't ever want to hurt him, but a relationship with him was just like starting a business with Cross—those kinds of things needed to be thought through carefully.

She looked up from her phone as I parked, scanning the building's façade for changes. However, the outside of Cross' building looked the same as it had, except for the dumpsters. Those were gone.

Cross met us at the door and took the boxes from my hands. He inhaled, and his eyes flashed to black for a second before he smiled at me.

"I've been looking forward to this sample," he said.

"Good. Let me know if I put enough blood in them."

His gaze swept over me as he shifted the boxes to one arm and settled on my bandaged finger. "I love that you made me something, but I never want you to hurt yourself." He took my hand and kissed the bandage. "Come in and let me put the boxes down so I can heal your wound."

Wound? It was a pinprick, but I didn't argue. I liked his concern.

As we walked inside the gutted building, Vena frowned. "I thought you'd be further along."

"You just saw it yesterday," I said to her. "How much did you think he'd get done?"

"It's not like Cross has to sleep. I thought this place would at least have some kitchen structuring done."

"I don't have the permits yet," Cross said.

"Who needs permits when you're a vampire?" she asked. "Just do your mind-whammy thing and get what you need."

"The wolves barely tolerate my presence as it is. Do you believe they would look the other way if I started influencing others? If this is to be a legitimate business, I need to show the wolves that I will follow human rules. I cannot expect their trust and continued acceptance of my presence if I treat humans as nothing more than a food source as so many of my kind already do."

"Fair point," Vena said.

We followed Cross upstairs where he placed the boxes on the table then took my hand and peeled the small Band-Aid off.

Since I was squeamish about my blood, I hadn't done anything crazy. Just a poke to my finger with a sanitized safety pin, which I'd admittedly been a baby about. Thankfully, no one had witnessed it.

Cross' lips closed around the tip of my finger, and my insides went hot at the touch of his tongue against my skin. While he licked, he held my gaze. I saw his hunger, but not for my blood. For me.

Breathing normal became a struggle.

"Since I'm in charge of the book section, I should probably put together a book of Everly for you," Vena said, reminding us both that she was present.

"Oh?" Cross said after licking my finger a final time. "And what would that book contain?"

"All her likes and dislikes. Obviously, hugs and finger-licking would be on the like side. But her history too. Childhood memories. Adventures she had. Her limited experiences."

I shot Vena a warning look.

"I'm not sure where your mind is going," she said primly, "but I'm talking about amusement parks. You never want to go."

I rolled my eyes at her and faced Cross.

"She's being extra today. Ignore her, and taste the food. I'm trying to figure out how much blood is needed to appeal to a vampire."

"Very little is needed," he said, picking up a bismark.

Vena covered her mouth and said something that sounded suspiciously like, "That's *not* what she said."

Ignoring her, I watched Cross closely as he bit into both selections.

"Your flavor is more noticeable in the bonbons. And I believe the bonbons would last longer than these, too. It will take time to build up our clientele, especially vampires."

"True," I said. "I didn't think of that."

"Now, why is the ever-present Vena causing our Everly trouble today? Problems with a certain wolf?" Cross asked, leaning back to study my best friend, who was looking decidedly annoyed.

"Yes, I'm having boy problems. You've lived a long time. You've had to see a wolf give up his goods a time or two. What will it take for me to get—"

"And it's time to go," I said.

She made a whiny face and pleaded with her hands. "Come on. Cross knows things. Hey, what about the dwarves? Know anything about the ruling family? We could talk about that."

Just as I was sitting, she added, "Cross can text me his advice later."

She winked dramatically at Cross and wiggled her eyebrows at me.

"I will tell you what I know of the dwarves if you vow to deliver the book of Everly to me by the end of next week. I need to understand her deep bond with you."

I snorted a laugh at her disgruntled expression even as she nodded.

"The current dwarven king, Curran, has ruled peacefully for fifty years," Cross said. "His wife's tomb lies within the mountain. She died giving birth to Princess Indri, now the heir to her father's throne since Prince Hakon has died."

"You know?" I asked. The news of the prince's death wasn't something found on any news stations. I knew because I'd checked.

"I do," he said. "Although I would prefer to spend my night watching you sleep, I need to prove my usefulness and gather information for Shepard. Is the prince's death why you're curious about the dwarves?"

"Yes and no," Vena said. "My parents and Miles are in lockdown in Dwarf Mountain because of his death. According to Shepard, the prince was young and in good health. That he died means foul play, and the king's probably investigating what happened."

Cross nodded. "King Curran will be adamant about finding the cause of Prince Hakon's death. Dwarves are known for their stubbornness, and Curran will not open the mountain until the case is solved."

"How long are we talking? A day or two?" Vena asked.

"However long it takes."

Vena frowned and looked at me. I saw the seed of fear in her eyes and leaned over to place a reassuring hand on her arm.

"No matter what happened to the prince, they won't want to stay locked in the mountain indefinitely," I said. "Just keep texting Miles and your parents. They'll answer as soon as they can."

"You're right," she said. "Even if they don't find the cause of death, they'll have to open the mountain to get food and supplies in a few days."

I feared what she would do if the mountain stayed locked for more than a week.

"Any other updates?" I asked Cross to get Vena's mind off the dwarves and onto something else.

He pulled out his phone and tapped it a few times then held it out for me to take. "These are the kitchen appliances recommended to me. If they meet your needs, I can order them."

My eyes widened as I looked at the commercial stainless steel gas range and ovens. "You want to get a Vulcan?" That was one of the best and most expensive brands.

"I take owning a business seriously. There is a reason White's is the oldest and longest-running gentleman's club."

"I almost forgot you started that," Vena said.

She hadn't. She was banking on the same level of success.

"I only ran it for a few years before I left. But I've learned that, if you set yourself up for success initially and don't cut corners, the business can go for centuries."

"As long as it gets me out of the nine-to-five grind, I'm in," Vena said.

Cross opened his mouth to say something but stopped to look at the staircase. "We have a visitor."

"As in Juicy's former patrons who want revenge for taking over their building?" Vena asked, slipping her hand to her shirt where her knife resided. "Or those little girls who sell cookies? I could go for a box or two."

"A wolf with a keen nose and impeccable taste," Cross said.

Shepard appeared a moment later. He looked at our cozy group sitting around the folding table before his gaze swept through the rest of the open space.

"What's up, boss?" Vena asked Shepard. "Come to check out our new digs?"

Shepard's gaze flicked to me briefly. "Cross has plans he wants to show me."

Vena popped out of her chair and gestured to the table. "Have a seat. We were just looking at the kitchen appliances Cross is getting for Everly. He knows a way to a girl's heart."

I narrowed my eyes at Vena, understanding she was stirring trouble in revenge for my stirring yesterday. She smiled back.

Shepard pulled the plans toward him, bumping the box of bismarks. His gaze caught on it, and he pulled the box closer to sniff the donuts.

His eyes flashed to me and then to Cross. "Why is Everly's blood in these?"

"The business is going to cater to all creatures," I said. "The bismarks and bonbons are experimental batches for vampires."

"And you're just going to cut yourself whenever you need to bake something?" His question was more growl than words.

"No. This batch is just for Cross. Eventually, there will be volunteer donors. Right, Cross?"

Cross nodded. "While I prefer Everly's blood, I don't want her to harm herself. There will be compensated volunteer donors."

"And the blood connection?" Shepard asked. "Are you going to protect the donors after?"

His tone carried a harsh, accusing edge. Why couldn't Shepard let go of his anger already?

Cross seemed unbothered by Shepard's attitude as he answered.

"It will be impossible for a bond to be created from what we sell. Once the blood cools to room temperature, it becomes safe. No vampire will be able to track the source."

I saw the doubt and mistrust in Shepard's gaze and felt sorry for Cross.

"I know you don't like vampires," I said to Shepard. "But perhaps, if they have a safe place to get blood ethically, things could change for the better. All creatures deserve a welcoming place."

"This is going to draw too many vampires," Shepard said.

Cross laughed. "In the beginning, it won't draw any. What vampire will want to step foot in here after what happened a few weeks ago? It will take time and a sense of safety for the ones we want to attract to arrive.

"Even then, they will know this isn't a place for a meal but rather just a tasty bite. So we'll hardly be flooded. The ones who do come in are the ones who are looking to elevate their lives. Those are the ones we can get information from—the ones who will help you deal with the vampire infestation."

Shepard looked thoughtful and grudgingly nodded.

"However, to get that information, I need you to help me expedite the building process," Cross continued smoothly. "The sooner we can open our doors, the sooner you can end your hunt and enjoy other pastimes."

I watched them silently stare at each other for a long, drawn-out minute.

"What do you need?" Shepard finally asked.

CHAPTER FIVE

"I NEED THE WORK PERMITS EXPEDITED IF POSSIBLE," CROSS TOLD Shepard. "The contractors are lined up and ready to work."

Shepard looked at the plans again and flipped from the first floor's business layout to the second floor's living space.

"What's this empty room in the middle for?" he asked, tapping a darkened square in the middle of the second floor that was about the size of the master suite's bathroom—which was excessively large.

"The contractors said space was needed to run various things, such as wires and ducts from the kitchen to the roof. That space will be used since I don't need a fourth bedroom."

"Do you even need three of them? Are you making new friends who might need a place to stay, or are you planning on having live-in feeders?" Shepard asked his questions without a hint of judgment in his expression or tone, yet I felt it all.

"Those are rooms for Everly and me," Vena said. "It's a backup place in case we ever run into trouble. Or if 'Brodier, Everly, and Vena's Eating Retreat' takes off and we want to ditch our crappy house to move in permanently."

I shot Vena a warning look as Shepard looked down at his

hands. I knew he was struggling to keep his reaction in check, not to Vena's horrible acronym for the business' name but to the idea of us living here.

In the weeks since our first shared kiss, not much had changed. Cross and Shepard had backed off their kissing-Everly war and treated each other civilly, which I knew wasn't always easy, especially with the ongoing vampire problem. But they were mutually benefiting from helping each other. That didn't mean their feelings for me had changed, though. Both made it clear through small and sometimes not-so-small actions that their interest in me hadn't faded.

And that was why Vena was poking at Shepard. At both of them, really. She knew why I was hesitant to start anything with either of them. I still didn't trust that their interest in me was genuine and not just some way to annoy each other. This was her way of pushing the subject.

"Let's stay on topic," I said. "First, the permits need to be approved. Then, the contractors need to get in here to do their thing.

"As for who will be using those spare bedrooms, it won't be Vena or me in the near future. I'm not ready to make any life-altering choices until after I get my degree. So, Vena, stop trying to stir up trouble, and Shepard, please don't worry about us and stay focused on the vampires."

"No warning for me?" Cross asked, watching me with a hint of amusement in his gaze.

"Don't order the wrong appliances or else?"

He laughed, and the way he tipped his head back was captivating enough that I quickly looked away.

"As you suggested, I'll stick with the bonbons for the vampire clientele. I've asked Miles for help figuring out what 'sweet' foods the other races like to eat. And since our initial core clientele will probably be humans, I'll work on some 'creature' themed treats for them."

"Please tell me that means you're going to make more fairy trash," Vena said, perking up.

"Only if you stop being a pain in my backside."

She saluted me and stood when I did.

"If there's nothing else, we'll get going," I said.

"I should go too," Shepard said. "I'll get you what you need, Cross."

Shepard followed us out and opened my car door for me.

"If you're headed home, would you mind if I follow you?"

"Is there a reason? I mean, not that you're not invited. I just know you have a lot on your plate."

His grey eyes were filled with something I wasn't sure I could or wanted to name. "You asked for an update on the vampire situation last night. I thought we could discuss."

"Sure. As long as you don't mind me baking while we talk. I'd like to make a few more test samples before our shift."

"Without your blood," he said.

"Without," I agreed.

That seemed to ease some of the tension in his shoulders. "I'll be there soon."

Shepard waited in the parking lot until he saw us drive away. When I glanced in the rearview mirror, I saw him walking back inside the building.

"Crap. He just went back in. Do you think he's going to give Cross a hard time?"

Vena grinned. "Probably. You're like catnip. Or whatever a wolf and vampire like. Blood and doggy treats?"

"You weren't helping the situation," I said.

"Your definition of helping would be to ignore it. You know I love you like a sister from another mister, but you all need a push toward each other. I'm that guiding hand."

"I'm not ready to make decisions about what I want romantically. I want things to happen naturally, and you're making it hard on everyone."

"Hard on?" She snorted. "That's what she said."

"Vena," I softly scolded. "I'm serious."

"Fine. But you're missing out on some prime action. And maybe you don't have to decide. Maybe you can have a three—"

"Stop!"

Vena smiled. "I'll leave that idea alone for now. But you can't honestly think you can string along two prime cuts of meat and nothing will happen."

"I'm not stringing anyone along. This isn't the time for… whatever is going on."

"It's never *not* the time."

"Vena," I said with a pleading groan. "Can we not do this right now? I'll make you fairy trash if you don't talk to me about Cross or Shepard for a week."

"Counteroffer. You make fairy trash, and I won't talk about them for twenty-four hours."

"How is that a counteroffer?"

"I'll throw in modest, nun-like behavior with Anchor tonight."

I glanced over at her to see if she was serious or not. "I don't think you can do it."

"Want to bet?"

"No. I want a clause in the offer stating what will happen if you break your promise."

She thought for a moment. "I will clean the bathroom for the rest of the summer."

"Deal." Either way this played out, I came out as a winner. "By the way, you still owe me a week of waking up to confectionary delights and one hot date at Enticed."

"You're right. I do. When do you want to go to Enticed?"

"Next Monday if you can get a reservation that soon. Maybe I can research some fae desserts there."

I parked in front of our house and didn't expect Shepard to arrive before we reached the front door, but he did.

"Done playing with your favorite vampire?" Vena asked.

"I was getting him in touch with someone who can expedite building permits."

"Thank you," I said.

He flashed a small smile at me. "You're welcome."

I headed to the kitchen with Shepard trailing behind.

"Don't forget about the fairy trash," Vena called as she sat in the living room with her phone.

As I washed my hands, I asked, "So, what's the update?"

"We're slowly clearing out nests," he said.

As I turned for the towel, he took the apron from the hook and looped the top strap around my neck, pulling me toward him to tie the strings behind my waist. The warmth of his arms and body enveloped me, and I felt a hint of his stubble as his jaw slid along mine.

"I'm sorry about earlier," he said softly next to my ear. "Vampires bring out the wolf in me. And even though I will admit Cross isn't like the other vampires, it's not easy to ignore instinct. But I'm trying."

"I know. And I'm grateful for it."

He pulled away, ghosting a kiss across my lips before he leaned back against the counter. "You know why I do it."

I mentally shook off the effect Shepard had on me and began pulling out ingredients.

"You said you were clearing out nests. That's progress, right?"

"It would be if every nest wasn't small and only comprised of newly turned vampires." He ran a frustrated hand through his hair until he caught me watching him. "I wish I could tell you this was close to being over. I wish I could–"

He looked down at the floor. I set aside the ingredients I held and moved closer to him.

"Could what, Shepard?" I asked.

"I want to go on a date with you, Everly. You can pick the place. Wherever you want."

I considered him, weighing how to decline without hurting him.

"This isn't about trying to get you to choose between me and Cross," he said. "This is about you deciding if you like me.

"I've been your boss and the alpha wolf keeping peace in D.C., but you've never had the chance to know me as just a man. My hobbies. What music I listen to. Who my parents are. Just the basic things a person would learn about the person they might like.

"If you're truly not interested in any of that, it's okay to keep drawing the line between us. But if you are interested—even if just a little—step over the line, Everly. I promise not to draw you any closer than you're willing to go on your own."

The intensity of his gaze and the memory of our last kiss burned through my previous resistance. It was obvious that he'd been thinking about this for a long time.

"Just a date? And no matter what happens, you know I'm not picking a side?"

He swallowed hard and nodded once.

"Okay," I said.

I didn't even see him move. Suddenly, I was in his arms, and his mouth was on the skin just below my ear.

"Thank you," he breathed.

The feel of his lips as he quickly kissed me there melted my insides.

"Fairy trash," Vena yelled from the living room. "That's what you're supposed to be doing."

I both loved and hated my best friend just then. On a higher level, she was absolutely right. On a hormonal one, I wanted to do to Shepard what she wanted to do to Anchor.

Shepard let out a low laugh and pulled back just a little.

"I apologize for distracting you."

I stared into his eyes, seeing his desire for me, his worry for D.C., and a loneliness he'd been hiding better than Cross.

Framing his face with my hands, I slowly stood on my toes and kissed him, just a whisper of my lips brushing against his.

Shepard didn't pull me any closer or deepen the kiss.

Testing to see if he genuinely meant what he'd said about letting me decide how far to go, I opened my mouth and licked his bottom lip. He growled, and his tongue met mine as his hands moved from my waist to my hips. Shepard's kiss in the safety of my own home robbed me of coherent thoughts. So did the hand that slid to my ass.

My hormones won over reason.

A small sound escaped me, and I grabbed his shoulders to lift myself higher. He growled again, and the next thing I knew, my feet were off the floor. My legs had a mind of their own because they immediately wrapped around his waist.

Squerk-squerk.

The sound registered a second before the spray of water hit my temple.

"Listen, I don't want to be the bad guy here, but there's going to be a whole lot of self-regret all around if you two don't quit it right there," Vena said, squirting us one more time.

Shepard ended the kiss sweetly then set his forehead against mine with his eyes closed.

"Don't move. I need a moment," he said.

Considering the tremors wracking his body, I took the warning seriously and held as still as possible as I panted for air and tried to calm myself.

Slowly, he released his hold on me. The slide down his body definitely didn't help either of us.

I felt him arch into me just a tiny, tiny bit and almost whimpered. I didn't though. He still had his eyes closed, and Vena stood sentry two feet away with the spray bottle ready.

"I'm sorry, Shepard. I shouldn't have–"

His eyes snapped open, and I saw the gold in them.

"Please don't apologize for giving me what I've been craving for weeks. The kiss and the date," he said, clarifying. "I'm free tomorrow. Any time. You can choose, or I can make plans for us, whichever you feel more comfortable with."

"I'll choose," I said. "You have enough on your plate."

"Taking care of you, Everly, wouldn't add to any burdens you might think I have," he said.

He stepped back and looked at Vena. "Thank you. I'll make sure Doc is here for watch duty."

Then he strode out of the kitchen.

"That was so damn hot," she said as soon as the front door closed. "Seriously. I videoed it. Want to see?"

I turned my back on her as she lifted her phone.

"Nope, I don't. I want to bake. Go watch TV or something."

"What? No way. I want to talk about how you want to bang a wolf just as badly as I do. Just wait. These dates are going to pull you even further in."

"Date, not dates. Vena, please. I don't want to talk about this right now."

The kiss with Shepard scrambled my brain and a bit of my heart. It left me feeling like there was a promise somewhere in there but that it also came with messy strings. Wolves didn't do casual. It was the exact thing I had been driving home to Vena for weeks now.

I wasn't ready for a relationship. I still had school, work, a new business venture, and…Cross.

"Seeing that lovefest and hearing Shepard talk about a date gives me the feels," Vena said, oblivious to my torment. "The feels of jealousy. Why do you get two men drooling over you, and I've got a guy who is avoiding me? What does a girl have to do to get a guy to have sex with her? I hung my gloriously used lucky panties in his locker. I wore my padded bra that hikes my boobs up like a pearl necklace. And I drop things all the time and pick them up, showing off this delicious ass. No response. Nothing.

All he does is run away with his snatch sniper, missing an easy mark."

"He was here last night, so he's not avoiding you. He bought you hiking boots when he saw yours falling apart, hand-sharpened your throwing knives, and took you on treasure-hunting dates. He likes you, Vena. You're just a little much."

"I'm perfectly enough much."

"Remember when MC was chasing you and throwing himself at you? How did you react?"

"I ran away," she mumbled.

"Is there a lesson here?"

She nodded. "Yep. No more chasing and no more beating around the bush." She snorted. "That's what he said."

I shook my head at her.

"You're right, Ev. I've been doing this all wrong."

"I'm glad you're being reasonable."

"Instead of beating around the bush, I'm going to be blunt. He needs to beat my bush, or he can say goodbye to my briar box for good."

I stifled a groan.

"Speaking of which, I think I'll take a few minutes before work to spruce up the hedges."

This time, I knew there would be no saving Anchor. He was on his own. I had too much going on with a different wolf. My lips still tingled from Shepard's kiss.

As if Cross could sense it, a text with two different color swatches popped up on my phone.

Cross: Looking at colors for the bakery. One reminds me of your hair and the other of your grey eyes. Which one should be our accent color?
Me: Maybe we should choose a color that will make people hungry instead?

Cross: Both of these colors make me hungry. And it'll feel like you're here even when you're not.

Damn. My heart was being pulled in two separate directions.

I thought of what Shepard had said about knowing him as a man and realized I didn't know Cross like that either. Asking him out would only be fair since I agreed to go on a date with Shepard. However, I suspected spending more time with Cross to start up the business had spurred Shepard into asking for the date. If Shepard found out I wanted to date Cross as well—

Squerk-squerk.

"Gah!" I swatted at Vena, who held the spray bottle with a smirk. "Aren't you mowing your grass?"

"Please, I keep this grass maintained like a golf course. I only needed a minor clipping. What's with the frowny face?"

I shoved my phone at her then grabbed a towel to mop my face.

"Interesting," Vena said when she read the text. "But why is it making you frown?"

"I just agreed to go on a date with Shepard. And Cross is making me feel—"

"You better not say guilty. You don't owe either of them anything."

"No. But I like them both. A lot. More than a lot."

"Excellent. Then keep it equal until you know for sure. If Shepard kisses you, you kiss Cross. If you go on a date with Shepard, you go on a date with Cross. If you eat Shepard's cannoli, you eat Cross' too."

I saw her point, but I didn't think I could treat my relationship with them so transactional like that. "No cannoli references, and I'll think about the rest."

"Nothing to think about. Just do it. Keep the playing field as even and as groomed as my downstairs."

I made a face.

She snickered. "It's glorious. You should see it."

"No, thank you."

CHAPTER SIX

I SMOOTHED MY WAVY HAIR AND STEPPED BACK TO CHECK MYSELF in the mirror. Dressed in a white button-up with a snug black skirt, I looked decent. My face was "pretty enough" even with a slightly small nose. Personally, I thought my eyes were my best asset. Vena claimed it was my chest. Sure, I was curvy, but nothing to bring a guy to his knees.

So why, then, were Cross and Shepard so persistent about me?

Shaking my head, I turned away from the mirror and picked up my phone to reread Cross' text messages. He'd been outright flirting this time. Plainly stating his interest in me. Sure, he'd hinted before and kissed me...and enjoyed sneaking into my bed. But he'd never been so straightforward.

Neither had Shepard. Until now.

Vena's advice to keep it fair had been replaying in my head. Screw being fair to *them*. What about being fair to me? I was slowly slipping into a situation I worried wouldn't end well for anyone. If I were smart, I'd walk away from both of them.

With a sigh, I pocketed my phone and opened my notebook to

work on the list of potential desserts I could make for Shepard to serve at Blur until Vena was ready.

On the way out, I grabbed the fairy trash I'd made. She radiated anticipation with each step.

"Please don't do anything I'm going to regret," I said.

She paused opening her car door and really looked at me.

"You okay? You sound...tired."

I got in behind the wheel and waved to Gunner, who was on guard duty again. Vena waited until we were on our way to turn and look at me.

"What's going on?" she asked.

"You say play the field, but what happens when one of them eventually wants me to choose? Bridges will be burned, and I'll need to say goodbye to a secure job or having my dream handed to me. Or both.

"I don't mind working for my dream, Vena. If I earn it myself, no one else will be able to take it away from me."

"Hey. Whoa. Where's all this negativity coming from?"

"What if I'm just a game to them? As soon as I said yes to a date with Shepard, suddenly Cross started playing his cards too."

Vena fidgeted before bursting out, "I'm sorry. That kiss was too hot not to share."

Stunned, I shot a panicked look at Vena. Cross and Shepard weren't the ones playing a game. My best friend was.

"You didn't," I said in disbelief.

"I just wanted to motivate Cross. He likes you, but he's playing it too safe."

"Dammit, Vena, not everyone needs to be a wrecking ball like you!"

The car went silent. Neither of us said anything until we were almost at Blur.

"I crossed the line, and I'm sorry, Ev. Really."

We'd been friends since forever. Like all friends, we'd had our share of spats, but when push came to shove, Vena always had my back. Always. And whenever I hurt, she hurt with me.

"I love you, Vena, but I need some time to stop being mad about this," I said honestly.

She nodded as I pulled into the employee parking lot.

Boulder was watching the back door and didn't seem to notice that Vena and I were unusually silent when we went inside and stowed our things in our lockers.

"Vena," Anchor said from behind us.

"Just the guy I need to talk to," she said, looking at him in the doorway. "This isn't working, Anchor. I need some time to think about whatever this is that we have."

We both stared at her, waiting for the punchline. Instead, she walked past him without even looking at him.

"Did I do something wrong?" he asked.

"No. We kind of had a disagreement before work. I think this is the fallout. She should be better by the end of her shift."

He nodded but looked worried. I wasn't sure how to reassure him. She was crazy about Anchor. Why would she want to keep her distance now? Was it what I'd said before? About it being forever? I didn't think so since she'd known that all along. Was she playing hard to get to draw him in, then? Or was it the stress of waiting for news from her parents?

I patted his arm and, on my way to find Shepard, dropped the fairy trash off at the bar. He was in his office, looking down at a clipboard on his desk. But as soon as I crossed the threshold, he glanced up at me with a smile that put me at ease.

"Do you have a few minutes?" I asked him.

"Always for you."

I let that comment slide. "You mentioned offering a curated dessert menu, right?"

He nodded. "Do you have ideas?"

"Some. But I'd like to know your thoughts before I get ahead of myself."

He sat back in his chair and gestured for me to sit as well. I took the guest chair across from him.

"I need to know your vision. Are we talking about a full range of options from pastries to cakes to pies to chocolates, or are you looking for a signature dessert? Or a dessert of the day, even?"

He looked thoughtful for a moment, his gaze resting on a printed menu on his desk. He pulled it free and looked at it.

"I didn't have a vision when I asked you about it, but you sparked an idea." He handed me the menu. "What if you come up with a dessert pairing for each item on the menu?"

"Each item on the menu?" While it wasn't a huge menu, that would be a lot of desserts.

"Let's see what you can come up with," he said as if reading my thoughts. "I'll ask Buzz and Detroit to create cocktails that pair with them. The top pairings will go on a featured menu that can be rotated so we don't have to have a lot of desserts on hand."

"I like that idea. It will take me some time to do the pairings, though. Can I take home some of the menu items to taste test while I experiment?"

He nodded. "Just tell Griz or Gator what you want before the end of the night. I'll let them know it's approved."

Standing, I was about to go to the employee room when Shepard stopped me.

"Have you decided where you would like to go on our date?" he asked.

I thought for a moment. Since I was on the fence about the date, I could turn this into a working date. "What if we try a place with a wide selection of desserts? We could see if any would work with our menu."

"Okay. I know a place. What time will you be free?"

"Is noon tomorrow okay?"

"It's a date."

My heart fluttered, and my stomach dipped. If I had to keep

dealing with these men, I'd be admitted to the hospital soon. Why did they both have to be so nice, responsible, and gorgeous? Those qualities were a love trifecta for me.

I fled the office so I could breathe again and found Vena in the employee room. She was focused on her phone, and a second later, I got an incoming message.

"What are you up to?" I asked, allowing my annoyance with her to fizzle out like it always did.

"Just asking for an update from Miles. I included you in the message. We should have heard from him by now, right?"

"Maybe. But if you were there, you'd be too busy looking at everything to pay attention to your phone, right? You saw the pictures. I bet you could explore the inside of the mountain for a year and not see everything. Your family is probably having the time of their lives."

"I just can't imagine the dwarves giving them too much freedom until they figure out what happened to the prince. Have you heard anything on the news?"

"We've been together the entire time. When have I watched the news?"

Before she could respond, Shepard and Anchor walked into the room. Anchor stood on the opposite side of the room from Vena and cast occasional glances her way.

"Assignments for tonight are as follows. Everly is on VIP, Pam upper left, Adrian lower left, Thomas lower right, and Vena upper right."

I winced. She'd be in the same section as Anchor. If she was trying to avoid him…

"Can Pam and I switch, please?" Vena asked. "I'm having some issues and want to be closer to the bathroom."

"Sure," Shepard said slowly. "Do you mind, Pam?"

"Not at all," she said.

Anchor's shoulders dropped as he walked out of the room,

and Vena avoided my gaze as she stood to leave. I watched her walk out and felt a thread of worry.

"Will she be all right for her shift?" Shepard asked quietly.

"She'll be fine."

Leaving the employee room, I prepped my station and got ready for a busy Saturday night. Though we were missing our dwarven regulars on the main floor, the fae maintained their presence in the VIP lounge in spades. Their natural appeal tugged at my senses, wearing me down as the hours ticked away.

"You look tired, my beauty," one of them commented as I delivered another round of drinks.

"Are you hinting I need to touch up my makeup?" I asked with a teasing smile.

He grinned at me. "I'm hinting that you should sit with us for a moment."

"Better not. I'd bore you in seconds."

"Now, that's impossible." His gaze drifted over me in an appreciative way that didn't feel creepy but more adoring. And that was the danger with fae; they could draw you in with a glance.

"Entirely possible. Do you know what I really want to ask you?" I asked, leaning toward him.

Interest and desire lit his gaze. "Ask me anything, pet?"

"What kinds of desserts do fae like to eat? Beignets? Dacquoise? Something simpler like an English biscuit? Or maybe like a Japanese cloud cake?"

He laughed, and the sexy sound wrapped around me.

"You truly are curious, aren't you?"

"I am. I've been wanting to eat at Enticed but keep forgetting to make the reservation. They have fae desserts, right? Not just desserts that cater to humans?"

"You are a delight," the fae said. "Give me your number, and the next evening you're available, I'll take you to Enticed myself."

"Tempting, but did you see that trim brunette with a pout

downstairs? She owes me a dinner there, and if I go with you first, she's not going to pay up, so I'll have to decline."

"For now, then."

I smiled and left their table. When I approached the bar, Detroit looked at me questioningly. I nodded to indicate that everything was fine and waited for him to fill my next order.

By the time the end of the shift finally arrived, my feet hurt, and my pocket held a neatly folded hundred-dollar bill in my collection of twenties.

"I can see why you don't want to count that downstairs," Detroit said, watching me.

I wrinkled my nose and handed him the bartenders' cut. "After Sierra's jealousy over how much more I make in VIP, I'd not rub it in with the others."

He nodded and continued to clean up behind the bar while I wiped tables. Vena wasn't anywhere in the main bar when I finally descended. Anchor was, though. He stood at the bottom of the steps, waiting for me.

"She didn't talk to you?" I asked.

"No talking. No teasing me by dropping things. Not even a glance. What happened, Everly?"

"I think sexual frustration combined with not hearing from her family and a best friend who was maybe a little firmer than she should have been got to her. I'll talk to her, okay? And nicely this time. I promise."

He nodded. "The fairy trash was good, by the way."

Everyone behind the bar seconded his sentiment, and I waved goodbye to them as I headed to the kitchen.

Vena wasn't at the time clock or waiting by the back door. When I couldn't find my keys, I had a teeny bit of concern she'd left without me. But when I opened the door and saw Shepard standing outside, he nodded toward my car.

"She's waiting for you. I am too."

"Why? Did something happen?"

"Yeah. My second-best server wasn't on her game tonight, and I'm worried about her."

"I'll let her know. Thanks for caring, Shepard."

"Always. Pick you up tomorrow at noon?"

"I'll be waiting."

A hint of gold flashed in his eyes. Pretending I saw nothing, I walked to my car and got in next to my silent best friend.

I waited until we pulled out onto the road to apologize.

"I snapped too hard at you, Vena, and I'm sorry. Anchor's worried about you."

She sighed heavily and looked out her window.

"Do you know why I've been pushing you to play with Shepard and Cross more lately?"

"Because you're horny and want me to get some if you can't?" I joked.

She gave a small laugh. It wasn't what I'd hoped for, but it was something.

"Sure, there's always that," she said. "But it's more, too. I'm crazy serious about Anchor, Ev. He's the one, and we're so close to giving in to what we both know is right."

"Uh...wow. Didn't see that coming. Then why did you tell him you needed some time apart?"

"So I don't jump him, obviously."

"Why aren't you jumping him if he's Mr. Right?"

She finally faced me, her expression sad.

"Because I can't leave you alone, Ev. I won't."

Understanding hit me hard. Werewolves mated for life. She knew what saying yes to Anchor would mean. They'd marry and start their family—at light speed if their make-out sessions so far were any indication. One of us would move out to give the other one privacy.

Knowing that I was holding her back from what she really wanted was a punch to the gut.

"Vena, please don't rob me of the chance to be the best maid of honor this world has ever seen just because my love life is moving at a snail's pace. Sisters cheer each other on; they don't hold each other back."

She sighed heavily.

"I'll think about it."

CHAPTER SEVEN

I WAS STILL THINKING ABOUT MY CONVERSATION WITH VENA WHEN I woke up the next morning. Having her admit Anchor was the one made me feel a little untethered. Life was about to change. Not only for her but for me as well.

For so long, I had taken comfort in knowing things would stay the same, at least until we graduated. That wasn't the case any longer.

But this was good. She found her other half, and it wasn't like I was losing her. It meant I had one more person to help keep tabs on her so she'd stay out of trouble.

"You're thinking too hard so early in the morning," a low voice murmured next to me.

I turned in bed and saw two beautiful light brown eyes tinted with amber staring back at me.

"Morning," Cross said. He tucked his arm under my head and pulled me against him to kiss my forehead. "What's got you frowning already?"

"Nothing bad," I said as I snuggled in, needing the comfort. "I'm just bracing myself for some life changes that might come sooner rather than later."

"I well understand life changes."

"I suppose after hundreds of years, you're a pro at it."

"Not necessarily. I wasn't prepared for the change in my life after a certain someone fell into a cave and bled on me. I never expected to fall for her or start a business with her either, especially after she dressed me in a brown corduroy leisure suit. And I especially never thought I would work closely with wolves for a common goal."

I leaned away to look at him. "It was Vena who dressed you in that suit."

He grinned. "My point is: Being open to possibilities makes changes less daunting."

"So much wisdom for eight in the morning. What are you doing here?"

He brushed a lock of hair from the side of my face. "Seeing what your plans are for the day."

"You could have texted me."

"Then I couldn't wake up with you and do this." He leaned in to kiss my lips, but I quickly stuck my hand between us.

"I need to brush my teeth."

I slipped out of his arms and stood with a stretch. His gaze swung to the bit of stomach the move had revealed, and I quickly dropped my arms to my sides.

"Let me get ready. We can talk over coffee." I grabbed clothes and fled to the bathroom.

Cross had asked me what my plans were for the day. This was the perfect time to tell him about my date with Shepard and ask some real questions, especially after Vena sent him the video of me clinging to Shepard.

While I dressed, I played the conversation in my head. Once I was ready, I returned to my room to find Cross leisurely sitting on my bed with his phone in his hand.

The t-shirt and jeans he wore sinfully hugged his body. My

pulse jumped a little as my gaze took him in, and I forgot what I wanted to say.

Vena was right; Cross dirtied up nicely.

Cross glanced up at me with a look of pure lust that matched my own.

His eyes flashed black as he stood.

"You tempt me when you look at me like that, Everly."

"Sorry." My gaze slipped away from him only to return.

"Tell me what you're thinking," he said, stroking his fingers over my cheek.

"I think I'm in over my head. A part of me still wonders if you like me as a person or if you like me because of who I am to you."

"Who are you to me?" he asked.

"Your buffer with the werewolves and maybe even the humans. The person who woke you who also happened to taste good too."

His hands framed my face, and his lips covered mine in a tender, heart-melting kiss that slowly grew more hungry with each stroke of his tongue. I was panting by the time he pulled back to study my dazed expression.

"I am grateful for your understanding of what I am and for your help to make peace with the wolves, but you are not a buffer to me, Everly. You are what I've dreamt of for centuries. You are my hope. I crave your presence in my life more than I crave a taste of your blood. The beat of your heart whispers promises of a happier tomorrow. Do you understand? My affection for you is genuine."

I nodded, still a little dazed from the kiss. That was the only explanation for my gaze dipping back to his mouth.

He chuckled and kissed my forehead again.

"Do you still believe you are in over your head?"

"Absolutely," I breathed. "Vena told me that she sent you a picture of me kissing Shepard yesterday. And now you kiss me today? I'm not sure what I'm supposed to do with that. I don't want to be caught in the middle between you and Shepard. Your position in D.C. is rocky at best. You can't afford to upset—"

He cut me off with a demanding kiss that had me grabbing his shoulders and holding on for dear life. Especially when his mouth left mine, and he started trailing kisses along my jaw and down my neck, which I blatantly arched to give him better access. I obviously had no sense of self-preservation. Yet, I couldn't and didn't want to stop.

"You are temptation itself. The trust you give me is…" His teeth scraped my skin, and I shivered before rubbing my hips against his. He had me against the wall with my legs around his waist before I could register.

"Everly." My name was an animalistic growl before he kissed me with a ferocity that tore me from reality and placed me in a world where only Cross existed. Cross and his mouth and the way he arched into me.

A whimper escaped my throat when I suddenly found myself standing alone against the wall. Disoriented, I looked around the room and saw Cross in front of my window, staring out.

"Your chaperone warned me that we would be interrupted if I continued," he said.

It took a few breaths for lucidity to return enough to understand who he meant.

"Ah." I cleared my throat. "A spoken warning is better than yesterday's spray bottle."

He glanced at me, his eyes completely black with a web of tiny black veins prominent in the pale skin around them.

"A spray bottle?"

I nodded before I realized what I'd given away—that I'd been so lost in Shepard's kiss that I'd needed to be sprayed like a cat in heat.

"Do you understand why I'm in over my head?" I asked softly.

The black faded from his face as he nodded. "I understand why you think you're in over your head, but I want you to know that I'm not asking you to choose between me and Shepard. Whatever time or affection you are willing to give me, I will gladly accept without any resentment. You have my word.

"Now, what are your plans for today?"

I hesitated before saying, "I'm going on a lunch date with Shepard."

"Make sure he takes you somewhere with delicious desserts. Preferably, outrageously expensive, too," he said with a hint of a smile. "He's been neglecting you of late with all the vampire hunting."

"Understandably, though," I said.

Cross nodded. "Perhaps you would have time another day for me then? I would like to take you out as well."

Remembering Vena's comment about keeping it equal, I agreed.

He crossed the room, kissed my forehead, and opened the bedroom door.

"Text me when you're available," he said. "I'll see myself out."

I watched him leave, rubbed my hand over my face, then tried a few calming breaths before going out to check on Vena.

Her door was open, and her room was empty. When I checked the living room, I was expecting to see her all-knowing smirk. Instead, I saw the back of Doc's head.

"Good morning," I said, trying not to feel embarrassment or panic.

He turned slightly and flashed a welcoming smile. "Good morning. Vena asked me to tell you that she left with Anchor but will be back in time for her shift."

"Oh. Okay."

It was good that she was with Anchor. It meant she'd spoken to him about her odd behavior last night.

I checked her location on my phone and saw she was in the

countryside. Likely another hunt. I wasn't sure if I should feel relieved she'd gone out with Anchor or embarrassed since that meant Doc had been the one to warn Cross.

Rather than thinking about either, I headed for the kitchen.

Since I'd forgotten to take home a few of Blur's appetizers the night before, I decided to use my creative energy on a creature-themed menu for the new business. The fairy trash was an easy yes. Opening my notebook, I looked at the possibilities I had jotted down. However, without input from Miles, I was a little unsure of what direction to go.

Thinking of Miles in lockdown sparked an idea for Blur, though. The dwarven regulars might need cheering up after their return from the mountain.

From what I knew, dwarves loved savory dishes like the lamb skewers with the herb dipping sauce. But they also loved Blur's signature drink, Effervescence, which had a fizzy, foamy texture.

If I took those two as inspiration, I might be able to come up with a subtly sweet lemon cheesecake that would satisfy their taste buds.

As I gathered the ingredients, I also took out a few others to make breakfast for Doc. It was a perfect time to get insight into a wolf's preference.

"Doc?" I called.

He stood by the counter in an instant.

"I'm making breakfast. Is french toast and bacon okay?"

"Of course. Thank you. Even regular toast is okay." He eyed the many ingredients on the counter with an arched brow. "How much are you cooking?"

"Test baking," I said as I pulled out a pan. "Are there specific foods wolves really like?"

He folded his arms and leaned his hip against the counter.

"We tend to eat more meat than humans," he said, echoing what Cross had said.

"But is there a food or traditional recipe that wolves would go out of their way to get? Or something that would be a treat that's only made on holidays? I'm trying to come up with recipes that would entice otherworlders into my bakery."

"The only taste we crave is that of our mate," he said. "But we eat everything humans do. What people don't always understand is how good our sense of smell is. We can determine who made the food. Many of us enjoy food more if it's made by a woman. Does that help?"

"A lot, actually. Thank you."

He smiled and was about to say something when his phone rang. He excused himself and moved to the other room to answer. I wasn't trying to listen while I made breakfast and a fresh pot of coffee, but I heard enough to know it was otherworlder business.

When Doc finally returned to the kitchen, I had plated the french toast and bacon and handed it over to him along with a cup of fresh coffee.

"Was that call about the dwarves?" I asked him, my curiosity getting the better of me.

Doc shoved a forkful of toast into his mouth and groaned. "So good." He finished chewing and answered me. "Yes. We're trying to stay in the loop as much as possible, especially since it has to do with the dwarf monarchy."

"Is there a problem?"

"Not necessarily."

I waited for more, and he chuckled. "I think I see why you and Vena get along so well. You're just as curious as she is. It's not my place to share otherworlder information, though. Be sure to ask Shepard about it when he picks you up later. I'm sure he'll tell you everything."

Doc's phone buzzed, and he set his fork aside to begin texting.

It didn't matter, though. He'd already distracted me from otherworlder drama with the mention of my date with Shepard.

A flurry of butterflies zipped around my stomach as I turned around and tried to focus on baking.

It did the trick, and when I removed everything from the oven a few hours later and glanced at the time, I realized Shepard would be there soon.

Rushing out of the kitchen, I flung open my closet and grabbed a pretty top, a cute skirt, and a matching panty and bra set that would make Vena proud. I closed myself in the bathroom to get ready.

By the time I finished a light application of makeup, I heard Shepard talking in a low tone that seemed to cut through walls, doors, and straight into my ovaries.

What was I doing? Get your head straight, I scolded myself.

I smoothed my hands over my sleeveless top and left my room. Vena would have approved of the amount of leg I was showing—and likely some under-cheek if I bent over. Not that I planned to bend over today.

My face flushed at the thought.

The conversation stopped, and Shepard's gaze found me as soon as I entered the room. I watched him inhale deeply and caught the glint of gold in his eyes as he smiled.

"You look amazing, Everly."

"Thank you. Was I interrupting?"

"No. Not at all. Are you ready?"

He held his hand out to me, and like a fairy drawn to silver, I moved forward until his warm fingers were curled around mine.

It wasn't until I was in Shepard's passenger seat that I realized I'd left Doc in our house.

"Oh, Doc?"

"Don't worry about him," Shepard said, leaning across the seat to grab my seatbelt.

The move put his neck close to my mouth. I wasn't a biter, but the thought of just a nibble tempted the hell out of me. So much so that my exhale escaped in a shaky whoosh.

A low rumble filled the interior.

"Everly, is there any chance I could steal a quick kiss?" he asked without moving.

"I don't think that's a good idea," I managed even as my libido screamed, "Please!"

CHAPTER EIGHT

ONE TOUCH OF SHEPARD'S LIPS AND I KNEW I WOULD LOSE MYSELF. Based on the slight tremor that wracked Shepard's body, he looked like he was having the same problem.

"Is it me you don't trust or yourself?" he asked softly.

"It's me," I said. "Definitely me."

"Wrong answer," he said a moment before his mouth was on mine.

The kiss melted my insides, creating a molten need for more. More of his lips on my skin. More of his taste. More touching. More of everything except clothes. We needed less of those.

My fingers had just drifted to his shirt when he caught my hands in his and set his forehead against mine.

"I hate myself for stopping this," he said, his voice pure gravel. "But I think you would hate yourself more if I didn't."

I gulped in one breath after another and managed to nod.

"Thank you."

He groaned and kissed the corner of my mouth lightly. I wanted to turn my head and steal another kiss.

"You're wrong, though," I said

"Wrong? About what?" He pulled back to meet my gaze.

I saw the gold in his eyes and felt even more guilt.

"I already hate myself. I know you can smell Cross on me. Every time I'm with one of you, it's like I lose my sense of direction. I can't tell the difference between up and down. You think this date—spending time together—will help me choose you, but it won't, Shepard."

He opened his mouth to speak, and I pressed my fingertip to his bottom lip. He nipped it. I felt the shock of that simple gesture all the way to my toes.

"You asked me to get to know you," I continued. "But isn't that so I can like you more and eventually say yes to everything you can offer me?

"I'm not stupid, Shepard. I know you're not pushing, but this is still a gentle nudge.

"The more I try to stay away, the more you're both there. And I like it, Shepard. I like it so much, and I hate myself for liking it. I want to say no to both of you, and I can't. You both keep drawing me in."

His fingers feathered over my cheek, and his gaze held so much adoration my knees felt weak with it.

"Don't hate yourself, Everly. I can deal with Cross' scent on you more than I can with you slamming the door on what I feel for you. Just keep spending time with…us. We're both okay with it."

I didn't believe him. Not for one second. But I wanted to.

My seatbelt clicked into place, and he moved away from me to buckle himself in.

"I hope you're ready for some serious desserts. You're going to like the place I found."

Taking a steadying breath, I smiled and asked about the restaurant, which turned into a nice conversation about the places Shepard and his people discovered during their search for vampire nests. He kept the vampire talk very minimal and unbiased. In turn, I asked questions about him as a person rather than a boss or the pack alpha.

He didn't really have any hobbies since his time was spent protecting the pack and running Blur. But he loved the color of the sky just before it stormed and admitted he'd taken an interest in me the moment I walked through Blur's doors for the interview.

"It took one hint of your scent to hook me," he admitted.

"Last fall? Why didn't you…"

"Make a move? I didn't want to scare you away, and I wasn't sure how you felt about my kind. You don't really talk about yourself at work. You're a very private person."

"Takes one to know one," I said.

He chuckled. "Very true."

"I have a question for you."

"Ask me anything."

"You said that a hint of my scent hooked you. Doc mentioned something similar about werewolves having great noses when it comes to their mates. How do werewolves typically find their mates?"

"It's not easy. We might smell a woman we think is right, but typically, the woman doesn't agree. My kind is rejected more often than they are accepted. Romantically, I mean."

"What if you know the one you're smelling is already interested in your kind? Would there be fewer rejections?"

"Depends on the woman, I suppose. Is there a reason you're asking?"

"I have an idea to help increase the popularity of our bakery and maybe help a few of your kind find their mates. What if women who are interested in a potential wolf mate each made a cookie that I could sell at the bakery? Wolves would be able to smell if they're interested in the woman through the cookie. If there's a match, they could meet up."

Shepard rubbed a hand along his jaw, not nearly as excited as

I was when I had thought of the idea. "It's a good idea. But it might work too well."

"Too well?" I chuckled. "Don't want your house overrun with women?"

"Space isn't the issue. There's enough room for everyone. But if Cross wants to attract otherworld beings like vampires, it wouldn't work if wolves are lining up for cookies. Vampires wouldn't dare enter with such a heavy wolf presence."

"I didn't think of that. I'll talk to Cross and see if we can work something out. Maybe it can be a special event instead."

Shepard pulled alongside a pothole-riddled road and parked near an alley. I looked around, trying to find a restaurant, but there was only a wig shop, a butcher shop, and a spice shop.

"Are we at the right place?" I asked.

"Remember how I said I found this place while searching for vampire nests?"

I nodded. "You must have looked hard because I still don't see anything."

"Because it's not in sight, which is why we thought it might be a nest."

He hopped out of the SUV and came around to open my door to help me down. Keeping my hand in his, he led me down the alley between two brick buildings.

The alley opened up to a small courtyard filled with metal bistro tables and chairs. A magical mix of fresh bread, sugar, and herbs scented the air there, and I read the sign above the propped open door. *Le Four Cachè*.

A chalkboard near the door displayed the day's menu.

"I love this place already," I said.

"I thought you would," Shepard said. "The woman who owns this is half fae, half human. She combines her love of both worlds into her menu."

"Why isn't this place packed?"

"Aibell doesn't care about customers too much. She loves her craft and gives leftover food to shelters and otherworlders who can't find employment."

"That's kind, but how can she afford to stay in business?"

"Her father is fae and can keep her business running for as long as she cares."

We entered the small restaurant that had mismatched wooden tables and chairs. Twinkle string lights crisscrossed the ceiling, creating the only light beyond the two windows in front.

"I'll be with you in a minute," a woman called from beyond a doorway that was draped with strings of beads. "Have a seat anywhere."

Shepard followed me to a table near the window.

"I can't decide between la soupe au pistou with fresh rosemary bread or the tomato and basil soup with goat cheese tartine," I said. All I knew was that I had to save room for dessert. The mille feuille and kouign amann were calling my name.

"What if we get both and split it?" he asked, hammering home just how perfect he was. Not only did he bring me to a place he knew I'd love, but it might be the inspiration for the bakery I needed.

"I'd like that a lot," I said.

A stunningly beautiful woman with white-blue eyes framed with dark eyelashes emerged from the beaded curtain. She smiled in welcome.

"What tempts you today?" she asked.

"All of it," I admitted.

She laughed. The sound was alluring enough that I felt the typical fae attraction.

"We'll take one of each special and share," Shepard said.

"Anything to drink?" she asked.

"Water for me," I said.

"Same," Shepard said.

She left us, and Shepard reached across the table to take my hand. His fingers barely closed over mine when his phone buzzed with a message.

I saw the annoyance flash over his expression.

"I don't mind if you need to check your phone, Shepard."

"But I do," he said. "I don't want anything to interrupt us. And if I'm honest, I'm a little disappointed that you're okay with it."

"I'm not the clingy type, Shepard. If that's what you're looking for, I'll just disappoint you. I'm more of the equal partner and mutual respect type."

He lifted my hand to his mouth and kissed my knuckles. "I like that you're not clingy and are independent. A little bit of a pout when I leave your side is just to boost my battered ego."

"Battered? How was—" I closed my mouth, understanding. He wanted to know he was wanted regardless of how I felt for Cross.

I held out my hand. "Phone."

He flashed me a grin and handed it over.

Doc: I think we might have a problem. Call me.
Shepard: You're interrupting your alpha's date with the
incredibly cute human who fed you a homemade
breakfast this morning and not your alpha. Is it really
important? If not, your alpha's attention is mine for the
next hour.

Shepard made a low sound that teased my senses as he read it and hit send.

"I wouldn't mind if you were a bit possessive," he said, the corner of his mouth tilting up.

"Possessiveness could become stifling after a while," I said, knowing damn well I was flirting with a man who would very much like to be possessive with me.

"Then let's have a safeword. I'll let you know when you go too far."

The room felt ten degrees warmer when his phone buzzed

again. It took him a few seconds to break the hold his gaze had on mine to check who'd messaged. When he read it, he growled lightly and stood.

"I'll be right back."

I watched him walk out with his phone and pressed my hand to my chest, trying to calm my thundering pulse.

Aibell emerged with two glasses of water.

"Whew. That's a lot of suppressed desire you have going on," she said, setting a glass in front of me. "Understandable. He's quite the specimen."

She leaned in a little and breathed in deeply. "If my father were here, you would be a meal he couldn't pass up. Unsatiated lust. I need to make a dessert that captures that. There isn't a fae alive who would be able to resist that."

She laughed lightly and ran a finger along my cheek before she set the other glass on the table and retreated.

Unsure if Aibell had just hit on me or not, I ran through the conversation a second time and realized she'd given me the answer to what fae wanted from a dessert. I just needed to figure out how to make it.

My phone buzzed as I was contemplating.

Miles: Shepard and Cross need to get to the mountain. Fast.
Me: Why?
Vena: Why?
Cross: I don't believe they would welcome me even if the mountain weren't locked down.

I waited for a response from Miles, but our lunch arrived first.

"Thank you," I said.

Shepard walked in as she turned away.

"I apologize. We need to take this to-go," he said, radiating urgency.

She took my food from me before I could sample a bite.

"What's wrong?" I asked.

"Can I explain in the car?" he asked.

"Of course."

I didn't ask anything else until we were on the road.

"Was it the message from Miles?" I asked.

"Miles messaged? What did he say?" he asked, proving that wasn't it.

"He said that he needs you and Cross to get to the mountain."

"Why?"

"He didn't say. If we're not leaving because of him, then why?"

"A body was found. Completely drained. He's from one of the coastal homes on the other side of the Chesapeake Bay. Doc has some concerns and needs me to go there."

"Oh. Let him know I'm sorry for the text I sent. I didn't mean—"

Shepard's hand closed over mine.

"Don't apologize for that. I liked it, and he understands."

My phone started to vibrate with an incoming call. Shepard released me so I could answer.

"Why isn't Miles answering, Ev?" Vena demanded. "What's happening in the mountain that he needs Shepard *and* Cross? What about my parents? Why do things keep happening to my family?"

My heart hurt for her because she wasn't wrong. First, her grandparents, then Miles, Anchor, and now Miles and her parents.

"You're getting a luck charm for your next birthday. I promise."

I heard a slight hitch in her breathing. "I'm serious, Ev."

"I know, but remember they're in Dwarf Mountain, not missing. The mountain is one of the safest places they can be right now."

"Then why send a plea for help?"

"Technically, Miles didn't ask for help. He just asked Shepard and Cross to get to the mountain. Don't forget…Miles is a book-worm. He might have found information that pertains to the vampires and what they are after. Either way, we'll find out. I promise. Until then, remember where your family is and who they're with. Do you really think a mountain brimming with dwarves will allow anything bad to happen?"

"Um, something already did happen, Ev. The prince died."

"Yes, but we don't know how or why. For all we know, he could have had a weak heart. All I'm saying is to wait for infor-mation. Let's meet at the house and figure out a plan."

"Fine." Vena disconnected.

My phone exploded with group texts from Vena to Miles demanding answers.

Me: Text Miles separately until he answers back, Shepard is dealing with another issue right now.

My phone went silent.

"Everything okay? Or is something else going on?" Shepard asked.

"Vena's worried. After Miles sent that text asking for you and Cross to go to the mountain, he hasn't responded."

Shepard reached out to take my hand. "Once I handle my situ-ation, I'll address the one with Miles. Don't worry."

Cross was already at my house when we arrived and opened the door for us.

"He still hasn't answered," Vena said as I entered. "Neither are Mom and Dad."

"I heard the dwarves were making plans for the funeral," Cross said as he moved a pair of chairs from the dining table to the living room so we could all sit.

Anchor and Vena sat on the couch with me. Cross sat on a

chair while Shepard remained standing, his hands resting on the back of a chair.

"I heard the same," Shepard said to Cross before looking at me. "I'll reach out to my contact and find out if he can tell me why Miles might be requesting our presence. Until then, you and Vena should both stay here with Cross and Anchor. Anchor, you can then take them to Blur for their shift later."

"Work?" Vena asked. "How can I work when I have no idea what's happening to my family?"

CHAPTER NINE

"I get that you're worried," I said. "But sitting here, doing nothing isn't going to get you answers any faster than going to work and casually asking questions."

"You have a point," Vena mumbled.

"So, while Shepard does his thing, you do yours."

"Fine," she said.

Shepard straightened and looked at me. "I'll make today up to you, Everly. I promise." With one last glance at me, he headed out.

I retreated to the kitchen with Cross, leaving Vena and Anchor to cuddle on the couch.

"What are the chances that Vena's family is in trouble?" I asked Cross quietly as I picked up my recipe notebook from the counter.

"If it were anyone else, I would say very little. However, you, Vena, and Miles seem to have an uncanny knack for finding trouble."

"Personally, I believe trouble has a knack for finding us, but whatever."

He chuckled and watched me add a note about fae desserts that evoke desire.

"And what type of dessert would that be?" he asked.

"For me, any dessert. But I doubt the way I desire a dessert is what the fae would be interested in. I need something that will remind them of what they want most."

"Sexual desire," Cross said.

"Exactly. Would you mind getting the takeout bag I left by the door?"

He retrieved the bag and placed it on the counter.

"I think these might give me a hint. Maybe. Does a half-fae need to feed like a full fae?"

"The traits inherited from the parents are always unique to the child," he said. "Some do and some don't."

"And what about half-vampires? All research says your kind is made and not born. Yet, you're not dead. You have a heartbeat. Doesn't that mean you can make kids too?"

With black eyes, he was in front of me, crowding my space.

"That is something I've questioned often in my long life. A woman who would love me enough to want to carry my child. To watch her grow round with life." He trailed a finger down the column of my throat. "I want it so badly it incites my bloodlust. I hunger for more than this lonely existence, but would I condemn my child to a life dependent on blood? A life filled with bias and prejudice and hate?

"Even if I knew such a pairing would result in a child who is human, do you think any woman would be willing to attempt such a thing with me? Look at my eyes, Everly. See how hungry I am for a taste of you. Would you hate me if I was unable to resist drinking from you when I hear you cry out in pleasure?"

My face flushed at the picture he was painting for me. Cross, consumed by lust and unable to stop himself from biting me. He'd safely sampled my blood too many times for me to fear it. All those little tastes had done the opposite. They'd shown me how good it could feel.

I tried to speak but had to clear my throat first.

"I'm not sure what answer you're looking for here. But I can say that having a kid is a big responsibility I'm not yet ready for. With anyone. I haven't even graduated or established the career I want. No matter who I want to have kids with, that's something that would be discussed at length."

He leaned in and set his forehead against mine, closing his eyes.

"When I'm with you, I feel like I'm a man again, not a monster."

I cupped his face. "That's because you *are* a man, Cross." I stood on my toes and pressed my lips against his, uncaring that his eyes were black and he was still fighting his hunger.

For a moment, he didn't move. Then he had me sitting on the counter with my legs bracketing his waist. His kiss was hot, hungry, and pure sensual heaven. I hooked my feet behind him and pressed him closer until I felt his hard length right where I wanted it.

He snarled against my lips, and his mouth moved to my neck. The scrape of his teeth against my skin had me tipping my head back.

"If I use the spray bottle, will you hurt me, Cross?" Vena asked.

I jerked and tried to pull away. Cross' arms banded around me as he scraped his teeth against my skin again.

Vena's worried gaze met mine. "If he bites you, what will Shepard do?"

I cursed, grabbed a handful of Cross' hair, and pulled his mouth off me. Or I tried too. He didn't budge.

Rather than attempting another tug, I ran my fingers through his hair and felt him shiver.

"Are you still with me, Cross, or did I lose you?" I asked softly.

He stopped kissing my neck. Breathing heavily, he stayed right where he was.

Vena stayed a few steps back, spray bottle held loosely in her hands.

"Don't be mad at me for interrupting," she said. "If you'd gone any further with her, she would have avoided you for the next three months, which would have driven you crazy. I've seen her do it. I'm just trying to protect you both from a hard time until I know she's actually made up her mind and not just listening to her runaway hormones. Which I do commend, by the way. A good time every now and again is an excellent mood boost. For most people. Just not Everly. You get what I mean?"

"I do," he said into my shoulder. "Thank you, Vena. You are a true friend."

"As soon as you detangle, I'll leave," she pressed.

He sighed, lifted his head, and took a step back.

His eyes were wild with black veins as he stared at me. I waited until Vena left to ask, "Are you angry?"

"With you? Never. With fate for making me what I am? Always."

"I'm glad fate made you who you are, Cross. If you weren't who you are today, I would have never met you."

He retreated one more step and offered me a hand down.

"Want to help me look up erotic desserts?" I asked with a small smile.

"After that kiss, I should probably stay away from anything erotic, but dessert should be fine. I'm happy to help."

Thirty minutes later, Anchor was distracting Vena in her bedroom when Cross' phone rang, interrupting our research. I didn't mind the interruption, though, since I had a notebook page filled with recipe ideas to test.

"It's Shepard," Cross said.

"Put it on speaker."

Cross answered the phone then placed it down on the counter between us.

"Hello, bestie," he drawled in a pronounced accent.

84

A soft growl came through the speaker, but it was hardly sinister. Even so, it made Cross grin.

"Be serious for a moment," Shepard said. "How long can a vampire live after their heart stops?"

"I thought you loved me," Cross said with a sigh. "Are you trying to find ways to kill me again?"

"I will if you don't answer the question."

"Why are you asking the question?"

"We found a body that has similar markings to what your old friend, Master, made on Gunther."

Similar markings? And he was asking how long it took a vampire to die after their heart stopped? It didn't take a genius to figure out why. Shepard was worried Master might still be alive.

My hand clutched the pen I was holding, and Cross reached over and stroked my back in soothing motions.

"How old is the body?" Cross asked.

"The body is a few days old," Shepard said. "Either someone is copying his methods, or Adriel is alive."

No. Not possible.

"How could he survive?" I asked. "I saw you fight him. Your hand was in his chest. He was dead."

Cross took the pen from my hand before it snapped in half. "While stopping a vampire's heart usually means death, Adriel isn't a typical vampire. According to what I've learned, he's known for getting out of impossibly tight spots."

"So it's possible," Shepard said.

"With Adriel, I believe it could be."

Shepard sighed.

"What aren't you saying?" I asked.

"I could smell Adriel's scent on the body. Either it's Adriel, or someone dragged his dead body around the crime scene to confuse us."

I shivered. "If he's alive, what about the people he's thralled?"

"Sierra is now under my control," Cross said. "Adriel would

have to try to break it, but I doubt she's of any use to him anymore. Even so, she's safely tucked away at Shepard's where he can't get to her."

"And Miles?" I asked quietly, aware that Vena was still in the house.

"That could be an issue," Cross said.

My stomach clenched with the implications.

"Let's table this for right now," Shepard said. "I have a few people I want to talk with first. I'll be in touch when I have more information."

"Can we keep this between us for now?" I asked before Shepard disconnected. "If Vena knows, she'll panic." I already knew Anchor could hear the conversation, but he wouldn't want Vena running off to find Miles. The best place Miles could be right now is trapped in a mountain so that Master couldn't get to him.

"The fewer people who know about this, the better," Shepard agreed. "If you don't hear from me, come to Blur for your shift like normal."

"Okay. Be safe."

"I will. See you soon."

When Shepard disconnected, I looked at Cross.

"If Adriel is alive, I'll ensure he doesn't stay that way for long," Cross promised. "How about we get back to erotic desserts?"

I shook my head. "I think I'll zone out in front of the TV for a little while." I had enough ideas for fae desserts, anyway.

Cross steered me to the couch and sat me down then handed me the remote. "I'll clean up the kitchen."

Before he finished, Vena and Anchor joined us to watch two old episodes of *The Other House*. Anchor was pretty chill with Cross. Both earned a dirty look from Vena when they laughed about the misleading facts about werewolves.

We had just turned off the show to get ready for our shifts when Anchor stopped us.

"Might want to wait," Anchor said. "Shepard's here."

He went to open the door before Shepard could knock. His grim face set Vena off.

"What? What happened?" she demanded, crossing the room to stand right in front of him.

He set his hands on her shoulders.

"I heard back from my contact. The king thinks Miles killed the prince. They allowed him to send the message because he claimed we can prove his innocence."

Her panic shifted to disbelief, which I shared.

"Miles wouldn't kill someone," I said. "He's even careful with fairies."

"I know," Shepard said. He turned Vena toward Anchor. She balked.

"We're going, right?" she insisted.

"No. *We* aren't. I need you and Anchor to stay here for two reasons. The first one is that I trust Anchor to help manage Blur and the vampire sweeps we've been doing. The second reason is that I'm worried about what will happen if your whole family is in the mountain.

"We don't know the situation. Until we do, I would rather have you on the outside."

She opened her mouth to argue, and he added, "We might need outside help this time, Vena. Who do you trust more than yourself to help your family?"

He had her there. She closed her mouth and stared at the floor for a long moment.

"Why does Miles think we're both needed?" Cross asked.

"The dwarven ring is missing," Shepard said.

The way he steadily held Cross' gaze, in addition to knowing that Master might be alive, was enough to send a chill through me.

"I'm not comfortable leaving Vena and Everly alone with only

Anchor as protection," Cross said, wrapping his arm around my shoulders. "No disrespect meant, Anchor."

"I understand," Anchor said. "My focus would fall to Vena first and Everly second. And Vena likes to do what she wants without considering the consequences."

"Vena is right here, asshat," Vena said, scowling at Anchor. "I can't believe you just said that."

"Are you offended because he's telling the truth or hurt because he's not seeing how deeply you care about us?" I asked.

She lost some of her anger. "The second one."

I nodded. "But you do know he's right, right?"

"Whatever. I get it. I'm a problem maker, not a solver, so I'll stay here, out of the way."

Anchor hugged her from behind, and she let him, which I took as a good sign.

"Everly can accompany us," Shepard said. "I'll message Doc and see if Sierra can cover your shift today and possibly tomorrow." As he spoke, he texted. "Pack for two nights. It shouldn't take more than that."

I looked at Vena, not liking that we were being separated.

"Go," she said. "I trust you to bring my family home. All of them, Ev."

I knew she was counting me as family, too, and went to hug her.

"I promise."

Fifteen minutes later, I was in the front seat of Shepard's SUV with Cross seated behind us.

"What are the chances of you finding a body with Master's scent after the dwarven ring goes missing?" I asked. "It means he's alive, right?"

"It's not something I would have thought possible, but the scent was fresh," Shepard said. "A few days old, not weeks."

I leaned my head back against the seat, trying to fight my dread.

"Whether it's Adriel or someone else, the problem is still the same," Cross said. "The vampires haven't given up on collecting the rings. We need to warn the fae that they're next."

Shepard tapped the steering wheel, seemingly deep in thought. "This must be why the vampires stopped supplying fae with humans. I wonder if they know the vampires are setting up to betray them."

"What does their supply have to do with the rings?" I asked.

"No matter what species we are, if we are hungry, we will focus on finding our next meal," Cross said.

A sick feeling settled into my stomach as I understood.

The vampires had cut off the fae's food source as a distraction.

Shepard used hands-free dialing to call a contact he'd labeled "Caution."

"Is that the same as 'use protection?'" Cross asked.

Shepard shot him a hard glance in the mirror. Cross grinned as a woman answered the phone.

"I knew you wouldn't deny me forever," the woman said with a sultry purr. "Tell me where you are, and I'll come to you."

"I'm on my way to see Curran about Hakon's death," Shepard said. "Their ring is missing."

"They should be more careful with their possessions. I would take great care not to misplace you." She made a sound that resonated in my chest and made my pulse race. "I dream of your taste, Shepard."

He fumbled with the call, trying to take it off speaker, and the SUV swerved.

"You're on speaker, Effora," Cross said. "Keep talking like that and your boy toy will end up driving off the road."

She laughed.

"Cross, I heard you were keeping unusual company. Perhaps I can interest you in accompanying Shepard in entertaining me. I've never had a wolf and a vampire at the same time."

I tried hard not to let my shock or jealousy show but knew Shepard caught me when he inhaled deeply.

"I think Shepard finds sharing with me a tempting invitation, Effora," Cross said. "But, respectfully, we'll need to decline. The missing ring must take precedence. We don't believe it was misplaced but taken."

"Taken? Who would—" She swore. "Does that bitch dare?"

"We know nothing yet," Cross said. "But Shepard will keep you apprised of what we learn. Guard yourself well, Effora."

Shepard disconnected the call.

"So she's tasted you?" Cross asked Shepard with a grin.

Shepard flushed scarlet, which I would have found adorable if I wasn't so worried about Adriel being alive.

CHAPTER TEN

THE HUGE DOUBLE DOORS OF THE MOUNTAIN ENTRANCE WERE SHUT tight as we parked in the insanely large parking lot at the base of the winding stairs.

When we reached the doors, Cross pulled on a thick rope. A low sound echoed inside the mountain, and a small chest-height panel opened right in front of me.

"Oh. Er, uh, I…um," a gruff voice stammered.

Cross nudged me back a few steps, and I saw a set of brown eyes gaze from my chest to my face then back again before Shepard stepped in front of me.

"Shepard Ulv and Brodier Cross, as requested by King Curran," Shepard said.

The panel slid shut abruptly. Metal clanked together as the massive lock retreated, and the heavy wooden door opened.

We stepped into the largest entryway I had ever seen. Not only was the gilded ceiling three stories high, but it had to be a quarter mile deep. Gold columns were positioned in rows to keep the massive space from caving in onto the white marble floor.

Four dwarves in silver armor guarded the door while a dwarf in gold armor nodded to us.

"The king has been anticipating your arrival, Alpha," he said. "I'm Tryn, the leader of His Majesty's personal guards. If you will follow me, I will take you to him."

I was not physically prepared for the trek through the mountain. It would have been paradise for Vena, but I was out of breath by the seventh staircase.

"Out of curiosity," I asked between panted breaths, "are there any elevators or escalators in this place?"

"There is only one elevator, which is designated for the royal family should there be a need to escape quickly." The guard didn't wheeze at all as he talked.

Having to traverse this mountain regularly probably kept him in shape, but I was ready to end the torture.

By the thirteenth staircase, we had entered the heart of the mountain where the dwarves lived. My gaze darted around as a market came into view. I spotted stalls for food, clothes, and jewelry. Children ran around as adults shopped.

The scent of grilled meats filled the air. Yet, for an entire dwarf population to be stuck inside the mountain, the space didn't feel stifling. Fresh air came from somewhere and carried away the grill smoke.

Once we passed through the market, I saw a few more areas designated for living and recreational space. Six dwarves played a game in a blocked-off section. It reminded me of basketball but was very aggressive with a lot of body-checking.

By the twentieth staircase, I could barely lift my feet to the next step despite seeing signs that we were getting closer to the royal family. The opulence had grown exponentially. Even the stairs were encrusted with jewels.

"Are you okay, Everly?" Cross asked as I stumbled on a sparkly step.

I blew out a breath and held the stitch in my side. "How much longer until we get there?"

"It's only a dozen staircases more," Tryn said.

I groaned. "Just leave me here. Come get me on your way out."

"I'll carry you," Cross said.

"You're too old," Shepard teased. "You'll throw out your back. I'll carry you, Everly."

"And I'm sure your youth is what attracted Effora," Cross said with a grin. "But let's not argue in the mountain. Shall we settle this the way the young do? Have you ever heard of Rock, Paper, Scissors?"

"You've got to be kidding me," Shepard said.

"I'll take that as a yes—unless you want to forfeit."

Shepard growled but held out his fist.

Cross held out his as well. "Begin."

Their hands blurred in motion for what seemed to be too long for a standard game of Rock, Paper, Scissors. Tryn looked on in the same confusion.

"You're cheating," Shepard said.

"I never cheat. I'm only faster than you."

"Stop," I said, realizing they could see what the other was doing because they were so fast. "Face back to back." I didn't care that they were playing the most ridiculous game two ring-bearers could play. It allowed me to rest for a minute.

Both men pivoted away from each other.

"Try not to get frisky," Cross said when their butts accidentally brushed together.

I didn't hear what Shepard muttered back, but it made Cross grin.

"Get ready," I said. "Go."

I looked at both their hands. "Cross wins with scissors to paper."

Cross squatted down in front of me, offering his back, and I wrapped my arms around his neck and my legs around his hips.

As he stood and walked past Shepard, he said, "Don't worry. You still have Effora."

"I will kill you," Shepard muttered.

"I heard you lack the penetration to see the deed done."

The dwarven guard made a choked sound and turned away. I lightly swatted Cross' shoulder.

"Behave. Remember where you are."

Shepard shot Cross a smug look and continued after the guard.

Cross clasped my legs, and I was acutely aware of his wandering fingers as he ascended each one of the remaining twelve meandering staircases.

My legs ached as he eased me to my feet outside a set of closed golden doors sentineled by another two dozen golden guards.

"I will announce you," Tryn said before slipping inside.

Shepard brushed my hair off my neck. "I'll carry you down when it's time to leave."

"Deal."

The doors opened wide, and our escort motioned us forward.

I wasn't sure what I'd expected, but the cozy living room decorated in gold and silver brocades wasn't it. An older man sat on an appropriately sized sofa along with a young woman. Both of them wore custom-tailored clothes that probably cost more than my rent. But I didn't envy them that when they also wore their grief like a cloak. It weighed their shoulders and their movement as they got to their feet to welcome Shepard.

"It is good to see you again, Alpha," the king said.

"I'm sorry it's under such circumstances," Shepard said.

The man nodded and sat again with a sigh, gesturing for us to do the same. His gaze swept over us, lingering on Cross.

"It is the cruelest of fates for a parent to outlive their child," Cross said. "You have my deepest condolences."

"You aren't what I was expecting." King Curran looked from

Cross to Shepard. "I didn't fully believe you when you said you would bring a vampire with you. I never would have thought the wolves would agree to a truce with vampires."

"We haven't," Shepard said. "The truce is with Cross alone, not his kind."

"And why is Cross the exception?"

"He doesn't feed like the rest of his kind," I said, needing to speak on Cross' behalf. "Not for sport or control or pleasure. And there's also this." I lifted Cross' hand to show the ring he wore.

His fingers lightly squeezed mine in affection, and I released my hold as Curran's gaze landed on me.

"We haven't been introduced," he said.

"I apologize," Shepard said. "This is Everly Reid, a friend of the Hunters and a human Cross and I both implicitly trust."

I would need to remind him of that the next time he questioned where I was going.

The king nodded to me. "You may call me Curran. This is my daughter, Indri."

She was lovely with dark hair and vivid blue eyes. She sat poised next to her father, but I could see it took effort to keep a calm expression.

"I'm sorry to meet you under these circumstances," I said.

Curran nodded and looked at Shepard and Cross again. "I would very much like to know why Miles sent a message to both of you. It wasn't what I'd expected when I'd allowed him to use his phone. I'd hoped he would message his accomplice."

"Accomplice?" I echoed.

"Yes, we wanted to believe he didn't act alone when he..." Curran's hazel eyes watered, and he cleared his throat. "When he poisoned my son."

Poisoned? Miles? It didn't make any sense.

Indri started silently crying, and I looked at Shepard. His hand covered mine, giving me comfort.

"Miles isn't the kind of human who would poison another person," Shepard said.

"His parents have stated the same, which is why I was willing to believe perhaps someone misled him. At his age, he would still have much innocence yet to lose. I'd hoped, for their sakes, he was coerced or tricked."

"Or thralled," Cross said. "With your permission, I would like to discover the truth."

Curran nodded and stood. "Come. For the safety of my daughter, we've locked him away."

Indri and the rest of us followed the king out the main doors, which opened at his approach. We didn't speak as we descended the stairs–only one set, thankfully–and took a hall that branched from the landing.

Within a few minutes, I spotted a silver guard in the hallway ahead.

"Open the door," Curran said.

The guards hurried to obey and stepped aside so Cross could enter the room first. I was two steps behind him and saw Miles sitting at a small table. With an angry gaze so unlike his usual teasing one, Miles watched us enter.

Shepard took my hand as Cross stepped in front of Miles.

"Stand and face the king, Miles," he said.

I appreciated the kindness in his tone and watched Miles' gaze immediately soften as he did what he was told.

"Miles, you will answer our questions honestly and fully to the best of your knowledge, including suspicions and guesses. Do you understand?"

"Yes," Miles said.

Cross gestured to Curran, indicating it was his turn.

"Why did you kill my son?" the king asked in a choked voice.

"Master told me to."

My stomach sank, and a chill raced through me.

"Who is Master?" Curran asked.

Miles cocked his head to the side as if confused. "He is Master."

"Master is a vampire also known as Adriel, who attacked during the Alpha challenge a month ago," Shepard said.

"When did Master tell you to kill the prince?" Cross asked. "Be specific."

"He came to me four days ago. He said I needed to follow my parents into the mountain and kill the prince."

The tears that had pooled in Curran's eyes quietly spilled over.

"Did he tell you why?" Shepard asked.

"He wanted the prince's ring."

"Where is Master now?" Shepard asked with an angry growl.

"In the mountain." Miles smiled, an odd tilt to the corner of his mouth. "He's been waiting for you."

"Is that why you sent a text asking us to come to the mountain?" Cross asked.

"Yes. Master wants all the rings."

Fear crept along the back of my neck as I understood what we'd done. We'd gathered two of the rings in the same place where Master had already managed to steal one.

"Did Master feed from you again since the incursion at the alpha challenge?" Cross asked.

"No," Miles said. His gaze finally shifted to me. "He's hungry for something sweeter."

Shepard swore softly and motioned for Curran to step out into the hallway. He waited until Cross joined us and the door was shut to speak.

"We have a lot to talk about, but not here. Please keep Miles locked up for now. He'll be safest here."

"Of course he'll be locked up. He killed my son."

"And as you suspected, he didn't act on his own. He was used like a puppet," I said gently. "You saw how Cross made him answer his question, right? The other vampire, Adriel, had the same control."

"No," Cross said. "He has more control over Miles. I can only make Miles do something within his nature without taking his blood. After drinking from Miles, Adriel can make him do anything. Even things he wouldn't normally do."

"So, would you blame the puppet or the puppeteer?" I asked the king.

I already knew who Miles would blame. He'd feel guilty about this for the rest of his life. And Vena...I didn't even want to tell Vena.

"I never should have given Hakon the ring." Curran made a choked sound and pressed a handkerchief to his eyes.

Indri wrapped an arm around his shoulders as Shepard led the way back to their living space.

"I don't understand what's happened," Indri said when the doors closed behind us. "Did a vampire ask a human to kill my brother because of the ring?"

"Unfortunately, yes," Shepard said.

Curran ushered her to the sofa. I sat on an intricately carved wooden chair that had a padded seat while Shepard and Cross remained standing.

"Adriel is an extremely dangerous vampire," Cross said.

"We thought he died at the alpha challenge," Shepard added, "but found evidence an hour before I contacted you that he hadn't. He's not like other vampires. He can change form into a cat. It allows him to move around in daylight and may be how he managed to sneak into your mountain."

"But why would a vampire want a ring?" Indri asked. "The ring's only purpose is to find minerals and gems."

Curran wiped his eyes before looking at his daughter. "There are things I have not told you. Our ring isn't as simple as it seems."

"None of them are," Cross said, holding up his hand to show his ring.

"Which is why we must protect them," Shepard said. "All of them."

"Yes. Of course. It is gravely troubling that a vampire wants them." Curran glanced at Cross.

"I agree," Cross said. "And I don't believe he is working alone."

"A month ago, we discovered the vampires had set up a blood center of sorts," Shepard said.

"They were keeping feeders, collecting their blood, and making it available to any vampire," Cross said. "It enabled them to remain hidden in plain sight within the Alpha's territory until Everly revealed their location."

Both Shepard and Cross glanced at me, and I could feel the weight of their warning never to do anything like that again. Did they honestly think I'd *wanted* to discover a hidden nest of vampires?

"Once we flushed them out, they went into hiding," Shepard said. "I thought they'd scattered. Instead, they'd regrouped and attacked the night of the Alpha challenge in an attempt to get my ring. However, my people, with Cross' help, ended the attempt quickly.

"We need to do the same now. With your permission, Cross and I will scour the mountain for Adriel."

"Granted," the king said. "But when you find him, I ask that you return him to me alive. I am owed a life and a ring."

"You have my word," Shepard said before looking at Cross.

"One of us should stay behind," Cross said.

"This is a mountain, not a grocery store," Shepard said. "I can't do it alone."

"What if you leave us with a couple of guards?" I said. "Cross can make sure they aren't under Master's control before you go."

Cross still looked uneasy but nodded.

Once he decided on two guards, plus Tryn, they left, and we were locked in.

"Thank you for trusting us," I said to Indri and Curran.

"Do we have any choice?" Indri asked bitterly.

"Daughter, please," Curran said with a sigh.

Before Indri could say anything else, I asked, "Where are Mr. and Mrs. Hunter?"

"We were unsure what to do with them, given the situation," Indri said. "Would you care to see them?"

"Please. I would like to explain what happened. They must be scared and confused."

Indri nodded and rang a silver bell with a ruby handle. A panel on the wall opened, and a butler entered. When Cross and Shepard had us locked in here, they hadn't known about the hidden door. Were we safe here?

"We're ready for dinner," Indri said. "Escort the Hunters, please."

CHAPTER ELEVEN

I SAT AT THE ORNATELY CARVED, GOLD-GILDED DINING TABLE THAT could easily seat thirty people and fought not to fidget. It felt weird with only the three of us, but my discomfort evaporated when the Hunters appeared.

"Everly!" Mrs. Hunter cried when she saw me. I stood quickly to receive her desperate embrace.

"It's okay," I said softly. "Miles will be okay."

She pulled back to look me in the eyes. "He didn't do it, Everly. He would never kill someone."

I didn't want to have this conversation with them, but they couldn't remain in the dark forever. So, I took her hands and met her gaze.

"Normally, Miles wouldn't," I said. "But he's not exactly himself."

She frowned. Behind her, Mr. Hunter did the same.

"Let's sit," I said. "This is going to take some time to explain."

I started from the beginning—Miles sending us on an exploratory hunt to check the validity of the information he'd provided. In some spots, I kept the details vague to protect Cross and to keep Vena from getting into trouble. But I stuck with the raw truth about Miles going missing and why we hadn't immediately called them.

Mr. and Mrs. Hunter listened silently, along with the king and the princess. I paused whenever servers brought in the next course but otherwise continued to the end. Or what I'd thought had been the end.

"We all saw him die. The connection Adriel had with Miles should have been gone. We thought it was. I'm so sorry."

Mrs. Hunter looked down at her untouched lamb steak.

"It's not your fault," she said. "It's not Vena's or Miles' either. It's ours for letting our kids believe we would have scolded them instead of helping them." Mr. Hunter's hand covered hers. Comforting her. "We've lost our parents; we won't lose our kids."

Mr. Hunter nodded. "I believe the rings are what my parents had been working on before they disappeared. Each ring possesses a special stone created to ensure the four races have equality."

I realized what he meant. The stones in the back of the book Vena and I had found had been labeled for each of the primary races. Those were the stones in the rings.

"Is that why the vampires are after the rings?" I asked. "Because they don't want equality between the races anymore?"

It didn't exactly make sense, though, since the vampires were definitely not equals. They hid in the shadows while the fae played in the daylight. Even the werewolves were carefully cautious about exposing themselves.

"In a sense," the king said. "And I think that's all I can safely say on the subject. As you've learned, it's a dangerous topic."

"Agreed," Mrs. Hunter said. "I do have a few questions for you unrelated to the rings or vampires, Everly."

"Ask me anything," I said.

"So Shepard is the Alpha werewolf?"

I nodded hesitantly, hoping I wasn't giving away something that should be kept secret.

"And he runs Blur along with his men, meaning they're all werewolves too?"

I responded with another cautious nod.

"And Anchor, the man you mentioned Vena is interested in, works there?"

Understanding settled with heavy sickness in my stomach.

"He does. He's really, really nice and perfect for Vena."

Mrs. Hunter smiled. "With her wild nature, she needs a strong, protective man who can keep up with her. We'll talk more about this later. Let's eat before this delicious food gets cold."

I ate in silence with the rest. My thoughts strayed to Cross and Shepard as I nibbled. The mountain was huge. How long would it take them to search every inch? Even though they were fast, traversing the staircases had to be tiring.

Indri rang the bell again and snapped me from my thoughts. The king stood with dry, red-rimmed eyes to bid us good night. He flagged his personal guard to go with him.

The Hunters stood, prepared to be escorted by another guard to their room, but not before Mrs. Hunter pulled me into a hug. "Stay safe."

"You, too."

When they were gone, Indri waved for me to follow her.

"How long does it take to get around this mountain?" I asked.

"With all the tunnels, mines, living and storage areas, it could take a dwarf a few days to navigate. Perhaps a wolf and a vampire could do it in a day."

Indri led me down a golden hallway and opened the door to a large room painted white with more gold details. A large sapphire-encrusted mirror was prominently displayed above a vanity.

"The sapphire room will be yours for as long as you stay. Your bag is already inside. The ensuite bathroom is stocked with necessities if you've forgotten anything. However, if you do need anything else, there is a rope bell near the bed. Someone will come as soon as they can."

"Thank you for your hospitality," I said. "I'm sorry we had to meet under these circumstances."

She gave a small nod. "Me, too."

Indri closed the door on her way out, and I breathed a sigh of relief.

Alone, I checked the time on my phone and saw we had been in the mountain for hours already. The summer sun had set an hour ago, not that I could tell since the mountain didn't come with windows.

Grabbing my pajamas from my bag, I went to the modern bathroom for a hot shower to relieve the ache in my legs.

Steam curled in the room as the water heated before drifting toward a vent in the ceiling. I stepped under the spray and let the water melt away my tension. My thoughts circled around what we'd learned and what I was supposed to tell Vena.

Although the king hadn't taken my phone, I hesitated to send an update until Shepard and Cross found Adriel.

Cleaned and rinsed, I shut off the water and toweled dry. A huge yawn popped my jaw as I slipped on my pajama tank top and shorts. I checked the door to my bedroom to make sure it was locked then shuffled toward the bed.

Just as I was about to pull back the covers, a chill stole through me that had nothing to do with the room temperature and everything to do with a tingling sense that someone was watching me.

Slowly, I turned around to find the room was empty. Yet the feeling was still there.

I reached over to pull the rope bell when a loud crash filled the room.

Startled, I whirled to face a leanly muscled man who stood below where the vent cover used to be. He was naked except for a familiar diamond collar.

Adriel.

My heart seized then went into overdrive.

His dark eyes turned darker as he sniffed the air.

"I love the smell of fear."

I scrambled to pull the rope, but he was on me, his naked torso pressed against my back as he pinned me to the wall beside the bed.

The protection charm I always wore around my neck flared but winked out before it could do any good. Adriel never even noticed.

"What's the hurry, Everly? I just want to play a little."

I fought against the panic bubbling up inside of me. How fast would Cross be able to reach me once I bled? Fast enough to stop me from dying?

"Listen to that," Adriel said softly. "The flutter of your pulse. Mmmm. So tempting. What is it that you fear, Everly? Me? Or perhaps you fear liking what I will do to you. Should I make you moan my name? We can record it so you can play it for the Alpha and Cross. I think that might upset them more than your screams. But I do crave your screams."

My body started to shake, and I hated my visible reaction.

He chuckled low in my ear and scraped one long nail along the length of my arm hard enough to leave a red mark but not hard enough to break the skin, knowing one drop of blood would alert Cross.

"I think we'll leave the screaming for next time." He spun me around suddenly to face him, capturing my wrists as he locked his gaze with mine. "Give in to your hidden desires, Everly. Let go of what is holding you back from enjoying everything this life offers."

His words echoed in my mind briefly before wrapping around me with a heaviness I couldn't resist. They pulled at me, flooding my mind.

What hidden desires did I have?

I thought of Cross then Shepard. They'd been tempting me with their presence for weeks. A vampire and a werewolf. Dangerous. Deadly. Yet, I wanted to do more than spend time with them. I wanted to taste everything they could offer me.

"Mmm. I can smell your desire. I knew I wasn't wrong," Master said, snapping me back to the present. "Kiss me, Everly."

My gaze dipped to the twisted smile tugging at his lips, and I felt nothing but revulsion.

"I'd rather walk across a field of broken glass," I said before thinking better of it.

He hissed in my face and twisted my wrists painfully. "Give in to me. Give in to your desire. I smelled it."

"Whatever you were smelling, it wasn't for you," I said through my pain and fear. His fingernails bit into my skin, and I attempted to twist my arms out of his grip, hoping it would scrape me hard enough to draw blood.

He snarled again and darted in toward my neck.

I screamed, giving him one of the things he wanted.

The door crashed open behind him, and he was ripped away from me but not before I felt his tongue and teeth on my skin. Snarls and growls filled the room. Something hit me from the side, and I crashed onto the bed.

When I sat up again, only Shepard remained in the room. His shirt was torn and bloody as he faced the door.

Something about the way he stood there, his chest heaving while radiating anger, called to me. I wanted to go to him. To comfort him.

Give in to your hidden desires...

I was halfway across the mattress when he turned toward me. His intense grey gaze met and held mine. I felt it all the way through me, like a seductive caress.

"Are you hurt?" he asked roughly.

"No."

His gaze drifted to my neck where I could still feel the rasp of Master's teeth.

"I can smell him on you, Everly."

"And you don't like it when I smell like someone else," I said.

Some of the anger in his stance melted away as he frowned at me.

"No. I don't," he admitted when I remained quiet.

"Should I shower again?"

He stared at me for a long moment before saying, "I'm going to ask Indri to check you for bites."

Give in to your hidden desires...

"Why ask Indri?" I drew my top over my head and tossed it to the bed beside me.

I didn't care that the door was smashed and standing wide where anyone could pass by. Only the way Shepard's gaze raked over my exposed breasts mattered.

He swallowed hard and shook his head slightly.

"You're right. He might have bitten me somewhere else," I said, hooking my fingers into the waistband of my shorts.

Shepard crossed the space between us and captured my hands before they descended more than a centimeter.

"Everly," he said, his voice carrying just the right amount of growl to make me breathless. Yet, I also heard the warning and saw his resistance.

"What's wrong?" I asked. "You threatened to strip me more times than I can remember just last month. Did you change your mind? Are you no longer interested in seeing me?"

I watched his pupils dilate and shivered in anticipation.

Give in to your hidden desires...

"Kiss me, Shepard," I said softly. "Show me you still want me like I want you."

He groaned and released my hands to cup my face. The kiss he laid on me conveyed every ounce of his hunger. I kissed him back with as much need, using my hands to push his shirt up his abs so that he would understand he needed to get rid of his top too.

He tore his mouth from mine and ripped off his shirt. I watched him toss the shredded material to the side and shivered with anticipation as he placed a knee on the mattress. My breathing hitched, and I reached for his shoulders. He made a pained sound as I smoothed my palms over them and down his chest.

Then he trapped my hands under his.

"What are you touching, Everly?" he asked.

"You. Your chest."

"And what do you feel?"

My face flushed. "Horny. Are you going to make me beg, Shepard? I didn't think you'd be so petty." Yet, I wasn't unwilling to beg. Anything to get him to touch me like I was touching him.

"You don't have to beg for anything, beautiful. I'd gladly give you the world without you needing to ask for it. But I'm worried this isn't you. The Everly I know would have noticed the blood soaking her palm. She would have been worried that I'd been hurt."

My gaze flicked to his bloody chest and skimmed over the wounds.

"That was before I saw how fast Doc healed on my couch after the fight. These scratches are already closing. I didn't think they'd bother you enough to stop this from happening. But if I was wrong…"

I tried removing a hand, but he caught it fast.

"You're not wrong. I'm just terrified this isn't you, Everly. Why now? A day ago, you weren't ready for this."

"A day ago, you asked me to give you a chance, Shepard. Do you know how many near-death experiences I've had this summer? I'm tired of overthinking everything and denying myself what I want."

"What do you want?" he asked.

"You."

His eyes glinted with gold. His body crashed into mine, knocking me back into the mattress. The press of his hot chest against mine was almost as good as the way he was tenderly kissing my brow and nose and lips.

Another growl escaped him as he opened his mouth and deepened the kiss. When his hand found my breast, I ground my hips against his hardness.

Give in to your hidden desires...

"Am I interrupting something?" Cross asked from behind me.

I ripped my mouth from Shepard's and smiled at Cross.

"No. You're just in time. Join us."

CHAPTER TWELVE

SHEPARD JERKED LIKE I'D HIT HIM AND PULLED BACK TO STARE AT me. His eyes were more gold than grey, and I could feel the fragile hold he had on his control with each tremor traveling through his body. The need to see that control shatter consumed me.

I reached up and stroked his cheek.

"Unless you'd rather he wait until we're finished."

He caught my hand, kissed my palm, and distanced himself.

I tried reaching for him, but Cross was right there, holding his shirt, which was still intact and blood-free. He had it over my head and my arms through the sleeves before I could protest. Then, to take the sting out of Shepard's rude abandonment, Cross kissed my forehead and looked into my eyes.

"Forgive me for this, Everly, but you must tell me what happened since the moment we left your side."

His words echoed in my mind, but they didn't weigh me down like Adriel's had. They wrapped around me lightly like a comforting hug, coaxing me to confide in him, which was easy to do.

"I had dinner with the king, princess, and Mrs. and Mr.

Hunter. Then…" I repeated everything—how I'd revealed Shepard and his crew at Blur were all werewolves, how I'd purposely not mentioned waking Cross or what Cross was, and finished right when they burst into my room.

"If you hadn't arrived when you had, I would be like Miles." I reached for Cross, running my fingers through his hair, so grateful he was a part of my life. My pulse sped as I thought of the ways he could become more a part of me.

Give in to your hidden desires…

"You *are* like Miles," Shepard said. His voice, laced with anger and regret, distracted me from Cross' tender gaze.

I frowned at Shepard, but Cross drew my attention back to him with another forehead kiss.

"You're right. You would have been like Miles. But I wouldn't have let you stay that way. When Adriel told you to give in to your hidden desires and let go of what was holding you back from enjoying everything life has to offer, what did you think of?"

"You. And Shepard. How much both of you tempt me with your touching and kissing."

Cross smiled, but his eyes didn't flicker black, which was a bit disappointing.

"So Shepard and I are your hidden desire?"

Shepard turned and left the room.

My gaze shifted from the empty doorway to Cross, and I tried not to show how upset I was that Shepard left. Cross still seemed to know, though. He smoothed a hand over my hair and kissed my cheek.

"He's not upset with you or abandoning you, Everly. He's upset with himself and Adriel. You've done nothing wrong. Would you like to sleep now?"

I thought about it for a moment then nodded. He helped me under the covers and kissed my brow again before meeting my gaze.

"Your mind is too strong for Adriel's words to work their magic for long. When you wake, you'll be yourself again. But I'm glad your hidden desires are no longer hidden from us, Everly. Do what you want of your own free will. Shepard and I won't mind. I promise."

He kissed me gently and told me to sleep.

I sank into oblivion without another thought.

THE WORDS "BE YOURSELF" and "desires are no longer hidden" played on a loop through my sleeping mind and were still in my thoughts when I woke the next morning. At least, I thought it was morning. With no windows in the room, it was hard to say.

The bed shifted slightly, and a soft-lit lamp on the nightstand clicked on. "Morning, sunshine." Cross kissed my temple. "How do you feel?"

"Fuzzy." Yet, even as I said it, the night before clarified in horrifying detail.

He coiled a lock of my hair around his finger. "To be expected. Do you remember last night?"

"Unfortunately. I still feel Master's teeth on me. He was about to bite me."

"Luckily, he didn't, or you would have been thralled, and this situation would be worse."

Worse?

I might not have been thralled, but I knew damn well Adriel had compelled me to act like a ho. I covered my face with my hands, remembering how aggressive I had been with Shepard right before I'd basically told him and Cross I'd be good with a threesome.

"It's bad enough," I said. "I can't believe I—" I groaned, not able to get the words out.

Cross chuckled and gently coaxed my hands away from my

face. "While I don't like that Adriel had compelled you, there is nothing wrong with giving in to your desires, Everly. You are allowed to live your life however you choose. And I'm grateful to be a part of your desires."

I didn't want to think about any of that now. The way I'd mauled Shepard would have to be dissected later. Preferably while surrounded by baked goods.

"Where is Adriel? Did you catch him?"

Cross shook his head. "I tracked him out of the mountain. Apparently, lockdown only means traditional exits are blocked, not air vents. The king has been made aware of this, and he'll take action to fix the problem so it doesn't happen again."

"What about the ring Adriel stole?"

"King Curran opened the mountain and sent his people out to search for it. They have a picture of Adriel in his cat form from the hotel's surveillance when Gunther was taken, so they know who they're looking for. Shepard and I will aid where we can. In the meantime, we can go home."

"Even Miles?"

Cross nodded. "Curran agreed to absolve Miles for his role in the prince's death but wanted to keep Miles here until Shepard fulfilled his promise. We convinced Curran it wasn't wise to keep a man who was under the thrall of a vampire in their mountain, so Shepard has been granted custody of Miles until we break the thrall."

I blew out a shaky breath. Our time in the mountain could have ended a lot worse, so I was grateful we could take Miles with us.

"I'll get dressed and be ready in a few minutes."

"Take your time." Instead of getting up, he folded his arms behind his head and watched me.

Trying to ignore him, I grabbed my phone from the nightstand and saw it was already mid-morning. A dozen messages from Vena waited, progressively becoming more demanding for information.

"Did anyone update Vena?" I asked.

"We've told her that everyone is fine, but we've been reluctant to say anything more until the matter of Miles was resolved. I came here as soon as Curran agreed to our suggestion."

"Okay. I'll text her right now. What's the plan now?"

"Once we leave the mountain, you and the Hunters will go with Shepard to his residence. On the way, Shepard will drop me off so I can begin my search for Adriel."

Me: Everything's been straightened out. Will give you the full story at Shepard's place. Meet us there in an hour.

Vena responded with a thumb's up emoji.

Placing the phone on the nightstand, I hurried to get ready. Cross watched me until I closed the bathroom door.

By the time I emerged, Cross had my bag packed, and a guard was waiting to escort us to the royal living space.

Curran and Indri were seated along with Shepard and the Hunters. Shepard's cheeks and ears flushed when he saw me. Thankfully, Curran distracted everyone by telling Tryn to fetch Miles.

Mrs. Hunter's hands were fisted on her lap as she looked at the king with teary eyes. "Thank you for letting us take our son with us. When he's himself, he'll want to see you." She swallowed hard. "I don't think he'll be able to forgive himself for his part in what happened."

Curran nodded, looking weary. "I don't fault Miles for what happened. Both of our sons were victims of a heinous act. This was the vampire's fault."

Mrs. Hunter agreed. "We didn't know a vampire could turn into a cat."

"Nor I," Curran agreed. "If I had, our mountain would have been more secure, and this tragic event might not have happened. So, let us part as friends and allies. Together, we can avenge my son."

When Tryn and another guard appeared, holding an angry Miles, Cross approached them and looked Miles in the eyes. "You will leave this mountain with Shepard. You will stay with him in his house and follow his orders. Do you understand?"

"Yes."

Both Curran and the Hunters flinched slightly at Miles' easy agreement to a vampire's order.

We left quickly after that and made the long journey down the main staircases.

"We'll follow you back to your house," Mrs. Hunter said to Shepard once we reached the parking lot. "We'd like to see where he'll be staying until…" Her eyes welled with tears.

"You are welcome to stay, too, for as long as you need," Shepard said.

After I climbed into Shepard's SUV, I messaged Vena.

Me: Your parents are coming too.
Vena: What? Why?
Me: Too much to explain over text. We'll talk soon.
Vena: You know I hate waiting.
Me: Play with Anchor for an hour.
Vena: He's been keeping his clam jammer tucked away.
I'll see what I can do.
Me: TMI

Reluctantly, I set my phone down and faced the current situation. I was sitting in the front seat with Shepard, who'd yet to say anything to me. Not that I'd said anything to him, either. In the back seat, Cross and Miles remained quiet, too. The next hour would be awkward as hell if we stayed like this.

Shepard seemed to have the same thought. He cleared his throat as he turned off the mountain road and said, "I apologize for last night, Everly. I didn't realize you weren't yourself."

Heat exploded on my face. "It's okay. I'd rather pretend it–"

"It happened, and Everly was herself," Cross said from behind me, robbing me of my chance to deflect. "Adriel didn't thrall her; he simply compelled her to reveal a part of herself that she's kept hidden from us. Compelling can't force someone to go against their nature; only thralling does that. And Adriel never had a chance to bite her, thanks to your intervention."

I shifted uncomfortably in my seat, wishing I was anywhere else but there. While I appreciated that Cross wasn't judging me for what happened, I wasn't sure Shepard felt the same regarding my behavior.

Shepard surprised me by reaching over and covering my hand with his. "As long as last night is something you wanted, there's no need for you to feel embarrassed or ashamed, Everly." He gave my hand a squeeze and then released me.

Disbelief sent my thoughts whirling out of control. What the hell did he mean by that? Was he saying he was okay with sharing me? Or that he was okay if I wanted to be with them both separately?

Unsure what to think, I turned my head toward the window and pressed my cheek against the glass, trying to cool the rising heat there. No longer caring if it was awkward or not, I embraced the silence and watched the scenery until Shepard pulled over in downtown D.C.

Cross got out but surprised me by opening my door and kissing my forehead.

"The only thing that has changed is your acceptance of your interest in us. Stop overthinking things and just live, Everly. One day, one moment, at a time. All right?"

I nodded, grateful for his understanding even as I mentally balked at what he was suggesting. He didn't give me a chance to cling to the limbo I'd been holding back for weeks though. He leaned in and brushed his lips against mine.

When he pulled back, his fingers feathered along my jaw, encouraging me.

Giving in, I kissed his cheek in gratitude.

His eyes flickered black briefly, and he flashed his crooked smile at me before he closed the door.

Shepard waited until Cross faded in the distance to speak.

"It's annoying to say this, but he's right. Nothing has changed. Well, maybe a little. What we did last night will fuel my dreams and make it more difficult for me to give you any breathing room."

I arched a brow at him, and he chuckled.

"Don't worry. I know not to smother you with my attention. Just know that you'll only need to look my way to get it."

"Thanks for the warning."

He continued to grin all the way to his place.

When we arrived, Vena and Anchor were already there. They stood side by side with an arm's length of distance between them. As if that would stop Mrs. Hunter from seeing what was insanely obvious—that Anchor was head over heels for Vena.

"You ready to gain Vena as a member of your household?" I asked as Shepard parked.

"Her parents won't object?" he asked.

"Doubtful," I said just before opening my door.

I caught Anchor nervously smoothing his hands over his thighs. Vena did, too, and I could tell by the look she cast his way that she wanted to eat him up like a bowl of ice cream.

"This is your *house*?" Mrs. Hunter asked, getting out of their car.

"My kind tends to live together," Shepard said, opening the back door for Miles. "Safety in numbers."

"Oh, I like that," Mrs. Hunter said. She looked pointedly at Anchor then at Vena. "Are you going to introduce us?"

"Mom, Dad, this is Anchor. Anchor, these are my parents, Dana and Garner Hunter."

"It's a pleasure to finally meet you," Anchor said, holding out his hand.

Mrs. Hunter melted at the uncertain smile he gave her as her husband shook Anchor's hand.

Vena gave me a look and shifted her gaze to Miles, who was standing amicably enough next to Shepard.

"I'll give you the cliff-noted version," I said. "Adriel isn't dead. He ordered Miles to poison the prince and then escaped the mountain, but not before revealing himself. King Curran doesn't hold Miles responsible and allowed Shepard to bring Miles here to keep an eye on him while we all help look for Adriel and the missing ring."

Vena closed her eyes, and I recognized the impending explosion.

So did Mrs. Hunter.

"Anchor, why don't you take Vena for a walk while we settle Miles in? Once she's calm, let's have a longer discussion about what happens next, okay?"

He nodded and took Vena's hand to lead her to the back garden while Shepard led the rest of us inside.

Mrs. and Mr. Hunter thanked Shepard profusely when they saw the room Miles would have and the people who were assigned to watch over him twenty-four-seven. Once they knew he was settled, we went to the dining room where a late breakfast was waiting for us.

"I heard your stomach growling since we left the mountain," Shepard said to me when I looked questioningly at him.

"Thank you."

"I smell bacon," Vena said, entering the dining room with Anchor. She looked calm, and I was sure that had to do with Anchor's arm around her shoulders.

The six of us sat at a table, and I listened to Mrs. Hunter gently question Anchor.

How long had they been dating? What were his plans for the future? Did he like kids? What did his parents do for a living?

It was a little funny to watch Vena squirm until she shot me a "you better help me end this, or everyone will suffer" look.

"Thank you for breakfast, Shepard," I said when everyone was finished eating. "And it was good to see you again, Mr. and Mrs. Hunter. Don't worry about Miles. He's in good hands."

I stood to punctuate that it was the end of our visit. Vena bolted out of her seat less gracefully.

"Isn't today your day off?" Mrs. Hunter asked, looking at both of us.

"From Blur, Mom, not from life in general."

Mrs. Hunter gave Vena a dry look but waved her away.

"Go ahead and escape. I think we'll stay for a while longer if that's all right with you, Shepard."

He agreed, and Vena and I retreated with Anchor, who drove us home.

I was grateful it wasn't Shepard. I wasn't yet ready to tell Vena what had happened with him, even though I knew I wouldn't be able to hide it forever.

CHAPTER THIRTEEN

As soon as I unlocked the house, Vena bolted inside. She had stewed in silence all the way home, but now, questions exploded from her.

"How is Master still alive? Shepard's hand was *in his chest*, Everly. There was blood. A lot of blood. He was a lifeless carcass. How can he go from carcass to poisoning people?"

"I don't know. Even Cross didn't have the answer to that," I said.

"We need the answer to end this. We need to figure out how he's still alive so we can figure out how to kill him for good." She retrieved her laptop and stationed herself in the living room. "It shouldn't take me long to research. It's not like cat-shifting vampires are common."

I left Vena and Anchor in the living room and retreated to the kitchen for a little quiet time. With my notebook and apron, I searched my cupboards and refrigerator to see what I had on hand.

My phone vibrated.

Shepard: Can we attempt a lunch date again later this week?

I stared at the message, trying to settle my thoughts about Shepard and Cross. The whammy that Adriel laid on me had opened my eyes and theirs. The attraction I felt for both Cross and Shepard could no longer be hidden or denied.

Both had said they'd be okay with me seeing the other. Both had said they'd give me the time I needed. And they both said it was okay for me to live a little.

Why not take them up on their offer, then?

Perhaps by following my desires, I could learn a bit more about them and myself. It could also be a test to see if either of them could actually share my time and affection without trying to stake a claim. I could also try to determine if I liked one more than the other.

Decided, I replied.

Me: Yes, I would like that.
Shepard: Can't wait.

Neither could I.

As soon as I found enough ingredients to make shortbread cookies, Cross texted.

Cross: Is it too soon to miss you?

I smiled at the message. For a vampire, he was cuddly and affectionate. Always taking opportunities to be in my bed when I woke up and kissing me whenever he had a chance.

Me: Maybe. But I don't mind. Did you find out anything about Adriel?
Cross: Nothing yet. The dwarves are stirring up the city

with their pursuit, so it might take me some time. But beyond missing you, I wanted to let you know the permits have been approved, the contractors have started, and everything you requested for the kitchen has been ordered and will be delivered in 5-7 business days.

I might have squealed a little at the thought of baking with shiny new Vulcan equipment. And I'd be the head baker. The space was all mine.

It was a dream come true. While I knew it was all due to Cross and not because of my skills or hard work, I didn't let that get me down. I would prove to him that taking a chance on me was the right decision.

Me: I'm excited to work with the new equipment, but isn't it too soon? Don't the contractors have a lot of work to do?
Cross: Crews are already working. They've assured me that they'll be done in time.
Me: That fast?
Cross: Padding their quotes with extra money helped.

I wanted to tell him not to rush on my account, but I knew the rush wasn't about me. Cross' vision to bring the races together could only start once the business was running. And then there was the whole need to get inside information to help Shepard flush out the vampires.

Me: Just don't go broke on my account.
Cross: If it's for you, I'd gladly be poor. But don't worry, Everly. I have means beyond the coins of which I still have plenty. Trust me.
Me: I do.

"I need to go to the Shadow Trade market," Vena called from the living room. "The internet isn't giving me the information I'm looking for. Everly, you in?"

I stepped into the archway so she could see me. "I was going to bake. Anyway, you know how I feel about that place."

"It's perfectly safe."

Anchor raised a brow at her.

"Reasonably safe," she amended. "Just stay in the front section."

"Is that where you're going?" I asked, knowing she'd be all over that place.

"Anchor can stay with you while I walk around," Vena said.

"I'd rather stay home and have Anchor go along with you."

She opened her mouth to try to persuade me, but Anchor put his hand on her knee. "We'll go after Doc gets here. He can stay with Everly. Why don't you get ready?"

Vena set her laptop on the coffee table and popped off the couch. "I'll grab my book list for our new place too. Cross let me know the contractors already started working on it, so I can scout for books while we're at the market."

I returned to the kitchen, happy that Anchor wasn't scared off by Vena's tenacity even as I acknowledged what that meant for our relationship.

A heavy sigh escaped me, and I realized it wasn't the first when Anchor asked if everything was all right.

"I'm fine," I said.

I focused on baking until Doc showed up. Vena and Anchor called out that they would bring home dinner then left.

"I'm not sure if you know this, but a person's scent changes with their mood," Doc said from nearby.

I glanced over my shoulder to find him leaning against the counter.

"Oh? Did you smell the hormones as they left?" I asked.

"No, I'm smelling your sadness. It's not like you."

"Not true. I'm human and female. There have been loads of times I've been sad. Just about every time I see a fairy or Vena eats my leftovers."

He chuckled. "I don't see any fairies, and your garbage is empty. What has you sad this time?"

I focused on the miniature meringues I was using as teeth in my elevated version of Dracula Denture cookies. The almond halves were adorable fangs. And everything together—the butter cookie, raspberry filling, and almonds—smelled and tasted divine.

"Life, I guess. Knowing that Vena and I will be graduating soon and thinking of what comes next for us."

"Change can be hard."

I nodded then glanced at him again. "Are you married, Doc?"

He grinned. "I'm telling Shepard you were interested in my current status."

I rolled my eyes. "He's less likely to have a problem with any potential interest I might have in you over Cross. Does it bother you when Cross comes over?"

"Yes," Doc said honestly. "It goes against every instinct I have not to go after him."

"Are you being metaphorical or literal?" I knew wolves had instincts, but I still didn't know very much about them.

"Literal. It's in our blood to kill vampires. It's what we were made for."

"Made?"

He shrugged. "You'll have to ask Shepard about our origins. It's a story only passed from father to son when we first change."

"Got it. Want to try my version of Dracula's Dentures?"

For the rest of the afternoon, I kept my emotions in check so Doc didn't question me again, and he kept himself entertained with a fictional werewolf romance book that Vena had brought home for "research."

I was showered and in my pajamas for the night when Vena and Anchor finally returned.

"What a shit show," Vena said, plopping onto the couch as Anchor went to the kitchen with the Chinese takeout. "Not a single person I asked had any information about a vampire who could turn into a cat, or about a vampire that wouldn't die even with its heart crushed."

"Rome wasn't conquered in a single day," Doc said.

Vena rolled her eyes. "Yeah, yeah. I'm being impatient. I know that. But I wasn't the only one. The market was crawling with dwarves asking the same questions I was."

Anchor returned with containers for both of us. I listened to her summary of their time in the market as I ate. She'd gotten a few leads on people who might be able to help her locate a black cat, but that was it.

With a food-happy sigh, I leaned back against the couch from my position sitting on the floor.

"You liked it?" Vena asked. "You're never going to guess where it's from."

"If you say something gross after I finished eating it, I'm going to punch you in the chesticles."

Doc made a strangled sound, and Anchor clapped him hard on the back.

"Nothing gross," she said. "I promise. It was a vendor in the Shadow Trade market. A stall in the front where it's totally safe. And just to be sure, I interrogated the lady selling them. Straight-up human-grade food. I guess it's good business there. After browsing all the unusual stuff, humans want something familiar."

"Makes sense," I said.

"There were a lot of other food stalls there...if you want to come with us tomorrow."

"Tomorrow?"

"Come on. Come with us. You and your girls are my lucky charm when it comes to getting information."

I made a face at her.

"Plus, we're due for a charm recharge. Especially with Master running around again."

I thought of my run-in with Adriel and how my charm had fizzled and knew she was right.

"Fine."

"Yay! You'll flip when you see how many dwarves are wandering around the market. They were glaring at people. A troll got offended and called one an ankle-biter and told him to toddle off. If Anchor hadn't been there, I would have had a front-row seat to a fight."

"Sorry to disappoint you," Anchor said.

"You're forgiven," she blew him a kiss. "It's your job to keep the peace."

I WAS CUDDLED up against something warm and firm. The hand gently stroking my hip told me this wasn't my body pillow.

"Cross?" I mumbled, not feeling the need to open my eyes yet.

"Hmm?" he hummed back, sounding just as relaxed as I felt.

"You smell delicious," I said, inhaling the scent of coffee and cinnamon.

"There's a reason, and it's on your nightstand."

I lifted my head and blinked my eyes open to see the most mouthwatering cinnamon roll plated next to a lidded coffee.

Reaching over him to get to the coffee first, I grazed his entire chest with mine. Yes, both of us were clothed, but that didn't stop the tingles from rushing through my body at the contact.

Cross' eyes flashed black, but he didn't make a move. Just allowed me to grab the liquid energy and sit back against the headboard.

A single sip told me it was exactly the right ratio of coffee, creamer, and sugar. A sigh escaped my lips, causing the veins around his eyes to darken as well.

"Sorry," I said, "but it's really good."

"I thought you might like it." He lifted the cinnamon roll plate. "This looked and smelled divine too." He cut into the gooey goodness and offered me a bite.

Normally, I was the one feeding people. This was a nice change of pace. Leaning over, I accepted the offering and moaned as soon as cinnamon, fluffy roll, and cream cheese icing hit my tongue.

"I'm delighted you're enjoying it."

"I can tell. Your eyes are getting a workout, and Doc probably thinks something is going on."

"He can hear our conversation. Plus, I already gave him the same wake-up treat as you, minus the cuddling. I offered, but he impolitely declined." Cross flashed a beautiful smile and reached over to touch the corner of my lips to wipe away a bit of frosting. He brought it to his lips to taste. "Delicious. Just like you."

I smiled at his flattery.

"Not that I mind the cuddles and sweet treats first thing in the morning, but is there a reason you're here today? Good news on Adriel?"

"Unfortunately, no news yet. However, Shepard is debriefing the fae queen in hopes of gaining her assistance. I told him removing her briefs would help if she actually wore any. He wasn't amused."

"He's with the fae queen?"

"Does that make you jealous?"

I slowly chewed the bite he fed me and shook my head.

"A person's feelings are their own. Affection can't be forced."

Cross smirked. "Tell that to the fae."

He fed me another bite and asked, "Do you have plans for the day?"

After swallowing, I said, "I'm thinking of going to the Shadow

Trade market with Vena. It'll be a good place to do some recipe research, and I need to get my protection charm charged. It fizzled when Adriel touched me."

"I know someone in the market who can help you with your charm. She's half fae and is skilled with protection spells. Can I give you her name?"

"Please."

Cross shifted the plate to his other hand and pulled out his phone. My phone, which was on the nightstand, buzzed.

"Will Anchor be going with you?" he asked.

I nodded and reached for the plate. Cross leaned over and kissed the top of my head.

"I have to meet with contractors, so I need to get going," he said. "Please be safe at the market. If you want my company, I can meet up with you there."

"I'll be fine."

With one last kiss, Cross left, and I relaxed.

Once I finished my breakfast, I climbed out of bed, grabbed my clothes, and closed myself in the bathroom. Vena was awake and waiting when I walked out. She gave my "fifty percent sugar and fifty percent sass" t-shirt a once over, grinned at me, then claimed the bathroom.

Doc stood at the sink when I walked into the kitchen with my plate.

"Did you eat the cinnamon roll or toss it?" I asked.

Doc frowned. "I ate it. It was really good."

I chuckled and washed my plate.

"Are you really going to the Shadow Trade market today?" he asked.

"Yes. Like I said to Cross, I need my charm charged, and it will be a great way to get ideas for the bakery. I have so many ideas already, but I know tastes vary and want to have a wide selection so that, no matter who walks in, they can at least find one thing they'll like."

I grabbed my shoulder bag and placed my small purse, a note-book, and a pen inside.

Vena entered the kitchen, sniffing notably.

"Why does this place smell like cinnamon? Where's the food?"

Doc pointed to a box on the counter. "From Cross."

Vena opened the box with a squeal. "He really does love me."

"Who loves you?" Anchor asked, appearing in the doorway.

Vena held up the cinnamon roll. "Cross."

Anchor made a disgruntled noise, which made Vena giggle.

Vena giggled?

"Let's go," I said. "The earlier we go to the market, the fewer people there will be."

CHAPTER FOURTEEN

VENA HAD BEEN RIGHT ABOUT THE DWARVES BEING OUT IN FORCE. They milled around the market, speaking with the vendors and shoppers alike. I overheard one asking about a black cat and another about missing people. The way they asked, using a tone I didn't associate with dwarves, bordered on rude. But then, my experience was limited to serving drinks at Blur and my very brief stay in the mountain.

I followed along behind Vena, aware of Anchor's towering presence behind me. He'd said he would be able to keep an eye on both of us that way.

The crowded market didn't make it easy to follow her when it was just the two of us. But with Anchor, things were different. People saw him and tended to move out of the way. It didn't make sense until I glanced back at him and caught his fierce scowl.

Shaking my head, I let my gaze wander the immediate area and caught a man watching me. I smiled politely and averted my gaze.

Anchor needed to stop drawing so much attention.

When Vena stopped at a table to ask about a locator charm, I glanced at Anchor.

"What is she planning to do with a locator charm?" I asked.

"Check every black cat in D.C."

I cringed.

"It's not a bad idea," he said. "She already promised to only go with me."

I nodded as Vena spoke to the vendor.

A stall one spot beyond where Vena had stopped drew my attention. Or, more specifically, the vial of glittery fairy dust on the table did.

"I'm going to go look at the next vendor's stuff," I said.

Anchor grunted his acknowledgment, and I stuck my hand into my bag to pull out my notebook as I approached.

"Hi," I said to the woman with the nubby horns on her head. "I'm wondering what that is." I indicated the vial and listened as she explained the substance was made of dew, sunlight, and a nymph's kiss. The contents were often used in spells.

"Is it edible?" I asked.

She gave me a curious look. "You want to eat it? Never heard that one. It's expensive and probably doesn't taste like much."

"It won't hurt humans or any of the races, though?"

She frowned in thought. "I don't think so, but I don't know of anyone who's eaten it."

I made a note to research more about the ingredients. It would be fun to make Fairy Trash with safe "magical" dust. Everyone loved novelty foods.

"Do you always have it in stock?" I asked.

We talked supply and price, which I wrote down before I thanked her and returned to Anchor's side. Vena had already made her purchase and was on to another stall. My gaze locked with the vendor at the table he was standing next to. It was all the invitation the goblin needed to start chatting me up.

After our run-in with Spawn when Miles had gone missing, I wasn't a fan of goblins in general. Their sharp teeth were a little freaky, which was a little ironic since Shepard and Cross could both have sharp teeth when their moods shifted, but neither one ever freaked me out.

While lost in my thoughts, the goblin handed me a flier.

"Thanks," I said just as Vena grabbed my arm to pull me away.

She plucked the pamphlet from my fingers and looked at it.

"Why does this look familiar?" she asked. Her expression immediately lit up. "Miles' place. I saw one just like it." She opened it up, and I saw it was filled with vampire propaganda, including a meetup place for people who were interested in learning more about vampires.

I glanced at Anchor. "Does Shepard know about this?"

"Later," Anchor said softly, his gaze not on us or the pamphlet.

We followed the direction of his attention and saw a dwarf arguing with a tall, beautiful woman running a vendor booth filled with jewelry.

"What's wrong?" I asked.

As soon as the words left my mouth, the dwarf's voice boomed loud enough for me to hear.

"I don't give a flying fairy's arse about neutrality. Answer my question, or I will drag you from this market by your lying silky hair, ye fang-loving whore."

The woman's creamy face flushed with her anger, and I watched the ends of her "lying silky hair" start to lift as if electrified.

Anchor swore under his breath.

"Be it once or a thousand times, it will not work, just as my attempts to speak the truth will never reach your deaf ears."

Anchor moved incredibly fast. Just as she finished speaking and pointed at the dwarf, Anchor stepped between them.

The air seemed to vacuum in and out again in a mini explosion that moved my hair and made my ears pop. I lifted my hands to rub my ears and bumped the man standing next to me, but I barely noticed as Anchor staggered back a step and met the woman's horrified gaze.

"There is a pact in the market," Anchor said. "Do no harm."

"I haven't," she said quickly. "Not truly. You'll be fine."

Vena bolted to Anchor's side, and I hurried to follow.

"What was that?" Vena demanded. "What did you do to him?"

The woman grabbed Vena's hand, holding it with a pleading expression. "Nothing that can't be undone with time and patience. Your boyfriend won't be able to–" She cleared her throat and gave Vena an apologetic look. "The spell will wane with each attempt and fade completely after one thousand."

Vena stared in horror at the woman.

I glanced at Anchor and saw his shock, then his slow smile, which he quickly covered when Vena turned to look at him.

"It'll be okay," he said quickly, pulling her to his side. "No harm done. She didn't break the pact."

"Screw the pact; she broke your lick stick!"

I hoped everyone around us heard lipstick.

"Only temporarily," Anchor said.

"Maybe we should take this outside," I said, very aware we were still the center of attention.

Vena's head whipped back to the woman.

"Undo it."

"I apologize. I cannot. Once cast, the spell is set."

Vena's look grew calculating. "Then we demand compensation for the pain and suffering we'll both endure until the spell's broken."

The woman nodded. "Name your price."

"Information on a vampire that can turn into a cat."

The woman laughed. "Everyone is looking for that, and no one knows."

"Then find out. You have twenty-four hours. Then, I'm reporting you."

"For what? I didn't harm–"

"He's a werewolf who was about to claim his mate. With *the Other House's* popularity, you can bet the media would love hearing about how a fae abused a werewolf."

I could see the woman wasn't buying Vena's bluff. Werewolves didn't do media exposure on purpose.

"And the Alpha won't be happy about an altercation in the market," I said.

"Very well. You have my word that I will exhaust all my resources in an attempt to find the information you want. However, I make no guarantees that I will discover anything, only that I will spare no effort."

"Deal," Vena said, handing over her phone. "Give me your number."

While they exchanged information, I shoved my notebook into my bag and pulled out my phone for the contact Cross had sent me, wanting to get out of there as quickly as possible.

Shocked at what I was seeing, I glanced between my phone and the woman's stall sign. Cross' contact was the same woman who had whammied Anchor's joystick. I cringed inside.

As Anchor shooed the dwarf away, I asked her, "Are you Asherah?"

Her eyes sparkled with leftover magic as she turned her gaze on me. "I am."

"A friend gave me your name. He said you could help me recharge my charm."

A smile replaced the scowl she had been wearing.

"You must be Everly," she said.

She beckoned me into her stall, which was filled with the most fascinating jewelry I had ever seen as Vena and Anchor remained in the main aisle.

As she walked around the counter, I took off my necklace and handed it to her.

She looked at it and tsked. "You bought that from Maude, didn't you?"

"I did."

"Never buy from her again. Her designs are uninspired, and she can barely wield the magic needed for protection spells. It's no wonder it fizzled out on you."

Maude was also more affordable than Asherah, based on the prices of some of the pieces I saw.

"I normally wear the charm under my clothes," I said. "So I'm fine with the design, and it really did work. I just let it run out."

Ignoring what I'd said, Asherah removed a beautiful box from under the counter. It was the size of two decks of cards stacked together and adorned with a silver weave with ruby and diamond petals.

She opened it, revealing a new necklace with the same design of silver, rubies, and diamonds. It was gorgeous and probably ridiculously priced.

Asherah smiled and pushed the box toward me. "It's got a full-spectrum protection spell on it with an additional booster to send would-be attackers on their way. And this box will recharge your necklace for you.

"Eventually, you will need to bring it back to me for a full recharge. But it will take years for that to happen."

"It's beautiful, and I love the charging box, but I doubt I can afford this."

She laughed again. "Who needs to afford anything when you have Cross as your lover?"

My cheeks heated, and Asherah breathed in deeply.

"Mmm. That's too much unsatiated passion for him to be your lover...yet. But don't concern yourself. Cross already sent payment for this set. It's a gift. He wanted the best, and this is the best."

She reached over and put the necklace on me.

I touched the charm nestled just above my cleavage and felt the buzz of energy. The spell was much stronger than on my previous necklace.

"Gorgeous," she said, stepping back. "I knew it would be. Cross has impeccable taste." Her gaze swept over *all* of me. "Impeccable."

She grabbed my old necklace and tossed it into a bin then placed the box in a gift bag, which she handed me.

"It might be best if you take your friend home before she attempts to use the scrying charm. It's more effective in a quiet place."

I glanced at Vena and saw she was dangling a charm over her phone.

"Thank you. For the warning and the necklace."

Even though Vena was preoccupied, she spotted my necklace right away when I exited the stall. "Someone spent some serious money."

"Cross bought it."

She snorted. "Shepard is going to love the rubies when he sees them."

I looked down at the necklace again and realized that I hadn't even thought about Cross having the ruby ring while Shepard had the sapphire ring. Cross had basically branded me.

But the necklace was pretty, and I could hardly be upset that he picked out something that reflected a bit of himself.

As we walked to the car, I texted Cross.

**Me: Just saw Asherah. She gave me a necklace and
charging box and said it was a gift from you. Are these
really diamonds and rubies? If so, is this necklace going
to protect me from human thieves?
Cross: They are real. I would never spend money on
paste jewelry for you. And don't worry about thieves.
The necklace will repel theft too.
Me: It's that powerful?
Cross: Asherah is that powerful.**

I cringed a little, thinking of the spell Anchor had intercepted and how Vena had confronted her. Good thing they'd settled amiably.

Me: More powerful than Master?
Cross: He is very powerful as well. But the necklace will still keep him at bay for a time.

My stomach churned at the thought of ever having to face Master again, and I hoped the necklace's strength would never have to be tested.

Me: Thank you for the gift.
Cross: My pleasure. If you're free later, come to the bakery and see the updates.

"As soon as we deal with Master, we'll deal with you, okay?" Vena said.

I looked up and saw we'd reached the car, and she was holding Anchor's hand.

"Waiting won't change how I feel, Vena."

But waiting wasn't something Vena did well.

"Your poor zipper ripper, though," Vena complained. "One thousand attempts is going to take time. I bet I can get rid of the curse in ten days once we start."

He groaned.

AT HOME, Vena's emotions fluctuated between outrage and determination as she attempted to use the scrying charm on her phone's map.

"It's not working."

"The vendor said you needed a calm state of mind to use it," Anchor said.

She tossed the charm to the couch cushion beside her.

"Well, it's not calm. It's annoyed. Why do my parents want to have dinner with us tonight?"

"Maybe because they just found out you're dating a werewolf and are insanely excited during an otherwise emotionally turbulent time?" I said dryly.

She wrinkled her nose at me then turned to Anchor.

"Do you know what would help calm me?"

The purr in her voice had me bolting to my feet.

"I'm headed to Cross' place," I said.

I had my keys in hand and was out the door before either could say anything more. The elderly man across the street was walking away in front of our house with his granddaughter as I left. She looked at me and waved. I waved back. Her grandfather didn't acknowledge me as I got into the car, but I was used to that.

Cross was waiting for me on the sidewalk outside the bakery when I pulled into the parking lot.

"Is this some kind of sixth sense thing, or did Vena tell you I was on my way?" I asked as he opened the door for me.

"Both," he said. "She sent a message, but I can feel when you're near, too."

"Handy," I said.

He escorted me inside, and I looked around at the changes. The broken bits of wall were gone, exposing some of the exterior brick. Skeleton walls made up of boards were being installed by some workers while other workers were running wires and metal tubes through finished sections of skeleton walls.

"Impressive," I said. "It's moving faster than I thought."

"I'm paying for speed."

"Speaking of paying, thank you for the necklace," I said again, touching the gems I'd purposely not tucked away. "I think it probably cost you more than I'm comfortable with you spending on me, though. Especially when you're already paying for all of this."

He gently pulled me into his arms.

"There is no need to worry about what's been spent. Once this place is established, I will earn more."

His soft brown gaze held mine, both reassuring and alluring.

"Okay, but please don't do something like that again without talking to me first. A plain necklace that's powerfully spelled is more practical than this one."

"I disagree. Rubies have inherent protective qualities, which make that necklace stronger." He pressed a finger to my lips when I would have said something. "However, I promise to discuss with you any future purchases that will affect you."

I nipped his fingertip and thanked him.

His eyes went full black.

Capturing his face, I brought his closer to mine and let my nose brush his as our mouths remained scant inches apart.

"Your eyes," I said softly.

He closed them. "I like the playful version of you, Everly. Very much."

Smiling softly, I brushed my lips against his.

"You say that now. Wait until I start something I can't finish."

He chuckled and groaned at the same time.

"I look forward to the experience."

CHAPTER FIFTEEN

CROSS HELD OUT THE CHAIR FOR ME THEN PLACED MY NAPKIN ON my lap before he claimed his seat.

"When you said lunch, I didn't think you meant this fancy, or I would have changed clothes," I said.

He flashed a smile at me.

"You're beautiful the way you are. If it makes you more comfortable, think of this as research. I heard the chef was a nymph and thought you'd like to sample the food."

Nymphs weren't very common at all, and I was curious what a nymph would serve.

My phone buzzed with an incoming text.

Shepard: I see you're at Muschi. Are you alone?
Me: No. I'm with Cross. How is the fae debriefing going?
Shepard: Not as well as I'd hoped. Anchor said you had gone to Cross' place, but when I saw you at the restaurant, I worried. Please stay with him or me.
Me: I will.

"Shepard?" Cross asked as I put my phone down.

I nodded. "He was worried I was alone."

Cross nodded and handed me a menu that was not in any language I had ever seen.

"Can you read this?" I asked.

"I'm a bit rusty in old fae, but I can manage."

"Then you'll have to order for me."

"How about a little of everything?"

"Maybe not everything. Pick the top five you think I'd like."

He ordered five appetizers, each of their soups, and five main meals. All in flawless, at least to me, old fae.

"How many languages do you know?" I asked after the server left.

"A few. Before English became a widely used language, traveling was often difficult. Using local guides was a necessity I often found difficult. So I vowed to learn the language of every country I visited."

"How many countries have you visited?"

"Sadly, only a dozen. But I hope that will change in the future." The way he looked at me said I could hop aboard the Cross Express and travel the world with him if I wanted to. The thought of exploring new places and eating new foods was tempting.

To prepare for the food's arrival, I dug into my bag for my notebook and a pen.

"I'll need the English equivalent name for these foods," I said as I placed the notebook on the table.

I saw a slip of paper poking out of it and looked at it.

Call this number if you want to know why a certain vampire won't die.

The number listed was in the D.C. area.

"What's wrong?" Cross asked.

I handed it to him. "I think I picked this up at the Shadow Trade market earlier today. There was a chaotic moment when Anchor stepped in to break up a fight. I bumped into someone who was standing really close to me. I think they slipped me this note.

"Every time we've gotten messages like this in the past, nothing good has happened."

"Agreed, but that was because you weren't confiding everything then. Let's call it together and find out what they want."

After looking around to ensure no one was sitting close by, I took out my phone and put the call on speaker.

A peppy female voice answered. "This is Amberly. How can I help you?"

"Hello, Amberly," Cross said smoothly. "I found your note about a vampire that won't die."

"You must be Everly's friend. Thank you for calling back so quickly. Yes, we have the information you want. Let's arrange a time to meet in person. Are you human? Non-human? What's your name?"

"Non-human. You can call me Cross."

I glanced from the phone to Cross when she didn't respond right away. He smiled softly.

"My employer has an opening in her schedule at 10 pm tonight," Amberly said without a hint of concern.

"And who is your employer?" Cross asked.

"Orphia Prince. I believe you're acquainted?"

"I am," Cross said. "And I'll decline the meeting on behalf of myself and Everly. Please tell Orphia to stop what she's doing. The rings aren't meant for her."

Cross disconnected the call and pocketed the note.

I was going to wait for him to explain, but the questions tumbled out unchecked.

"Who's Orphia? If you know her, why does she want to meet

with me? And what the heck did you mean the rings aren't meant for her? Are you saying she's the one who's been trying to get them, not Adriel?"

He chuckled and reached for my hand, playing with my fingers as he spoke.

"Orphia is a woman I mistakenly once viewed with affection. She is a vampire, but not like me. She has no wish to co-exist peacefully with any of the races. Her only desire is complete dominion over everything."

I captured his hand. "When you say you viewed her with affection, what does that mean? Ex-wife? Ex-lover? Master?"

"In her mind, perhaps all of those."

"And in yours?"

"An ex-lover."

He met and held my gaze, waiting for my reaction. However, I wasn't sure what reaction to give. Was I jealous of an ex-girl-friend who was working with someone like Adriel? Absolutely not. However, it definitely concerned me. But more concerning was the fact that Cross' apparently emotionally unstable ex wanted world domination.

"And the rings?" I asked. "Are those part of her world domina-tion plan?"

"Yes. I left England to escape her centuries ago when she'd made her interest in my ring known, which is why you found me in that cave."

"So you hid your ring, but what about the rest of them?"

"I have no control over the others. The rings—one for the vampires, one for the dwarves, one for the fey, and one for the werewolves—were never meant to be possessed by one person. Together, they could end the world we all know. However, without mine, her attaining the others would be useless."

He lifted my hand and kissed the back of it.

"Rather than allow Orphia to steal any more attention from our lunch date, I would prefer to focus on you. After we finish here, there's another cafe I wanted to take you to so we can review their aesthetics. The interior designer I'm working with called it a moody blend of modern and gothic. And after we look at the cafe, there's a baking supply store I wanted to take you to."

"All of that sounds amazing," I said.

He released my hand while I focused on the food's arrival, setting aside the problem of the rings and his crazy vampire ex for now.

While I sampled everything, Cross made notes for me. Once I was full and had sampled everything, he paid the bill, and we left.

"Thank you," I said as we walked to the car. "Some of those dishes were amazing."

And some were downright disgusting, but he already knew that from my reaction to tasting them.

"You are more than welcome, Everly. I hope it helps in your quest for the bakery."

"Understanding flavor preferences definitely helps."

We were still half a block away from my car when something dark darted out from under it.

I stared at the black cat in the middle of the sidewalk. It arched its neck, showing its sparkly collar, and Cross inhaled deeply. A second later, Cross and the cat were gone, and I was left alone.

Understanding Cross had taken off to chase Adriel, I grabbed my phone out of my purse to call Shepard.

"I wouldn't do that," a voice said from behind me.

I turned to look at a business-dressed man who didn't look well. His briefcase was open, and rumpled papers hung out of the dividers. But what really worried me was his slightly askew tie and the small spot of blood staining his collar.

"What do you want?" I asked, even as my thumb swiped the screen to unlock it.

"I have a message for you. Reconsider the meeting, or she will meet with someone else." He lifted his hand, and I retreated a quick step before seeing an actual printed photo in his hand.

My mom's smiling face as she looked at my grandma filled me with fear so intense I could barely breathe.

"Take it," he said.

With trembling fingers, I plucked my family free from his grasp.

"Call her back before it's too late."

He turned on his heel and walked away.

I lifted my phone and took three pictures of him. Then I took two long, calming breaths before sending his picture to Cross and Shepard.

Me: This guy might lead you to Adriel. He just threatened me with a photo of my family.

Cross was in front of me less than a minute later and hugged me.

"Forgive me, Everly," he said. "I shouldn't have left you alone."

"It's okay. I'm guessing you didn't catch him?"

"No. Adriel disappeared into the sewer just as I received your message."

Cross released me and pulled out his phone. Mine buzzed.

Cross: I have Everly. Stay focused on gaining the help we need. I'll coordinate with Doc to send your people out to guard Everly's family.

He sent another text I didn't receive then pocketed his phone and took my shaking hand in his.

"Doc will make sure they're safe."

"How? They already took a picture of my family, Cross. What if they're not there?" As I spoke, I found my mom's contact number. Cross stopped me.

"If you call them now and they are unaware, your current state will worry them."

He was right. I needed to be calmer, no matter what. I took several cleansing breaths before calling them on speaker.

My mom answered on the second ring.

"This is a surprise," she said. "Is Vena causing trouble again?"

Her easy-going voice relieved me, and I forced myself to smile.

"Always," I said. "She has a boyfriend now, though, so I don't think she'll be pulling me into her shenanigans for much longer."

"Nonsense. You two have been inseparable for over a decade. That's not going to change because of a man. What's he like? Do you like him?"

"I do. He's good with her. Hey, Mom, I was wondering if you've been watching the news lately."

"The news? Why?"

"There are a lot of people going missing, and I'm just worried about you guys."

"Oh, sweetie. You don't need to worry about us. Those people that are going missing are from the city. You need to keep yourself safe."

"I will. I promise. Does grandma still have that necklace that Vena gave her?"

"Of course. She never takes it off."

"Good. Make sure she doesn't. Give everyone my love."

"I will. Love you, too, sweetie."

Cross waited until I disconnected the call to ask, "What necklace?"

"After Vena's grandparents disappeared, she bought my grandma a tracking necklace. She didn't want me to lose my grandma like she lost hers."

Cross hugged me again. "That won't happen. Trust Shepard's people. They will keep your family safe."

His phone rang, and I listened to his one-sided conversation after he answered.

"Shepard knows what he's doing." Cross smiled briefly. "I've never thought otherwise. Thank your men for Everly and find a way to move them." He paused. "Agreed. They're unlikely to give up." He listened again. "Thank you."

He pocketed his phone and rubbed some warmth into my cold hands.

"Shepard had the forethought to have people watching your family since we left the mountain. The thralled humans who were watching your family have been removed, but to prevent this from happening again, Shepard's people are going to move your family temporarily. They'll win an all-expenses paid trip from the radio station your father favors. Expect another call from them soon."

I let out a shaky breath and nodded.

"Is there anyone else that Orphia might use against you?" he asked.

Vena's family was still safely tucked away at Shepard's complex, and Vena was with Anchor. Other than them and my family, there wasn't anyone nearby.

"Vena and I have friends from school, but they're backpacking in Europe this summer."

"I think they'll be fine then. Orphia won't expend unnecessary energy abroad."

He kissed my forehead.

"Are you willing to allow me to distract you for the rest of the day?"

"Please."

CROSS CARRIED the bags inside the new place like they weighed nothing, but I knew otherwise. He hadn't held back while shopping.

Construction crews were still on site even though it was getting late. They barely stopped working to swivel their heads in our direction to see who'd arrived.

"Let's set this in the storage area for now," he said. "Then I'll take you to dinner."

While he walked away, I looked around. The transformation was amazing, considering the short timeframe. All the walls, including the kitchen and bathroom walls, were there now, allowing me to visualize the space. More wires and plumbing were being added.

My phone buzzed with a message.

Mom: Our bags are all packed. I still can't believe your dad won. How crazy is this?

I smiled, recalling my mom's excited call hours ago when I'd been shopping with Cross. She'd shared that they'd "won" a two-week cruise for my parents and grandma. My mom was beyond excited since they both were self-employed and could leave immediately.

Me: I'm so excited for you. Please send me lots of pictures so I know you're having fun and are okay.

"Your parents?" Cross asked as he joined me.

"Yep. They're all packed and ready to go." I smiled at him. "Thank you for this."

"You're welcome. I hope your mind can be at ease now that they're safe. I want you to enjoy dinner." With a hand on my lower back, he led me from the building.

"Where are you taking me?"

"It's a surprise."

A short drive later, we arrived in front of one of the higher-end restaurants downtown that took reservations months in advance.

A valet opened my car door and took my car keys.

"Enjoy your evening," he said before he whisked off in my old car.

I looked at Cross. "Am I dressed okay for this place?"

He looked at our outfits, casual summer and hot vampire wear, and shook his head. "No. But I've reserved a private room. It doesn't matter what we wear."

"A private room? When did you reserve it?"

"When you were shopping earlier."

I shook my head. "How? This place takes months to get into."

"For some people, perhaps."

He led me to a side path accented with pretty twinkle lights. A man wearing a full tuxedo stood outside the entry and welcomed us as he opened the door to an entryway decorated in rich blues and silver. Another man, dressed in a matching tuxedo, asked us to follow him and led us down a hallway with four doors. He opened one on his right, and I stepped into a room twice the size of my bedroom. It had the same design as the entry and was lit with a chandelier over a long table set for two with white candles stationed along its length. A champagne bottle sat waiting in a silver bucket filled with ice.

The man pulled out the chair for me and pushed it in when I sat down. He then poured the champagne, filled our water glasses, announced that the first course would arrive soon, and left.

"Are there no menus?" I asked Cross.

"Not here. The chef prepares his signature dishes."

The idea intrigued me. A static menu would be nice for non-adventurous folks who stuck to what they liked. However, for foodies who got bored easily, I could offer a "baker's choice" selection that changed monthly or even daily. It would allow me to test new items to see what would stick and what might need to go—not just for the bakery but the dessert and drink pairings that Shepard was thinking of offering too.

"What are you thinking?" Cross asked.

I realized I was staring vacantly at him and grinned.

"Sorry. I liked the idea of signature dishes. We should try something like that at our place."

He reached across the table and took my hand. "Our place. I like the sound of that."

I knew how much he liked it when his eyes flickered with black. His soft smile, along with his darker eyes, did things to my libido.

"Even though I'm not ready to move in yet?" I asked.

"I have no reason to rush you, Everly. I have all the time to wait."

Hearing that made me sad. While I appreciated his patience, I also understood what he meant. He had no lifespan. At least, not a natural one. I was the one who was aging and had a time limit, which brought about another set of concerns.

"Have you ever lived with a human? For a lifetime, I mean."

Cross looked down at our joined hands and played with my fingers lightly.

"I've never wanted to until you," he said.

"What happens when I turn seventy?"

His gaze lifted and locked with mine. "I will hold your hand just like I am now and continue to love you for the rest of your life."

It was my turn to look away.

"I frightened you."

"No. You just gave me a lot to think about."

The door behind him opened, and Shepard strode in.

"What are we thinking about?" he asked.

CHAPTER SIXTEEN

CROSS SMILED AS SHEPARD TOOK THE EMPTY SEAT BESIDE ME.

"Everly is going to think about moving in with me."

My gaze ricocheted between Shepard and Cross. Was Cross purposely antagonizing Shepard? I thought they'd moved past that.

Neither one seemed upset, though.

Shepard simply nodded and leaned back in his chair.

"It makes sense she's thinking of future living arrangements now that Vena seems committed to Anchor. It won't be long before Everly is alone in that house, and that's not something either of us want. If she plans to run the bakery, which requires waking early, living above it would save her time in the mornings."

I couldn't believe what I was hearing.

"With those extra bedrooms you have, I wouldn't mind staying over too and getting away from everything myself from time to time."

The amused tilt to Cross' lips grew more pronounced.

"Extra rooms? I thought you and I could share."

I untangled my fingers from Cross' and stared at the pair, unsure what to think of the teasing.

The door opened again, and the server entered with an appetizer and another place setting for Shepard. When the door closed behind him, I was again the center of their attention.

"Not that I mind, but why are you here, Shepard? Did something happen?"

"I wanted to make sure you were all right. Doc arranged everything for your family so they'll be safe. They won't be alone, even on the ship. A mated pair is going as well, discreetly keeping an eye on them."

"Thank you. That makes me feel better. Can you afford to send any of your people away now, though?"

"The pair is expecting, so they don't mind leaving D.C. right now. And not having to watch your parents' home actually helps. I can reassign those people to search for the man who approached you earlier and to the market. I heard what happened this morning and how close you were to being hit by the spell."

"What spell?" Cross asked.

"Remember that chaotic moment I mentioned? Anchor stepped in to break up a fight between a dwarf and a woman who specialized in powerful protection charms,"—Cross nodded subtly that he understood who I was speaking of—"and got hit by a spell meant for the dwarf. I wasn't in any danger at all."

"What happened to Anchor?" Cross said.

"Nothing," I said, fighting not to flush. "He'll be fine."

"He's currently impotent," Shepard said. "According to Anchor, it will wear off after a certain number of…er, attempts."

I'd expected Cross to laugh because, truthfully, it was a little funny. But he wasn't laughing. He was staring at me with an expression that would have chilled me if I'd thought it was directed at me.

"You're overreacting," I said to Cross. "Even if the spell had hit me, it wouldn't have been a big deal."

Cross' eyes went completely black and stayed like that as his gaze shifted to Shepard.

"We agree that having Everly hit by that spell would have been devastating; however, the danger to her wasn't in the spell but in the moment's distraction." He withdrew the note from his pocket and handed it to Shepard. "She discovered this in her bag while having lunch with me."

Shepard took the note, saying nothing as he scanned the brief message.

"We called the number. An old acquaintance of mine, Orphia Prince, wanted to meet with Everly. We declined. When we left the restaurant, Adriel was there in his other form. I gave chase."

"And that was when the man appeared?" Shepard asked.

"Yes."

"So, who is behind all of this? Orphia or Adriel?" Shepard asked.

"Adriel follows Orphia. He's after the rings for her," Cross said.

The rings.

"I believe she'll continue trying to lure Everly to appear like she did when Adriel lured her to that club." Cross looked at me. "You cannot fall for her tricks. No matter who she uses or what she does. Do you understand?"

"Why me?"

Cross and Shepard shared a look before Shepard said, "She understands we would do anything to get you back.

"I'll let Anchor know about this slip-up," Shepard said, pocketing the note. "I'll also ensure he isn't the only one keeping watch over Everly and Vena."

Uncomfortable with the current mood, I quickly changed topics.

"How did your meeting with the fae go?"

Shepard flushed and tugged at his earlobe. Cross chuckled.

"What? Why are you laughing?"

"Do you recall Shepard's call on the way to the mountain?" Cross asked. "He had to meet with the fae queen, who has long lusted after your Alpha."

My Alpha? I glanced at Shepard, noting the increasing color in his face.

"Was she too handsy?" I asked.

Cross' laugh echoed in the room. The door opened behind him before either of them answered, and the server delivered the first course.

Once he was gone, I waited expectantly for one of them to clue me in.

"I'm betting it wasn't only her hands he had to fend off," Cross said.

"I'm sorry you had to go through that, Shepard. I know what unwanted attention feels like." Both shot me a worried look. "I meant serving at Blur."

"Ah. Yeah, it was uncomfortable, but at least, she listened to the problem and acknowledged that the vampires need to be stopped. However, she isn't convinced that the problem is serious enough to break their neutrality yet."

Cross tapped his fingers on the table as he gazed at the food.

"Fools," he said before sighing and looking at me. "Let's focus on dinner. The rest can wait until later."

It turned out to be a nine-course meal. Each course was paired with a wine, and even though each serving was appropriately sized smaller, I was full by the last dish.

The waiter arrived with the bill.

"I think it's time to get you back home." Shepard stood and held out his hand to help me stand.

"Thank you both for everything today," I said.

"It's my pleasure. Always," Cross said. He looked at Shepard. "Less pleasurable with you, but we can work on that."

"But it was a pleasure for me, Cross," he said as he walked me out the door, leaving Cross with the bill.

I heard Cross' low chuckle trail after us, and Shepard grinned. Once we were outside, we waited for our vehicles.

"With everything that's happened today, I've asked Vena to pack you a bag and bring it with her to the complex," he said. "It would be safer for you both to avoid your house for a while."

"Does that mean we're imposing on your personal space again?"

"It's never an imposition to have you there, Everly. Since Vena's parents are already there, I believe Vena will stay with them."

If her mom had anything to say, Vena would be sharing a room with Anchor, but I didn't say that.

Shepard followed me in his SUV, and we reached his complex in no time. The lights were still on in the massive building as we parked near the front entry door. Six kids ran out of the building, carrying nets and jars.

"What are you hunting?" Shepard asked as we approached.

"Fireflies."

"And what will you do with them after?"

"Release them. Mom said I couldn't use them as nightlights."

Shepard tousled the boy's scruffy brown hair. "We protect, not harm."

"I know."

"Good. Have fun with the others. But stay near the house and guards."

Only when Shepard said "guards" did I notice men stationed around the house.

When the boys ran off, I asked, "You didn't use to have guards outside, did you?"

"No. With the current situation, I want to ensure we keep an eye on the pack."

"And the kids are safe out here?"

"There are men stationed out in the woods, too." Shepard took my hand and walked me inside. "Even though we're not in an ideal situation, it's important for kids to still be kids. Until something makes that change, I'll give them as much freedom as possible while still ensuring their safety."

We walked through the entryway, and the woman behind the reception desk, off to the side, gave us a curious but friendly glance as we passed. The halls were fairly quiet as we navigated our way to Shepard's suite.

From staying with him before, I knew the room was broken into two sections with a living area and a small kitchenette. On either side of the living room was a door—a guest room and the master suite. Shepard's room also had a private patio overlooking the wooded park.

It was like being at a resort.

"Make yourself at home," Shepard said. "I'll get your bag from Vena."

Alone, I brushed my teeth with a new toothbrush waiting on the counter then showered.

When I emerged, wrapped in a towel, Shepard stood in the bedroom. His hand fisted the bag he held as his gaze swept over me. Fine tremors ran through him.

Thoughts from the last time I'd seen his control fray collided with my normally sensible thoughts. I liked that I made him struggle.

"Nice necklace," he said.

I touched the gems, unsure what to say, and watched him inhale deeply.

"You're worried I don't like that he gave you something. Don't worry. I'll never deny you the protection you need, Everly. Even if it's from him."

Shepard closed the distance between us and caught me up in his arms. Holding me, he kissed my damp neck lightly, adding the scrape of his teeth. "Just...please don't pull away from me."

I wrapped my arms around his waist and let myself melt into

his hold. He growled against my skin but didn't press for anything more than simply holding me.

"I'm not pulling away from you, Shepard. Dating two people is new to me, and I don't want anyone hurt."

He released his hold around me to smooth back the wet hair from my face. "Is that what we're doing, Everly? Dating?"

My stomach dipped. "Isn't it?"

His slow smile melted my insides. "I hope so."

He kissed me tenderly. It stole my breath and made me want to hop up and wrap my legs around his waist.

When he broke away to look at me again, I exhaled shakily.

"I think I need to understand your boundaries, Shepard. I don't want to accidentally do anything that would lead you to believe I'm ready to be mated to you. Is the line sex, or is it before that?"

He swallowed hard, and I watched his eyes change from grey to gold.

"Are you asking because of Cross, or are you not yet ready to commit to any relationship?"

I thought about it. The idea of a solid relationship wasn't off-putting. Maybe because I found someone worth liking. As soon as I had that thought, I knew it was right. Yet it wasn't a single someone but two of them.

"It's about Cross. I like you both," I said.

Shepard let out a long breath and smiled slightly.

"I need you to translate your reaction for me," I said.

"I can handle that you want Cross, too. It's the idea that you're not yet ready to settle down and want to date other men..." Another tremor ran through him. "I think we've progressed too far for me to handle that well."

"But you're fine with me seeing Cross?"

"Playing nice with him to be with you isn't a sacrifice. It would never work if he were like the rest of his kind. But he's different and keeps you safe when I can't. So I'm willing to make him the exception."

His sincerity burned through me, and I rose to my toes to brush my lips against his.

"So what does that mean exactly for the line? Is it at third base or second?"

"There is no line," he said roughly before kissing me hungrily.

All my teasing thoughts fell away under his barely-checked aggression. His hands roamed under my towel, along my sides, igniting my need for more. I tugged at his shirt until my fingers slipped under to tease over his sides in return.

He growled and picked me up without breaking the kiss.

My back pressed into a mattress, and I wrapped my legs around his waist. It had the opposite effect than I'd been hoping for.

He broke off the kiss and looked down at me.

"You're addictive, Everly. I understand what you want and will do my best to respect it." He kissed the tip of my nose. "Change. I'm going to shower and cool off."

He left me, and only after I listened to the door close did I try sitting up. The towel had come loose and needed an arm to keep it pinned in place. I didn't have to worry, though. The bag he'd brought was right next to me.

On *Shepard's* bed.

I opened it and found the silky nightgown. While I didn't mind the nightgown, I noticed Vena hadn't provided underwear, and the length of the pajamas would probably just barely cover my backside.

Whatever. It wasn't like I was doing anything but getting under the covers. Tossing the towel aside, I put on the nightgown and climbed into bed.

I woke up hot, sweaty, and cocooned tightly. It wasn't the blankets restricting my movements but two arms that criss-crossed over my stomach. One was heavier than the other. I followed those arms to the men on either side of me.

Shepard was turned toward me. His exhales tickled my neck.

On the other side, Cross faced me as well. However, he wasn't sleeping. When our gazes connected, he saw my disbelief and smiled at me.

"How did you get in here?" I whispered, not wanting to wake Shepard for Cross' sake.

"Not even a pack of wolves could keep me from reaching you." He pressed a kiss against my temple. "And being in bed with a sleeping wolf is icing on the cake."

I couldn't believe Cross. Part of me wanted to laugh. The other part was freaking out that Shepard would wake up.

"I can hear you," Shepard mumbled, sounding more bored than angry. "You're not as quiet as you think you are."

"Quiet enough not to rouse your pack," Cross said. "Speaking of arousing, your sleeping heart rate is quite high this morning. You like me in your bed, don't you…"

Cross' arm moved to pet Shepard's hip through the blanket. Shepard's eyes snapped open, and he shoved Cross' hand away.

"Find your own bed."

"I'm willing to share mine if you share yours." Cross wiggled his eyebrows.

Shepard rolled his eyes before shoving him from the bed. "Go, or I'll call the guards."

Cross stood and leaned in to kiss my neck. "I hope the next time I'm in bed with you, you'll skip the underwear again, Everly."

"Run fast," Shepard said then whistled sharply.

Cross chuckled and blurred out the patio doors.

"Is he going to be okay?"

"Yes. Everyone knows not to kill him."

"Not to kill, but what about harm?"

"He'll recover quickly." At my concerned expression, Shepard smiled. "He'll be fine. What are you hungry for this morning?"

CHAPTER SEVENTEEN

WHEN WE ARRIVED IN THE MAIN DINING HALL, THE HUNTERS, Vena, and Anchor were still there. So were Gunther and another man, but they sat at another table farther away. Otherwise, the room was empty.

Based on the Hunters' empty breakfast plates and Vena's tortured expression, I knew they'd been there a while, and she needed a break from her boyfriend's interrogation.

"Hi, Mr. and Mrs. Hunter. How's Miles?" I asked as I joined them.

"As well as can be expected," Mr. Hunter said. "He's eating and drinking but angry about his forced captivity. He keeps asking about my parents' research and the book they'd found before their disappearance."

The same book Vena and I had found hidden at their house.

"He's nicer to us than the other people here," Mrs. Hunter added.

"As soon as the vampire controlling him is dead, he'll be back to normal," Vena said. We all knew that was a lie, though. He would never be the same again once he realized what Adriel made him do.

Shepard sat beside me and passed me a plate with eggs, bacon, and toast. I dug in.

"Any progress in finding the vampire?" Mr. Hunter asked, looking at Shepard.

"Unfortunately, no. I have men out, night and day, searching. Adriel's scent is familiar to some of them, and it's helped pick up a trail here and there, but they always end abruptly."

"If he's a cat, he can jump and climb," Vena said. "Are they looking on top of buildings, too?"

"And the sewers," I said after swallowing my bite of food. "Cross mentioned he went down one yesterday."

"You saw him yesterday?" Vena said with an edge in her voice.

"Yeah. He used himself as a distraction to get me alone so one of his minions could tell me I needed to meet up with Cross' ex." It was simpler to say she was his ex in front of the Hunters than to admit she was an evil vampire after all the rings. After all, I wasn't sure how much Shepard and Cross wanted to share about them.

"His ex? The same one who'd sent your look-alike to our house as a gift to Cross?"

"I guess." I'd forgotten about that.

"Ew. Why does she want to meet up with you?"

"She wants to use Everly as bait to force Cross to give her what she wants," Shepard said.

"His ring?" Mr. Hunter asked, proving why the Hunters were so successful at tracking down information.

"Yes," Shepard said after a moment. "It seems Adriel is working for her."

"Damn," Vena breathed.

My phone buzzed with a message. Thinking it might be Cross, I checked it and found a text and video from the number on the note.

Amberly: Stop searching for answers you don't need.
The only solution is to meet with Orphia.

The video was dark when it started, but then a hand moved away from the lens.

A woman wearing white pants and a flowy top lay on a bed. Her hands and ankles were bound, and a black ball gag covered her mouth as she struggled against the two men pinning her.

I couldn't see their faces, which were buried against her neck. But I knew them. The black leather clothes. The sparkling collar. The cat ears.

Her muffled screams silenced the conversation at the table.

"Ev?" Vena said.

I watched Pet lift his head and turned to look at the camera. His lips were red, smeared with blood. Master lifted his head and grabbed Pet's face, kissing him passionately over the woman whose screams turned into a moan.

Shepard took the phone from me.

"Everly," Vena said, waving a hand at me. "What was it?"

"A message from Cross' ex," I said shakily. "It said to stop looking for answers we don't need and to meet with her. The fae woman from the market won't be calling you back with information."

"What?"

Vena grabbed the phone from Shepard and swore under her breath as she watched.

Shepard dialed his phone and stood abruptly to move a few steps from the table.

"We have a problem," Shepard said. "No. Focus, Effora. The vampire we're looking for has taken one of yours." He paused, listening to whatever the fae queen had to say. "I'll send you the video, and you can decide for yourself if you're still neutral."

He hung up the phone just as Vena finished the video.

"This just proves we're moving in the right direction," she

said. "My scrying stone is working. I can locate all the black cats within a three-city block radius of where I'm scrying. It's not ideal, but it's something. Anchor and I can go out and keep looking."

"I'll join you," Gunther said, standing. "It's better to go out in pairs."

"He's right," Anchor said. "I was distracted at the market, and that's how the note got into Everly's bag."

"That's not your fault," Vena said, passing my phone to Shepard so he could send the video to himself.

"I'll meet you out front," Gunther said to Anchor, leaving with the other guy.

Vena nodded and frowned at me. "I thought Asherah was crazy powerful. How did they get her?"

"According to the queen, fae and vampire 'relations' aren't uncommon," Shepard said. "She thinks it's consensual."

"That did *not* look consensual," I said.

"I agree." He handed me back my phone then wrapped an arm around my shoulders, comforting me.

"The woman in the video, Asherah, was supposed to be looking for information on Adriel," I said to Mrs. Hunter. "I think that's why they took her."

"We need to know how to kill him," Vena said, "Or finding him won't do us any good."

"Then while you and Anchor are out scrying, we'll do what we do best and start researching," Mr. Hunter said.

"But we'll need our laptops and a few other things from home," Mrs. Hunter said. She turned to Shepard. "Is it safe for us to go?"

"Without knowing where Adriel is, nowhere is safe right now," Shepard said. "Until this matter is resolved, the safest place for you and your family is here. Since Everly needs to pack for a longer stay, too, I'll take her home, and then we'll run to your place to pick up what you need."

They agreed, and while Mrs. Hunter started a list of what they'd need, Shepard and I left. Gunther nodded to us on our way out to the parking lot. When we sat in his SUV, he sent a message to Cross, asking him to meet at my place.

I smiled.

"What?"

"Nothing. I just like that you didn't pull one of your guys and asked Cross instead."

"He's useful, especially when it comes to you. And I'll always keep my word."

He started the SUV and took my hand once he was headed down the tree-lined drive. The ride was quiet with both of us lost in our thoughts until he parked in front of my house.

He paused before getting out and watched Cross and the neighbor girl, Harper, play catch on the sidewalk. Although she and her cranky grandpa lived across the street, I didn't interact with her often. Still, she was a cute kid, maybe six years old.

She waved at us when she saw me, all smiles and teeth.

I glanced from Cross to Shepard and saw he was still staring.

"You okay?"

"He keeps surprising me."

With a grin, I hopped out and met Cross and Harper.

"Can you play hide and seek with me today?" she asked me. "Grandpa keeps wheezing cuz of his allergies."

"I'm sorry. I can't today. I'm actually here to pick up a few things and leave."

"Where are you going?"

"A friend's house."

She looked from me to Shepard, who seemed even larger next to the girl.

"Is that your friend?" she asked.

"Yep."

"I'm her best friend," Cross said.

"Naw. That's Vena," Harper said, still eyeing Shepard. "I don't think you'd be good at hide and seek."

"Why not?" he asked.

"You're too big. You won't fit anywhere."

He nodded. "True, but I'm excellent at finding people. When we have time, we'll play."

Her eyes lit. "Really?"

"Really. But for today, why don't you go back to your grandpa's house."

"Only if you promise to come back and play."

"I promise, but it'll be a few days before I can."

"Fine," she said with a sigh.

We watched to make sure she went into her grandpa's house okay before going into mine.

Grabbing my largest suitcase, I filled it with everything I thought I'd need for a week, including my recipe notebook and favorite whisk.

"I don't think you need that," Shepard said, eyeing the whisk.

"Maybe not, but I have room in my suitcase. I'm a stress baker if you don't know this about me. It's my happy place. Some people have a hoodie or blanket that comforts them. I just need a kitchen and my whisk."

"Then, by all means, bring the whisk. Ready to go?"

I took one last look around the house and nodded.

Shepard loaded my suitcase into the back of the SUV while Cross and I got in.

I swiveled in my seat to look back at Cross. "What were you doing when Shepard messaged you?"

"Checking in with the project manager at our place. Since I spent last night looking for Adriel, and I knew today would likely be more of the same, I stopped by in person.

"It's really taking shape. The inspectors approved the rough-in work, and they're ready to move on to drywall while the

HVAC people finish on the roof. So we're on track to have the appliances delivered and installed on Saturday."

The news was exciting and the only ray of sunshine in an otherwise rather bleak week.

As Shepard got in and started the engine, my phone buzzed with a message.

Mrs. Hunter: Here's the list of what we need. If you can't find something, call me.

"Who is it?" Shepard asked as I scanned the list.

"Mrs. Hunter. She sent a list."

She wanted books, their laptops, Mr. Hunter's slippers, her housecoat and lap blanket, his spare reading glasses, her coffee cup warmer…the list went on.

Shepard and Cross both glanced at it over my shoulder.

"Do they normally pack like that when they go on their excavations?" Shepard asked.

"No. They're minimalists when they're in the field, but when researching at home, they have their comforts. It drives Vena nuts because they tend not to sleep much when they fall into a research rabbit hole. She worries about their health." I didn't add that Vena's worry started after her grandparents had disappeared.

When we reached the Hunters' place, I decided "divide and conquer" was the only way to go.

"Cross, would you mind getting the books while I get the rest of the stuff?"

He agreed, and I jogged up the stairs to collect the other items. Shepard trailed behind me, holding everything I found as I went. When we returned downstairs for the coffee warmer and slippers in the study, Cross was sitting in the reading chair, flipping through the pages of a familiar book.

"What are you doing?" I asked.

"Checking to see if there's anything useful," he said.

"What is that?" Shepard asked.

"The book that Cross helped Vena and me find. The book that Miles has been asking for. It mentioned the stones your rings are made out of. Vena and I read it. It's just a bunch of old stories about encounters between humans and otherworlders.

"It was what Vena's grandparents were researching when they disappeared. We're not sure why, but they hid it."

"You're right that it doesn't seem to hold anything useful. Yet, it does seem important. It's best to return it to his hiding place then." Cross slipped it back into the hidden desk compartment.

Thankfully, Mrs. Hunter hadn't asked for the gemstones book or that awful scrotum map, which was also hidden in the desk compartment.

Shepard's phone rang. He handed his pile of supplies to Cross and briefly looked at the number before answering on speaker.

"How can I help you, Effora?"

"I could think of several ways we could help each other. Perhaps you'd be more interested if I looked like a certain little blon—"

"If you don't have anything useful to say, I need to go."

The flush staining his cheeks was adorable.

"So impatient. I love it," the fae queen purred. "I was just calling to say that I've spoken to Asherah, and she's fine. A little love play, as I suggested. And before you ask, yes, I inquired about Adriel's whereabouts. She couldn't say, though."

Shepard's flush increased, but based on his expression, I doubted it was due to embarrassment this time.

"Effora, they targeted Asherah because she was trying to help us locate Adriel."

"And I find that fair. We've promised to stay neutral, after all. They were decent enough to ensure she had a good time being taken by them."

"I want to talk to her."

"Excellent. Come to my place tonight. You can talk to me first; then we can all have a chat."

Shepard surprised me by hanging up on her. I glanced at Cross. He wasn't smirking as usual, though.

"She's good at mind games. Don't let her get to you," he said to Shepard.

"I don't care about the mind games. I care that she's purposely avoiding choosing sides even at the expense of her own people's safety."

"I've already tried reaching out to Asherah and haven't heard back from her yet." He rapid-fired a text and looked at both of us. "I've asked my people watching the Shadow Trade to let me know if they hear anything about Asherah. If she's fine as the Queen says, she'll be back soon."

He pocketed his phone and took back the items from Cross. "Do we have everything?"

After double-checking the list, I nodded, and we left.

When we were back on the road, I noticed Shepard tapping on the steering wheel.

"Cookie for your thoughts," I said.

He glanced over briefly. "I thought it was a penny for your thoughts."

"I like cookies better. What's on your mind?"

"Safety. I have extra guards around the complex but haven't made any changes at Blur. Since Adriel and Orphia are getting more aggressive, I think it's best if you don't go to work tonight. You'll be safer at my place."

"I'll be safe at Blur, too. Your staff is already ninety percent wolves, and I don't want to stay at home while everyone else is doing their part. I can at least make sure you're not short-staffed at work by being there."

"You forget that Blur has already been attacked once. It could happen again."

"I didn't forget. It was attacked by vampire minions, not

vampires. Vena and I were able to fend for ourselves by barricading ourselves in your office. And I'm wearing a new protection necklace that's a thousand times better than my old one.

"Actually, this might be a great opportunity," I added.

"Opportunity for what?" he asked.

"If Adriel really wants to meet with me, he would probably rather take the chance at Blur than at your house. Then your guys can capture him, and we can put this all behind us."

"I'm not using you as bait," Shepard said.

"It's not a horrible idea," Cross said. "I can be backup."

"We're not using Everly as bait," Shepard reiterated. "But if you insist on working tonight, you're in the VIP section, Cross will monitor outside, Anchor will remain the VIP bouncer at the stairs, and Vena will work in the section closest to Anchor."

I quickly agreed.

CHAPTER EIGHTEEN

After storing my things in my locker, I headed upstairs to the VIP section. Two wolf-sized men came from Shepard's office with tool belts slung on their hips. When they passed me, I glanced down the short hall to find they'd replaced Shepard's door.

Walking over, I looked at the heavy steel door with a ridiculously large bar lock on the inside. This door might have been useful in a bank or a panic room, but not in a club.

"It's reinforced and will keep out anyone trying to get in," Shepard said behind me, making me jump. He placed a calming hand on my shoulder. "Didn't mean to scare you."

"I didn't hear you," I said then pointed to the door. "Tell me you didn't get this installed because of our talk in the car earlier."

"I could. But it'd be a lie."

"Shepard, this is over the top."

"No. It's what I should have had in the beginning to keep my staff safe."

I eyed him. "As long as it's for everyone."

"I'm about to announce it in the meeting."

Knowing he had already assigned me to the VIP section, I

went to the staff meeting with him anyway, wondering how the others would react to the door.

When we were assembled, he doled out the section assignment for the night.

"Just a quick announcement before you go to your section," Shepard said. "Considering past events and current public safety concerns, I installed a reinforced door in my office. If another break-in happens or you feel unsafe, go to my office and secure the door. Please watch out for your fellow coworkers so they get to safety as well."

Thomas raised his hand. "Do you think we'll get attacked again?"

"No. I've added extra security measures to minimize that risk. The door is a backup. Any other questions or concerns?" No one spoke up. "Alright. Let's have a good night."

When we filed out, Vena slid up next to me. "Did something happen that I don't know about?"

"A surge of protectiveness. It's either the door, or we have to stay at home."

She wrinkled her nose. "Ordinarily, I might not mind staying at home, but not if I'm forced to."

"Same. Find anything today?"

"Other than a lot of regular black cats, nothing. I hope I don't get bad luck with all these black cats crossing my path."

"You know that's not true," I said. "Black cats are like all the other cats. Stop giving them a bad rap."

"I know. The one I want to find and stake him a thousand times is influencing my bias."

With a wave, she jogged down the VIP stairs. Anchor was already in place at the bottom, and I watched her stop to run her hand over his shoulder.

"Just curious, but how soundproof is Shepard's office now?" she asked.

Rather than hear an answer I didn't want to know, I got my section ready.

Patrons began trickling in after Army opened the front door. A group of dwarves headed toward Thomas's section, and several human couples claimed spots near the outer sections to listen to music.

It didn't take long for the VIP section to fill and for me to lose myself in the rhythm of serving drinks with a smile. My section was the only calm one in the house, though. Several times throughout the night, minor altercations occurred where Shepard, not Doc, respectfully asked dwarven patrons to leave.

"What's going on?" I asked Detroit after the fourth time.

"They're angry."

"Yeah, I got that from the fist shaking. Why are they mad?"

"Shepard promised to hand over their prince's killer and hasn't yet."

"He promised to *help* find him. And it's only been three days. D.C. is huge and filled with people. What do they expect? A miracle?"

"Yes."

I sighed, feeling bad for Shepard. He was getting so much unnecessary pressure from the dwarves. Didn't they realize he wanted to find Adriel just as badly as they did?

By the end of the shift, Shepard looked tired and ready to throat punch someone, which made me a little nervous for Cross as he walked in from the employee exit. He ignored Buzz and Tank's soft growls and sat next to me at the bar.

"Anything?" Shepard asked him.

"No. It was quieter out there than in here," Cross said. "You should warn Curran his people are causing trouble. They won't make finding Adriel any easier."

"You want me to call a grieving father and complain that his people are what? Upset their prince is dead?"

"He's a father, but he's also a king responsible for the safety and welfare of his people. Silence isn't helping him. Allow him to decide how to handle the situation."

I tugged on Cross' sleeve, silently urging him to shut up. He grabbed my hand and kissed it in an old-world way that melted my heart a little.

"Ignoring a problem doesn't make it go away," Cross said, looking at Shepard again.

"Obviously. If it worked, you wouldn't be here."

Cross smirked, and Shepard rolled his eyes then looked at me.

"He's here to take you home since Vena already left with Anchor and I have to patrol after this. Maybe you can help him leave faster so he's less annoying."

I shoved my tip money toward Buzz and stood.

"Be careful. I'll see you when you get back."

Shepard surprised me by reaching over the bar, cupping the back of my head, and kissing me. He was there and gone before I registered the intensity of his goodbye.

Cross tugged on my hand to gain my attention.

"Let's get you home."

We sat in the car, and after waiting for Pam to pull out of the lot first, I followed her onto the road and turned toward the pack house.

Cross took my hand from the steering wheel to kiss it. "I prefer kissing you after you've baked. Your scent is as sweet as you are."

"Are you saying I stink after my shift?" I asked with a laugh. Because after a night of hustling, I knew I wasn't the freshest bun on the rack.

"I love all your scents," Cross said. "Especially—"

Glass exploded inward from Cross' window as a car t-boned us at an intersection with a green light. The impact whipped me against my door. My head smashed into the window.

My vision blurred with the blinding pain, and a high-frequency ringing filled my ears as the car came to a standstill.

Dazed, I brushed glass off my shirt and wiped my face. My fingers came away bloody.

I blinked at the wet redness and then looked over at Cross. He was slumped at an odd angle in his seat, his door having crumpled in on him. Blood ran from a large cut on the side of his face, which was turned toward me.

"Cross?" I could barely hear myself over the ringing in my ears and touched his face with my bloody hand without thinking.

His eyelids fluttered, but he didn't open them.

"Cross, please…" I said louder.

My door was ripped open, and someone grabbed my arm. Energy swelled from my necklace. It surged through my skin like a barrier and knocked the person off their feet, sending them flying back twenty yards.

The thumping in my head grew more pronounced, and my vision swam as I looked from the prone body to Cross.

"We have to go." I reached for him again, aiming for his arm but touching his face instead. My feeble attempt left a bloody smear across his mouth.

His eyes fluttered open as my vision tunneled.

I felt Cross hold my hand even as someone grabbed my other arm again. Another wave of energy spread as the necklace protected me. Cross' lips brushed my fingers.

A low growl, almost drowned out by the ringing in my ears, filled the car. Metal groaned.

Then Cross was at my door, gently lifting me out of my seat. He pressed his lips to my temple, and I felt his tongue. He said something I couldn't hear, but it didn't matter. Cross was awake and had me. Everything would be fine.

That thought evaporated when he took off. My stomach roiled at the sudden speed at which he moved, and I gagged. His mouth returned to my head as everything went dark briefly.

Whether it was the blank spaces in my consciousness or the

fact that Cross ran fast, we were inside a building in a matter of minutes.

A hotel.

Over the ringing in my ears, I heard Cross' deep voice issuing orders for towels and clothing.

The next time I blinked my eyes open, he was holding me in a shower.

"Hang in there," Cross murmured, pressing his lips against my temple again. The stroke of his tongue stung at first, but as the burn eased, the darkness reclaimed me.

I woke up in Cross' arms. The sunlight made my eyes water, and my head hurt, so I closed my eyes and snuggled closer to Cross.

"Morning, sunshine," he said. "How do you feel?"

My head ached. So did my neck and my left shoulder. A lot.

"Like roadkill." Then I remembered why and winced, which made my head pound harder.

"I stopped the bleeding and healed the wounds," he said. "That won't help any bruising, though. I'm afraid I'm only good at healing cuts."

"What happened?"

"We were targeted last night. The crash was a calculated attempt to take you. Thankfully, you had the necklace that protected you long enough to give me time to recover."

"Did they try to take your ring?"

"No. It was a human minion. I don't believe the person who sent them expected me to be in the car after you left Blur. So they likely only had orders to take you.

"Shepard is tracking them down now. I'm sure we'll get an update soon. Until then, how can I make you feel better?"

"Water for now. Pain reliever if you have it."

He leaned away and laughed softly when I made a noise of protest.

"Sit up a little," he said.

As soon as I attempted to move, my body aches increased. Cross immediately helped me upright and handed me the glass.

"Shepard and I would also like a doctor to look at you. We're concerned about how hard you hit your head."

"So am I," I said after taking a cautious sip. "Concussions are no joke. Had one before, thanks to a past adventure."

"Is that a yes to the doctor then?"

"Sure. I can make an appointment."

"No need." Cross reached for his phone and sent a message. "She'll be here in a few minutes."

I paused to blink at him. "This hotel has a doctor?"

The corner of his mouth tilted upward.

"Not exactly. She's an acquaintance of mine."

Acquaintance? It'd been over two months since I'd fallen into his cave and woken him. But I'd never heard him talk about anyone else. Just other vampires he'd met trying to gather information. Yet, I knew he also needed to feed and had "friends" for that. So, was that what this doctor was?

"Rather than guess, ask," Cross said, sounding amused.

"Okay. What do you mean by an acquaintance? Is she someone you feed from?"

"No, she is someone I met through one of my kind, who, like me, does not believe humans are simply a food source. He uses her to obtain human blood ethically, without the need for a feeder."

"Is she safe? She's not related to the bad vampires, right?"

"No, she has no relation to Orphia's group. She's the sister of a recently turned vampire. Very trustworthy and understands our kind better than most doctors."

A knock sounded on the door, and Cross got out of bed to

answer it. He was wearing a pair of shorts. I looked under the covers to see I was wearing my underwear, and that was it.

I pinned the cover to my chest as he opened the door and let a tall brunette in. Her gaze immediately found me.

"She had a head injury that bled a lot on the way here," Cross said. "I healed that, but her head still hurts."

The doctor checked me over, keeping it all professional. She shined her light in my eyes, asked me basic questions, looked at my side, which hurt, then gently probed my neck before handing me some pain relievers. I downed them right away with a large gulp of water.

"I don't see any sign of concussion. Either you're lucky, or Cross' healing ability helped that out, too. There's still so much about that we don't understand."

She stood as she put her things away in the case she carried.

"If anything changes... headaches, nausea, blurred or doubled-vision, call me right away."

"We will. Thank you," Cross said.

She nodded, and he walked her to the door. After he closed it behind her, he turned and caught me rolling my shoulders.

"Want me to rub them?"

"Please. It feels like I went hiking with Vena again and fell into a cave."

He chuckled and settled in behind me.

His hands were magic. Or maybe the meds kicked in. Either way, I sighed happily twenty minutes later.

"That's so good," I said with my eyes closed.

His lips skimmed my shoulder, adding to the pleasant relax-ation. His thumbs found a particularly tense spot, and I moaned. I felt him lean forward a second before his teeth scraped my skin, scrambling the signals from relaxing to something more.

I tipped my head back to rest on his shoulder and looked up at him. His gaze swept over my face, and he kissed my forehead, nose, and throat, right where my pulse fluttered.

"You're right. I think you started something I can't finish," he said, his voice low.

"Can't or shouldn't?"

"Shouldn't?"

"Says who?"

He groaned and shifted our positions as he pushed the sheet down to kiss each inch he exposed. His soft breath against my skin and the feel of his skilled hands teased me as they drifted to my breasts.

It wasn't that all my aches had magically disappeared; it was that his touch helped distract me from what lingered after the massage and the meds.

Dipping his head down, I felt a whisper of air on my nipple right before he took it into his mouth and gently sucked, his tongue rolling and flicking over the sensitive nub. I threaded my fingers in his hair and arched into his mouth with a moan.

He growled, the low vibration lighting me up on the inside. The sharp points of his teeth pressed against my nipple as he drew it deeper into his mouth. When he released it, we were both breathing heavily.

"You're delicious," he said.

"Then why did you stop?" I asked, fighting my blush. "You were making me feel better."

The dark veins around his already black eyes spidered out further.

"I might not survive this."

He gripped my underwear and slipped them from my body. His fingers traced over my folds and gently circled that place that made my eyes roll back. One of his long fingers slipped inside of me.

I forgot time and space as he slowly unmade me. With each of my mumbled pleas, I could hear Cross, who was always so cool and collected, coming unglued with me. His whispered words of endearment were heavily accented and rough. And his teeth...they scraped relentlessly at my breast and collarbone.

"There," I breathed. "Right there."

His finger stroked over that magical place inside of me. He knew exactly where to touch with the perfect amount of pressure. There was nothing clumsy about his pursuit of my orgasm. In fact, in just a space of a few scant minutes, I was on the cliff and plummeting fast.

He kissed my neck as I saw stars and slowly returned to myself.

I felt his body melt next to me. He pressed a kiss to my lips and forehead.

"I'm never letting you go, Everly," he said.

CHAPTER NINETEEN

AFTER CROSS FETCHED CLOTHES AND OTHER NECESSITIES FOR ME from whatever source he magically seemed to have at his beck and call, I closed myself in the bathroom. A quick look in the mirror confirmed I didn't have visible bruising on my face.

When I left the bathroom, Cross handed me my phone. "You might want to respond to Vena before your phone explodes, or she does."

Glancing at my phone, I saw there was a string of texts asking if I was okay.

"I assume she knows what happened."

"Yes. I let her know not to worry."

Vena wasn't the only one who texted. My parents had sent a few pictures of them enjoying their vacation already this morning. Grandma's joyful expression made me smile as I saved the pictures and checked my other messages.

I opened a group message with Shepard and Cross and saw the back-and-forth conversation between the pair. While I was passed out, they'd worked to piece together what had happened and coordinated a search. If I hadn't known they had started as enemies, at least on Shepard's side, I would have thought they were…not friends but perhaps colleagues working together seamlessly.

"What's this about the GPS locator?" I asked as I kept reading.

"Shepard found it on the underside of your car. We think that's how Adriel found you outside the restaurant. It explains the crash as well."

Frowning, I thought of my poor car that I'd paid off. "Other than a vampire trying to kill me, I now have to deal with insurance and finding a new car."

"Don't worry," he said. "I've already notified your insurance and have a solution to your car problem."

"Do you ever sleep?"

"I don't need sleep, remember?"

"I remember. Just doesn't seem right that you're active around the clock."

"You'll like me for that later."

"I like you either way." My phone buzzed again. "I'd better text Vena."

"Let her know you'll see her in a half hour. I'll need to get you to Shepard's so I can join the search."

After I sent her a message, we headed to the hotel lobby and out the front door where a middle-aged man wearing a full bellhop uniform opened the door for us. A valet was waiting just outside the door and handed Cross a key.

"All ready for you, sir."

Cross took the key and gave it to me.

"What's this?" I asked.

"A key to the SUV."

I looked from him to a shiny new and ridiculously expensive SUV sitting in front of us.

"Cross, is this the solution you mentioned?"

"Yes, but I didn't buy it for you, so no scolding me about expensive purchases. I bought it for our business. You'll need it once the bakery opens and you need to deliver desserts to Blur."

"It's a company car?" I asked, making sure I heard him right.

He nodded. "For our business."

I felt like I was being played—that he'd purchased this SUV for me. But if I was really going to use it to haul around supplies and possibly catering orders, I knew I couldn't turn it down. The business and I would need it then.

"Did you have to get the bright red color with polished chrome work?"

"I wanted it to be a safe vehicle. It comes fully loaded with all the extra safety features. The red will stand out in traffic." He shrugged. "The chrome was a bonus."

Ah. There it was—the reason behind the purchase. He wanted me to be safe.

I leaned over and placed a kiss on his lips.

He smiled at the innocent peck. "What was that for?"

"For you being you."

He gave me a kiss back. "That's for you, and there are plenty more." Walking to the driver's door, he opened it. "Would you care to drive, or would you like me to?"

Even though I was still sore and a little leery about driving again, I sat in the driver's seat. It was better to drive now and leave whatever bits of fear I might have behind me.

Driving the SUV came with a learning curve. My old car didn't have nearly as many bells and whistles. It certainly didn't have leather seats with a heater and A/C built in.

Once I figured everything out, I drove out onto the street.

I let off the gas through every intersection to look both ways. It wasn't enough to anger the drivers behind me, but I knew it was just residual fear I'd have to shake.

By the time we arrived at the pack house, I felt a little more at ease driving, but I still had to unclench my fingers from around the steering wheel. Cross set his hand on my leg.

"You did well. Now, are you ready to reassure everyone?"

I looked toward the main doors where Vena, Anchor,

Gunther, and Shepard waited. The fact that Anchor held Vena's hand was probably the only reason she hadn't stormed the vehicle.

"Ready," I said.

Cross moved so fast that the sound of his door closing registered at the same time he opened mine for me. I smiled at him as he took my hand and helped me down.

"Probably not very reassuring when you have to help me like this," I said softly.

He chuckled and kissed my forehead.

"You've had your time with her," Vena said. "Hand her over."

Cross led me toward the group but veered at the last second toward Shepard.

"I'm leaving her in your care."

"Thank you for getting her out of there quickly last night," Shepard said. "And for keeping me in the loop."

Cross nodded, gave me one last long look, and then disappeared.

"When I said hand her over, I meant to me," Vena said.

Grinning, I looked at my best friend and opened my arms.

"Come on. Give it to me."

"That's what she said," Vena said before slamming into my arms hard enough to rock me backward. Even as I winced at the impact, I wasn't worried she'd knock me over. Shepard didn't have the same faith in her.

"Careful," he warned.

She made a dismissive noise at him and hugged me hard.

"You really worried me," she said into my hair.

"You should be worried. My driving is better than yours, and someone still hit me. You're so screwed."

Vena snorted. "Not for another nine hundred and fifty-three times."

"Ugh. You need therapy. Let go of me."

"No." She hugged me harder before she actually let go of me.

"I want to wrap you in bubble wrap and put you in a closet somewhere."

"So I can come out of the closet?" I asked with a grin. "You know you're the only girl for me."

It was her turn to groan, but I saw the glint in her eye that told me some of her fear was letting up, thanks to my teasing.

"I want you safe. And since bubble wrap is too fun to pop, I'm going to put my efforts into finding the asshole who keeps hurting the people I love instead. Behave while I'm gone, and clean your room." She waved to Anchor and Gunther. "Come on, boys. Let's find a cat to skin."

"Ew," I said.

She blew a kiss at me and walked away with the other two.

I faced Shepard and saw the worry reflected in his gaze.

"I'm fine," I said. "Promise."

He wrapped me in a gentler and yet more intense hug than Vena's.

"When Cross called me and told me what happened…" A fine tremor ran through Shepard.

"I'll admit it wasn't fun to be hit by a car, and I never want to do it again, but I really am fine, Shepard. The doctor looked me over and everything. No stitches, thanks to Cross. No concussion. Just a few aches that aren't too bad."

He sighed and kissed my temple without letting me go.

"Bubble wrap does sound like a good idea."

"I hear it's not very sexy or breathable."

He grunted a small laugh.

"Was everything okay here? No attacks or anything?"

He pulled back to look at me and shook his head. "Everything was quiet."

"Good. I'd rather Adriel stay focused on me."

"I'd rather he die," Shepard said.

"Yeah, well, I guess there's that too. How are the Hunters? Miles?"

"The Hunters are exceptionally quiet while researching. Vena made me promise to ensure someone delivers food and drinks, or they won't feed themselves. Miles has been increasingly agitated. Cross offered to compel him again tonight so he rests. I think the Hunters will take him up on the offer."

Shepard's hold finally loosened.

"What are your plans for today?"

"Whatever you want. Today, I'm yours."

I smiled.

"I'm a little hungry. Why don't we make me and the Hunters a snack to carry us over until lunch?"

Shepard led me inside to the kitchen where other women were already gathering to start lunch. I grabbed two apples and sliced them along with some cheese, nibbling as I worked. When I was done, Shepard and I brought the plate to the Hunters, who were in their room next to Miles' room.

I knocked on their door but knew not to wait for them to open it. Most likely, they didn't even hear it. Their hyperfocus when researching was like nothing I had ever seen before.

Opening the door, I found them both at a small table. Papers, books, and maps were splayed on every surface available in the room. Mr. Hunter had a magnifying glass and was peering at a map while Mrs. Hunter scrolled through a website on her laptop.

"Time for a break," I said, scooting things over on the table to make room.

"Just a few minutes," Mrs. Hunter said distractedly.

I would bet anything she didn't even register who came into the room or why I told them to take a break.

I slowly slid the plate under her nose, stopping her. Her startled gaze snapped to me.

"Oh. When did you get here, dear?"

"Just now. It's time to take a break and eat something before I have to get Vena to intervene."

"You can put the plate down. I'll eat while I work. Thank you for bringing it."

"If I leave and come back in an hour, I'll find sweaty cheese and brown apples. Eat." You too, Mr. H."

He mumbled something.

I shoved a slice of apple at him. He took it and slid it into his mouth, not looking away from the map.

Sighing, I put down the plate to confiscate the map and laptop.

"Eat, and I'll give you your things back," I said.

"I don't remember her being this bossy," Mr. Hunter said.

"That's because Vena normally does it," I said. "Eat. And while you're eating, you can tell us if you've discovered anything."

"We've discovered a lot of dead-ends," Mrs. Hunter said, accepting the plate from Shepard. "Oh, and we heard from your parents. They are having a marvelous time. Your grandma took a selfie with a handsome young man. She said she would bring him back for you."

"Not necessary," Shepard said.

Mrs. Hunter smiled at him. "Good to hear."

I poked Mr. Hunter's arm when he picked up a book. "You're not done eating."

He sighed. "I concede. My wife was right, though. We've reached a lot of dead-ends. But..." He scooted from the chair and hurried over to the bed to weed through a pile of papers. Pulling out something that looked horrifically similar to the sheep scrotum map, he opened it.

"This might explain how a vampire can turn into a cat."

Shepard accepted the nasty, weathered scrap. I peered around his arm to see there was writing on it.

"Is this fae?" I asked.

"Yes. Old fae. I was able to translate it loosely. Basically, it's saying that a powerful fae, and I'm talking really powerful, would have the ability to turn humans into shifters. Since vampires were once human, I suspect it would be the same principle."

"And that's how Adriel is different?" I asked. "A fae made him into a shifter?"

Mr. Hunter scratched his head. "I'm not fully convinced. Power like this is nearly unheard of, and who of the fae would grant such a gift to a vampire? Especially one as twisted as I've heard Adriel is? I need to research some more to make sense of this."

"Maybe Adriel coerced someone to give him shifting power," I said.

"It's a possibility," Mrs. Hunter said, even as Shepard said it was impossible.

"A vampire can't control a fae."

"A deal then, perhaps?" Mr. Hunter said.

Mrs. Hunter shook her head. "The fae are stingy unless it benefits them. I can't see Adriel having anything that would entice a powerful fae to give such a gift."

Mr. Hunter sighed. "We'll keep researching."

"After you eat," I warned.

He took his plate and shoveled some of the food into his mouth.

"I'll need to call Effora about this," Shepard said. "Excuse me."

Since I wanted to hear the conversation, I followed Shepard out to the hall and to his suite. He brought out his phone and called Effora, placing it on speaker.

"Hello, handsome. How may I please you today?"

"You can please me by telling me what you know about creating shifters."

"Creating them?" She gasped throatily and then burst out laughing. "Darling, when I said it was lunchtime, I meant real food, not me."

Shepard and I looked at each other in question.

"Effora, this is important. Can you put your snack aside for now?" Shepard asked.

"And deny my meal?"

"Delay. Not deny."

"You always were good at edging me, Shepard. Very well. Eloise, darling, I'll feast with you momentarily. That's a good girl." Effora sighed. "Lots of good energy in that one. But she is gone. Now, what do you desire, Alpha?"

"What do you know about creating shifters?" he repeated.

"Not much. Why? Are you thinking of adding an extra animal to your menagerie? A lion, perhaps."

"Effora, I believe a fae gave Adriel the power to shift into a cat."

"That's a serious allegation," she said even though her tone remained playful.

"It is. I have King Curran and the dwarves breathing down my neck and vampires who are on a killing spree. I need answers."

"If you allowed me to breathe on your...neck, you'd have more answers and fewer worries."

"And if you don't want to take this call seriously, then I'll hang up."

"Oh, very well. I'll look into it for you. Why don't you pop in tomorrow so I can debrief you?"

"I already know what you mean by debriefing, and I'll pass. Call back when you have useful information."

He hung up only to get an incoming call from King Curran. Shepard swore under his breath.

I patted his arm. "I'll see about lunch," I said and left him to his call.

CHAPTER TWENTY

THE WOMEN FROM EARLIER PAUSED THEIR CONVERSATION TO GREET me when I returned to the kitchen. They had a neat assembly line going where the plates moved down the line of the prep counter and finished on a tray that slid nicely on a baker's rack.

"Need any help?"

The woman laying out the plates handed me a stack.

"You can take over for me for a few minutes so I can run a plate to Bear. He was out all night and just came back. I want him to eat before he passes out."

Another woman passed her a plate piled with sandwiches, and she hurried out.

"I don't know how much longer they'll last like this before they collapse," one woman said with a shake of her head. "If it weren't for what happened the last time, I think Shepard would have already reached out for help from the other packs. After all the pack leaders left, the number of missing persons started to climb."

Another woman added, "I heard the city officials are worried they won't be able to keep this quiet for much longer. They should just say vampires are overrunning D.C. and to stay indoors or run the risk of joining the hundreds already missing."

"The mass panic would just give the vampires more opportunity to take more people," the first one said. "We need help. Who knows how many of those missing people have already turned?"

The others hummed in agreement, and my stomach twisted with worry.

"I think it's worse than we know," a third woman said. "I heard from Gunther that they went into some tunnels, looking for the black cat, and it was empty. No homeless people."

"Maybe the city moved them," another said.

We could all hear the doubt in her voice.

"Maybe," the first woman said as the one who'd delivered food to Bear returned.

"Here." She handed me two plates as she resumed her place. "You should take these to Shepard before he passes out, too."

I nodded and accepted the plates, feeling guilty for not considering Shepard's lack of sleep after reading the group text between him and Cross.

Back in the suite, I found Shepard in his kitchenette, hands braced on the counter and head hung low. At the sound of my entrance, he looked up. How had I not noticed the dark circles under his eyes?

"I brought sandwiches if you're hungry," I said.

"Thanks." He took the plate from me and consumed a quarter of a sandwich in a single bite.

"Did the call with Curran not go well?" I asked.

"He's pressuring me for details I don't have and is angry, like I am, that the fae queen isn't being more forthcoming with help of any kind. Information, manpower, whatever…we'd take it."

He took another bite, visibly frustrated.

"Do you think she knows something and isn't telling you?" I asked.

"Has Cross ever told you how his kind came to be?" Shepard asked.

I shook my head.

"The first vampire was a human who betrayed his fey lover. She cursed him to an existence of loneliness where he would hurt the people he loved and they would run in fear of him.

"Not all fey can cast that level of curse. It was done by a queen several generations ago."

Considering a fey lifespan, I knew that meant a very, very long time ago.

"The queen then never imagined her curse would have such a devastating effect on humans. The man killed untold numbers, which was bad enough. But some of them didn't die. They became like him, hungry for blood.

"To prevent the spread, that queen's successor cast a new spell on her loyal human lover. He would protect humans from the vampire threat, and for his efforts, he would be rewarded with enhanced senses and another, stronger form."

"Your kind," I said in understanding.

He nodded.

"What the Hunters found was the story of our beginning, and they're right in that Adriel's so-called "gift" likely came from a powerful fae. It's also unlikely that such a spell has escaped the queen's notice. I just wish I knew who she was protecting."

He sighed heavily and finished his sandwich. I could see his exhaustion tugging at him even as his phone buzzed with a message.

I leaned over to look at it.

Doc: The tunnel on the north side is empty too.

"Does Cross know it's this bad?" I asked.

"He knows. He's helping search too."

"Good. Then, tell Doc to coordinate with Cross while you take a nap."

I was already nudging him to his room.

"And why do I want to nap?" he asked with a teasing smile.

"Because your pack needs a rested Alpha. And I'll cuddle with you."

"You should have led with that." He chuckled and allowed me to escort him to his room as he texted Doc and Cross.

"This isn't the date with you I had planned," he said as he handed me his phone and pulled me into bed with him. "You better still be here when I wake up."

I held his arm around my waist and closed my eyes.

"Go to sleep, Shepard."

His breathing evened out within moments, and I eased my phone out of my pocket to set an alarm so neither of us would be late for our shift later.

I didn't need to worry. Before the alarm woke me, I felt the bed shift, and the warm body that had been next to me was gone.

Glancing behind me, I saw Shepard pulling out a dress shirt and black pants from the closet.

"Did you sleep at all?" I asked. "I think I melted into the mattress."

"I slept enough. If you need to sleep more, go ahead. You have another thirty minutes."

"There's no point without you next to me," I said, just to watch his eyes spark with gold.

I sat up, and my sore muscles protested the movement. Shepard caught my wince.

"You can stay here if you're not up for work."

I shook my head and stood to stretch. "It's better if I keep moving. I'll atrophy if I don't."

Walking over to my suitcase, I found it was empty. Shepard pointed to the closet. "Your things are in there and in the dresser."

"When did you have time to do that?"

"Lisa did it. I hope you don't mind. She takes her den mother role seriously."

"I don't mind." I looked in the closet to find Shepard's clothes pushed to one side and my things on the other.

"I'll meet you at the entry when you're ready," he said. "I need to speak to a few people. Unless you need something now."

"I'm fine."

He kissed the top of my head as he passed by while also tying his tie. "I like having you here," he said then left the room. A moment later, I heard the door to the suite close.

I knew I had time to spare, but I also knew Shepard would want to get to Blur sooner rather than later, so I hurried to get ready and was at the entryway in fifteen minutes.

Shepard was off to the side, talking to four men. When he saw me, he ended the conversation, and they took off in two trucks.

"Ready?" I asked.

When he nodded, I held out the key to the new SUV. "Want me to drive so you can communicate with people?"

"If you don't mind."

"I don't mind at all."

As I suspected, as soon as we sat in the car, Shepard's phone went off every few minutes with some kind of issue or request. I wasn't sure how he was going to manage Blur and deal with everything else going on.

Pulling into the lot, I saw Boulder guarding the back door. I said hello before following Shepard inside. Shepard headed toward the main bar while I went to the lockers to store my things. Gunther was there, putting on his apron.

"How are you doing?" I asked him. "I heard you were out looking in tunnels earlier."

"I'll look in every tunnel and sewer if I have to. I'll find Adriel even if it kills me."

Gunther was probably the smallest and leanest of the wolves.

He'd had a drinking problem in the past, which might have been the reason Adriel had kidnapped him instead of trying a stronger, sober wolf. But since then, Gunther had changed while I wasn't paying attention. The beaten-down guy was still present, but he looked determined. Possibly stronger.

"You haven't been drinking," I said.

"Not a drop. Not until Adriel is dead."

I studied him momentarily, wondering what he'd do once Adriel died. Would he go back to his old ways? Before I pondered too long, Gunther went to the dish station, and Vena popped up beside me.

"What are we daydreaming about? How hot your men are or how stewed cat tastes?"

"Ew!"

"I've been telling her we're not cooking cat," Anchor said.

Vena looked as if she was about to say something, but Anchor hugged her to him, smothering her face into his chest. She didn't seem to mind that he cut off her words or air supply.

"She found a pamphlet about troll stew in her parent's research pile. One of the main ingredients is cats. She hasn't been able to think about anything else since then."

"Not true," she said, her voice muffled. "I've been thinking of plenty of other things, and if you don't let go of me, I'll give all of Blur a first-hand view of those things."

He let go and smiled down at her, running a soothing hand down her back. "I'll be at the bar."

"Get the latest intel while you're there."

Once he was gone, Vena turned to me. "I feel like I haven't seen you in forever."

"You saw me earlier today."

"For-eh-ver!!"

"Miss you, too."

We stowed our things in the locker and headed out to get our assignments for the night. Shepard once again put me in VIP. If

Sierra had been working, she would have likely complained, but everyone else took it in stride.

The shift started out as usual—well, the new usual anyway. There were more dwarves and more grumbles toward the wolves but the same drink orders and appetites from the servers' standpoint. Not that I had to deal with any of that. It's what I saw when I passed close enough to the glass wall to see downstairs.

The VIP section was once again a mix of influential humans and fae. The humans were low maintenance. As long as I watched the level of the drinks they were sipping and approached whenever they were low, they didn't need me, which meant I could focus on the fae.

Usually, I kept my distance. Tonight, I had other plans.

I struck up conversations and, under the guise of gossip, tried to gain any nugget of information that might be helpful to the search for Adriel and vampires. Hearing their points of view regarding the increase in vampires and missing persons was interesting. They weren't as unconcerned as their queen.

"My great-grandfather mentioned a time like this in his memoirs. He wrote that he encountered a lovely human woman with tempting curves and bright hair—much like yourself—who was so struck by grief from losing her husband that he couldn't coax a single orgasm from her."

"A travesty, for sure," I said.

The fae's gaze intensified. "You have no idea how tempting you are. Come home with me, and allow me a chance to spank the mockery from you."

"It wouldn't work," I said lightly. "My roommate has tried on multiple occasions. Spankings aren't my thing. And it would take a lot more effort than a polite request to get me to come home with you."

I saw one of the humans finish his drink. "Duty calls. I'll be right back."

I moved to leave his table, but he caught my wrist. His pull, which I hadn't even noticed while talking to him, buzzed under my skin briefly before the charm under my shirt warmed and dispelled it.

"What would it take, Everly?" the fae asked.

"Since I don't even know your name, probably a white kidnapper van crammed full of desserts that I haven't yet tried. But seriously, you have two seconds to let go, or Detroit will jump the bar and toss you down the stairs. Blur has a strict no touching the staff rule."

He glanced at the bar, released me, and lifted his hands in surrender.

"I deeply apologize for frightening you."

"You didn't." With a nod of farewell, I made the rounds for more drinks.

When I returned to his table, he was gone but had left a note on a napkin with his name, Niroog, and his number. He'd even been helpful enough to include a pronunciation for his name.

"Knee-rook," I said softly before folding the napkin and sticking it into my pocket along with the hundred he left for a tip. Although I had no intention of calling the number, it never hurt to have it just in case I needed fae intel.

Shepard appeared at the top of the stairs as I cleared the table. He had his phone pressed to his ear as he strode toward his office. It wasn't unusual to see him take calls. What was unusual was that he didn't look at anything else as he moved. Eyes forward. No looking at me, Detroit, or the tables.

I glanced at Detroit, who was staring after Shepard with an equally troubled expression, and hurried over.

"What did you overhear?" I asked.

He took the dirty glasses from me to add to the dishtub behind the bar and shook his head.

"Don't try lying to me, Detroit. Spill it, or I'm telling Vena that you know a shortcut to ending Anchor's impotence spell. You know what that means? She'll be in your ear non-stop asking for your help, and when you admit that you don't know it, she'll still come at you with all sorts of ideas and ask your advice."

Detroit looked positively horrified at the idea. "You have a mean streak that makes up for your height deficiency."

I shrugged and leaned in. He sighed and leaned closer to whisper in my ear.

"The police discovered a mass burial at a place outside of eastern D.C."

My stomach twisted with what that meant, and I gripped the bar. An arm wrapped around my waist and spun me around.

I blinked up at Shepard, who leaned in the way Detroit had. However, with Shepard, it felt completely different. He turned his head toward my ear to speak.

"My tether is frayed, Everly. It would be safer if you didn't get this close to anyone else."

Hearing the tremor in his voice and understanding his frayed composure wasn't just due to another man being close to me, I wrapped my arms around him, giving him the hug he needed.

He made a sound, hugged me in return, and then released me.

Detroit was on the far side of the bar as Shepard walked away. He shook his head at me. "I should have picked the Vena option."

I grinned and went back to clearing my table.

CHAPTER TWENTY-ONE

After Blur closed, I went to Shepard's office. He was talking on the phone while Cross listened.

"Is he still talking about the mass grave?" I asked quietly.

"You heard about it?"

"I threatened to sic Vena on Detroit if he didn't tell me."

Cross grinned and closed the distance between us to kiss my cheek. "Clever, Everly. And, yes, he's talking about the site. I get the honor of escorting you while Shepard and his crew head to the scene. Are you ready?"

"Yep. Just have to grab my things from my locker. What about Vena?"

"Anchor will take her back to the complex."

Shepard ended his call and kissed my forehead. "I'll be home later. Don't wait up for me." He turned to Cross. "Thank you for taking her, but this doesn't give you an invitation to my suite."

Cross simply smiled at him and took my hand. "You know I never need an invitation."

Shepard narrowed his eyes at Cross, but I could see there was no heat behind the gaze. "Go on. I have to get the guys on the road."

When we headed downstairs, only Boulder bristled this time, but it was because we had to pass close to him to get to the lockers.

He immediately stepped back, mumbled an apology, and fled to the main floor.

"You make an impression," I said teasingly.

"When you're this handsome, it's hard not to," Cross teased back.

"Did you just call yourself handsome?" Vena asked, bumping him out of the way to get to her locker.

"Your hearing did not betray you."

"Geesh, and people call me conceited."

"I'm not sure who the people you are referring to are, but I'd disagree with them. You are much more like a fishwife. Loud and abrasive."

"Aw. You brought back your pet name for me." She held a hand to her heart. "I thought you'd forgotten."

Anchor and I shared an eye roll and shooed them out to the parking lot.

I let Cross drive to the pack house so I could check news feeds for information regarding the mass burial while not watching intersections. Unfortunately, I didn't find anything online. Whatever was happening at the gravesite was being kept a secret for now. Just how many other things were kept from the public?

Cross kissed me sweetly after he parked the car in the lot. "I'll see you soon."

I nodded and headed past the guards at the door.

The few people I saw on the way to Shepard's suite just nodded in greeting but didn't try to strike up a conversation.

Once inside his rooms, I showered, dressed in pajamas, and headed to bed, only to find Cross there, waiting for me. He was wearing lounge pants and a t-shirt that looked suspiciously like Shepard's.

"You're poking the bear," I said.

"Poking the wolf, actually," Cross said. He patted the mattress. "Don't worry. He knows I'm here."

"Does he know you're wearing his pajamas?"

"No. That's a surprise for later."

I shook my head at Cross' antics. "Just don't poke too much. He's under a lot of pressure."

"Never fear. I've lived a long enough life to know when I tiptoe near someone's limit. He's fine."

Cross opened his arms. "However, I'm not fine. I'm starved for your attention."

I crawled into bed and found myself wrapped in his arms a second later.

"What do you think is going on with the mass grave?" I asked once I settled in.

"Not to frighten you, but I think this is just the tip of the iceberg." He kissed my head before turning off the light. "Enough dark thoughts for now. Go to sleep. I know you're still a little sore from the accident."

"I am," I said. "But it was good that I had to work. It kept me moving."

"Well, if you need any other activities to keep you moving, let me know. Otherwise, time to sleep."

The feel of his fingers running through my hair followed me into my dreams.

Before I even opened my eyes, I knew Shepard had taken Cross' place. Cross held me like he couldn't believe he was holding me, but Shepard wrapped me in his arms like he was afraid I'd escape.

I dragged my hand over the arm caging me from behind. A soft growl reverberated through him, and he tightened his hold when I reached his hand.

"Squeeze any harder, and I'm peeing your bed."

He chuckled and immediately released me.

"Be right back," I said, climbing out of bed.

I took an extra moment to brush my teeth before I left the bathroom.

Shepard welcomed me with open arms and held me just as tightly, burying his nose against my neck and breathing me in.

"I guess things weren't good last night?" I asked.

"Things went from horrific to bleak," he said. "We found five more—I don't even know what to call them other than body dumps." He sounded so sad and tired. "So many people, Everly. It explains why all the nests we found seemed newly turned."

"Because they were?"

He nodded. "Cross is trying to establish trust with the newer ones he comes across to find out where and how they were turned. There are older vampires out there hiding, just like Adriel and Vivian. Cross thinks his ex is behind this. If she is, she has a network of people helping her."

"You mean humans?"

"There's no other way for her to stay so hidden."

"What can I do to help you?"

"This," he said, snuggling me closer.

"While you might like this, it's not actually getting anything done. What if I agree to meet with her and bring you and Cross with me? She didn't seem bothered by the idea of Cross and me meeting with her before."

"No."

That was it. Just one word. It should have annoyed me, but honestly, I was a chicken and didn't want to meet Cross' ex either.

"Then what are you going to do?"

Shepard lifted his head and looked down at me as I twisted to look back at him.

"Make it harder for them to stay hidden. Too many people

have been found to keep this quiet. The police will make a public announcement today.

"Things are going to change quickly," he said. "I want you to promise you won't go anywhere alone."

I smoothed my fingers over his cheeks, noting the stubble.

"Thank you for worrying about me," I said. "But I'm not asking Detroit to walk me to the bathroom at work."

Shepard scowled at me. "You know that's not what I was asking."

"Not yet. But the more you worry, the more you'll unconsciously smother my freedom. What I'm willing to promise is that I won't turn off my tracking and will let you know wherever I'm going whenever I leave, okay? I swear I'll be mindful of the higher danger and not do things that will cause you to worry."

I saw the disagreement in his gaze and kissed him lightly. When he opened his mouth to argue, despite the kiss, I kissed him again. With tongue.

He growled and flipped us to pin me underneath him with my hands caged above my head. His gaze held mine for several beats before it swept over my face, lingering briefly on my lips.

"I was going to tell you that won't work to get your way, but I'd be a liar."

He cut off my soft laughter with an aggressive kiss.

He released me and his hands rode up my sides, skimming my breasts. A second later, he had my shirt off and groaned as he kissed his way down my neck and to the valley of my breasts. I threaded my fingers in his hair, drifting in the sensations he was weaving.

I was so distracted by his mouth I didn't notice his hands at my waist at first. When I did, I lifted my hips, showing him my trust.

His growl vibrated through my chest a second before I lost my last bit of covering, and his mouth was on me. My hold on his hair shifted from a caress to an anchor as he proved his hunger for me.

I came so hard and fast from his mouth alone that I saw stars.

Panting and in a daze, I stared blankly at the ceiling while I waited for my pulse to slow. Shepard kissed my inner thigh then swept me into his arms to carry me to the bathroom. He set me on my feet as the shower warmed, and he stripped. My gaze unabashedly took in all of him. The muscled limbs, sculpted shoulders, and abs. I fought not to drool.

When he turned to me and held out his hand, I eagerly took it.

I loved showering with Shepard. He washed me with a singular focus, watching my reaction to each soapy caress. I liked everything, but I really loved the way he rubbed my scalp as he shampooed my hair. I was a puddle of relaxation when he finished washing me. It didn't stop me from stealing the soap from him, though.

His pupils dilated as I ran my slick hands over his chest and down his abs. He claimed my lips for another intense kiss as I wrapped my hands around him and did my best to make him forget his name.

I swallowed his groan and didn't stop kissing him until he stopped twitching. Panting, he leaned his forehead against mine and slowly washed my stomach. Once I was clean again, we left the shower, and he leaned against the shower as he watched me dry my hair.

"What are your plans today?" Shepard asked, sounding much more relaxed.

"I was going to see if I could make the promised dessert for Blur in your kitchen here."

"Perfect. I'll be around, coordinating search efforts and taking calls. Let me know if you need anything."

He kissed my forehead and left to get dressed.

I spent most of the day in the kitchen, helping the women cook and listening to their conversation. They were worried, which I understood since their mates were out there hunting things that could kill.

Once the women cleaned up lunch, they let me take over the kitchen to make lemon ricotta cheesecakes for both the pack house and Blur. By the time the cheesecake had set, I had to get ready for my shift.

Shepard was in the suite when I walked in.

"Any news?" I asked.

"We're still searching." He finished buttoning his shirt. "I heard you helped in the kitchen. Thank you. Are you still up for your shift tonight?"

"Yep." I gathered my things and headed to the bathroom. "I'll be ready in a few minutes."

"I'll wait for you at the front again. I need to speak with my guys."

I hurried to dress and grabbed the cheesecake from the kitchen on my way out. Shepard was outside like he said, watching a line of trucks pull away.

When he saw me, he took the cheesecake, inhaled appreciatively, and placed it in the SUV.

"I think Chef Griz will be impressed," he said.

"I hope so. I thought it would go great with the lamb skewers and herb dip."

Shepard answered calls and coordinated his people's search efforts as I drove us to Blur. It sounded like the few locations they tried earlier were busts.

Two black SUVs followed us when I pulled into the employee lot.

"Trouble?" I asked.

"Yes. It's the liaison," he said with a defeated sigh.

"Liaison to what?"

"Your kind. He is the go-between for your higher-ups and otherworlder higher-ups. I'll have to talk to him."

Communication was normally a good thing, but one glance at

the black-suited men who got out of the SUVs told me they might not be very good at communicating with words. However, the back door opened, and a different type of man stepped out.

His honey-blonde hair brushed the collar of his tailored suit. He radiated a manicured flawlessness that didn't seem human because it put me at ease and made me want to please him.

"Is he fae?" I asked.

"No. He's human. The liaison is always a human that the fae gift with immunity from outside influence and an ability to calm. The side effect is a confidence that draws other humans in, which is probably what you're feeling right now."

Shepard opened his door. "Don't worry. Hugh is harmless enough and good at his job, even without his gifts. Let's see what he has to say."

They disappeared inside before Shepard opened my door. He carried the cheesecake and held it away from Boulder, who was sniffing appreciatively as he held the door open.

"That smells delicious."

"It might become part of the menu," I said. "That's if Chef likes it."

Shepard handed it off once we were inside, kissed my forehead, and left to meet with the liaison. I veered to the kitchen where Griz and Gator were prepping for the night.

"I brought lemon ricotta cheesecake as promised."

Griz stopped chopping onions to inspect it. "Looks and smells light and refreshing." He cut into it with a clean knife and placed a slice on a plate. "Visually appetizing."

I felt like I was in class, but I knew Griz didn't mean it like he was grading me. He was telling me what he was both looking for and finding.

Picking up a spoon, he dug it into the cheesecake. "The right density." He sampled the bite and nodded. "Light and refreshing as it looks with a balanced amount of sweet and tart.

"Well done, Everly. I think this is a perfect pairing for the lamb skewers. Let's offer it to regulars who order lamb skewers during tonight's service. Head out to the bar. Buzz has something for you to try, too."

I couldn't help but smile. It was one thing to get compliments from friends and family, but it was another to get it from someone who took cooking seriously and understood the complexities of taste and texture.

My joy faded a little when I walked out to the main bar and saw Buzz and Tank both quietly standing there with their heads cocked and vacant stares. Buzz held a finger to his lips and slid a drink toward me as he listened to whatever was being said upstairs. I silently sat on the barstool and sampled the pretty purple drink.

A short while later, the liaison walked down the stairs with his guards and left.

Buzz sighed and looked at me. "No need to threaten me with Anchor's overzealous mate. I'll tell you anything you want to know as soon as you tell me what you thought of the drink."

"It's good. Too fruity to drink a lot of, which is good because it's strong." I took another small sip. "Lemon, blackberry, and mint?"

He nodded. "To pair with your cheesecake. See if you can sell them as a set."

"You got it. Now, what'd you hear?"

"Shepard explained the trouble he's having getting the fae queen to help. The liaison is setting up a meeting for all the leaders. Shepard, Curran, Effora, and Cross—even though vampires have never been included before."

The way he said it told me what he thought about that, but I wasn't offended. Prejudices were hard to shake. That Cross could walk into Blur without being attacked or chased was major progress.

"How long will Shepard have to wait to hear back from him?"

"Not long. The liaison doesn't play." He gave me a reassuring smile, and I slipped off my stool to get ready for my shift. That was how Vena found me by the lockers when she came in.

"Hey, my sister from another mister," she said. "Did you miss me?"

She wiggled her eyebrows and hugged me.

"You're in a good mood."

"I am. We took a break after scrying to work on Anchor's spell."

"La-la-la-la," I said, covering my ears.

She laughed and pulled my hands down.

"It's fine. No details. I promise. Well, about that anyway.

"The scrying stone is really begging to be crushed. We haven't had a decent lead yet. I'm thinking of heading back to the market. You want to come with?"

"No, thanks. That would probably send both Cross and Shepard through the roof."

She made a face. "Will your keepers allow you to walk D.C. with me to look for the cat?"

"Doubtful," I said as we went upstairs.

Shepard put Vena in VIP and me at the bottom of the stairs so I could sell the dessert drink combo to the regulars, which proved to be a success.

We were out of cheesecake within the first hour, and other patrons were full of questions about whether desserts would be common now. They were interested, and I listened to all their thoughts and feedback, making a ton of mental notes.

I was still riding my success high when a commotion broke out at the door several hours later.

"Feeders!" Army yelled from the door.

Every wolf inside Blur bolted for the main door.

CHAPTER TWENTY-TWO

"GET TO THE EMERGENCY EXIT AT THE BACK OF THE STAGE!" Thomas yelled to the people in his section.

Vena appeared out of nowhere, grabbed my arm, and shoved me toward the stairs as the first feeder emerged from the swarm of bodies at the entrance.

"Get to his office," Vena said as I scurried up the stairs.

I'd seen how the first feeder's gaze had swept over the escaping people as if searching for something or someone.

We reached the office and bolted ourselves in. Pam was only a few seconds behind us, proving she'd listened. She joined me at the glass wall, and we watched the chaos below.

"I really need to find another job," she said softly. "Working for werewolves is getting too risky."

My gaze swung to hers, and she gave me a shaky smile. "Figured out they were werewolves after the last break-in."

It made sense, considering the way Shepard and his guys were subduing the feeders.

The main area had just emptied of all Blur's guests as they fled out the back exit when I saw a blip of movement near the stage door. It zipped from intruder to intruder, not interfering with the fight, just getting really close.

A second later, Cross stood in the middle of the room.

We couldn't hear what he said, but all the fighting stopped.

"That can't be good," Pam said.

"It is. Trust me. It's very good he's here."

"Who's here?" Vena asked from her place by the door.

"Cross. He stopped them all from fighting."

"Good. That means we can find out what's going on."

She didn't open the door, though. We waited until they'd gathered and surrounded the compelled humans before leaving the office's safety. Shepard met us at the bottom of the stairs.

"It's safe to clean your stations and shut down for the night. We'll keep them on the dance floor until the police take them away."

As the servers cleaned, both Anchor and Shepard stood a little outside of the ring of wolves. When I wiped down a table near the dance floor, I heard Cross tell Shepard one of the compelled had a message.

"What's the message?" Shepard asked.

"We will never have a night of peace until the rings are handed over."

Shepard's jaw clenched. "Do you know where these people are from?"

"The one I spoke to is from D.C., but I'm sure the police can give you all the addresses once they run each person through the system."

I occasionally felt Shepard's gaze on me as I cleaned, but the police's arrival distracted him. They removed the people with little fuss, and I finished my section and sat next to Pam at the bar to count my tips.

"It's a sad night," she said, looking at her tiny stack of cash. She went to pay the bartenders, but Tank and Buzz refused the money.

"Keep it," Buzz said.

Pam didn't argue. Instead, she said a quick thanks and headed out through the back.

"Think she'll quit?" Tank asked.

"Maybe. Is everyone else okay?" I asked.

Tank nodded. "Thomas and Adrian headed to the kitchen, and we made sure to block it."

I nodded and slid off the stool. "Tell Vena I'm by the lockers. Have a good night."

After clocking out, I put my apron away and tucked my tip money inside my purse. As I waited for the guys, I glanced at my phone and saw I had two messages.

One was from my grandma. She sent a picture of my mom on a lounge chair, holding a mimosa in her hand.

The other was from an unknown number. There was no message, just pictures of my trashed house. My hands shook as I swiped through the pictures. Both the interior and exterior of the house were covered with graffiti. The windows were smashed. The furniture was ruined beyond repair. Our clothes were ripped to shreds. My kitchen looked like a hurricane had hit it, and I was pretty sure someone had defecated on the counter.

"What's wrong?" Vena asked as she came over. "You look like you're going to pass out or kill someone."

I handed her the phone, unable to speak without succumbing to emotions I didn't want to unleash here.

"They fucking trashed our house!" Vena yelled.

She was loud enough that I was sure every wolf and vampire within a five-mile radius heard her. So it was no surprise when Shepard, Cross, and Anchor strode through the kitchen door a few seconds later.

Vena handed the phone to Anchor. Anchor quickly passed off the phone to Shepard so he could hug, or maybe restrain, Vena. She turned to feral mode as Shepard called a crew to go to our house and pack what was salvageable.

Anchor whispered something in her ear, and she exhaled a defeated sigh, then nodded. Detaching from him, she hugged me.

"We'll get the bastards." After releasing me, she followed Anchor to the back lot.

"I'm heading to the station," Shepard said to Cross. "Call if you need me. It's going to be another long night."

Before he left, he kissed me gently. "I'm sorry about your house, Everly. I should have had someone guarding it."

"You needed people looking for the vampires, not babysitting an empty house. It's not your fault."

"Don't worry about the damage or replacing things. I'll take care of it. Just stay with me or Cross until I can deal with it."

"Focus on the vampires. I'll be fine."

I felt queasy about the whole thing. Violated even. But I hadn't lied. I would be fine…after a good cry session in the privacy of a warm, comforting shower where there were no witnesses or sensitive ears.

After he left, I convinced Cross to drive me to his hotel room for the night.

"Did the feeders have any other messages?" I asked after Cross closed the door to the room.

"Only the one. They didn't seem to know anything else."

"Do you need to get out there, too? I'll be fine here. I'll lock and bolt the door."

"My only job tonight is to take care of you and to stay in touch with Shepard. And since I take my job seriously, you'll find everything you need in the dresser and in the bathroom."

"What do you mean?" I asked.

"Take a look."

I headed to the dresser to find it filled with clothes in my size, in styles I would have picked out for myself. They were all cute and comfortable looking.

My lower lip trembled at the thoughtfulness, fueling my

already overwhelmed emotions. Cross stepped behind me and hugged me to him as he kissed my neck lightly.

I patted his arm instead of speaking. After taking a steady breath, I stepped out of his hold and went about my nightly routine. Then, I crawled into bed with Cross, who was waiting for me with open arms.

* . ☾ * .

A SHOWER of gentle kisses over my face and down my neck slowly woke me.

I made a pouty sound. "Sleep…"

He chuckled.

"I'll feed you if you open your beautiful eyes."

I did and saw the room was just barely lit by a crack in the blackout curtains.

"What are you going to feed me?" I asked.

He sat up and took a plate from the side table.

"Eggs Benedict with hash browns if you're interested."

"I'm interested."

I hurried to sit. He kissed my forehead and handed over the plate. While I took my first bite, he propped pillows behind me so I could eat in bed.

"Would you like to hear the latest news?"

"Please," I said, feeling decidedly royal with the breakfast and the personal news update.

"The police are identifying the people found at the dump sites. They aren't just from the D.C. area. Although many were homeless, some were people traveling, and some were from surrounding areas. Only a very few were residents who'd been reported missing. The number of missing persons still unaccounted for concerns Shepard and the liaison.

"Shepard has told Hugh that the problem is too big for his people alone, even though he's calling in for reinforcements.

Don't worry. Not whole packs. Just extra members from packs because he doesn't want those cities left defenseless.

"Because of the extra manpower needed to continue the hunt, Blur will be closed for the foreseeable future."

I stopped eating to stare at Cross.

"You won't be idle. There's still plenty of work for you to do at our place."

It wasn't just Blur closing that had me feeling like my world was falling apart.

"I know. It just sucks knowing I won't have any income." Especially since I was officially homeless after last night's break-in.

"There's more," Cross said, watching me closely.

"Go ahead. Pull the Band-Aid off quickly and tell me."

"The mayor has publicly announced there's a 'health crisis' and has asked citizens to watch for strange behavior and to report any missing persons, even if it's a neighbor that hasn't been seen in a few hours."

I let out a long breath. "I wouldn't want to be the police right now. I can imagine the calls they're getting."

My phone buzzed softly from its place on the chair positioned near my side of the bed.

"The police aren't the only ones who've been getting calls. Vena and Anchor returned to your house earlier. They helped the cleaning crew pack whatever was salvageable. Based on her colorful texts to me, it's not a lot."

Having lost my appetite, I handed Cross my plate so I could lean over to grab my phone. His hand slightly touched my hip, and I caught his heated gaze when I straightened.

"I like when you look at me like that," I admitted.

His eyes went black.

"And like that."

He groaned and kissed my forehead before standing.

"You tempt me, Everly, but I must return you to the wolves for the time being. Shepard spent the night searching for answers and needs me to take over so he can rest."

I nodded and accepted the clothes he handed me.

Cross had impeccable taste and had picked out a shirt that modestly flattered my curves. I felt cute when I walked out and gained his appreciative stare.

That feeling slipped away as I drove across town to the complex and my thoughts swirled with what had happened in the last twenty-four hours. I had no home. No job. No car of my own. No spare money to live off of, never mind any to replace what I'd lost. I still needed a huge chunk of money for my final year of college. And vampires were after me and those I loved because of the rings.

What in the fairy feces was I supposed to do?

I'd worked too hard to become independent to be okay living off of either Cross or Shepard. And going back to my parents wasn't a viable option. At least, not for me. It would be like giving up.

By the time I pulled up in front of the complex, I was angry to the point of tears. Cross didn't say anything, but I could feel his worried glances as I parked.

Shepard opened my door as Cross got out.

"Everly, I'm so sorry," he said, wrapping me in a hug.

"Did something *else* happen?" I asked.

"No. Nothing. Just your house."

Just?

But wasn't he right? Sure, what we'd lost would be hard to replace, but Vena and I were both still here. It could have been worse. So I nodded, hugged him back, and tried to push away my negative thoughts.

After a moment, I let go. "You head to bed."

"What will you do?" he asked.

"Don't worry about me. I'll probably check in on the Hunters, call my parents, talk Vena down from whatever new way she wants to kill vampires, and bake something."

He smiled and gave me one last hug before I shooed him away. When I looked back, I saw Cross was already gone.

As Shepard went to find his bed, I knocked on the Hunters' door

"Come in."

I peeked in to find them still researching.

"How are you both?" I asked as I stepped inside and closed the door.

Mrs. Hunter leaned back and rubbed at her tired eyes. "We've exhausted all our contacts and found no new leads. There are no records of any fae gifting a vampire with another form, so we cannot know what it would take to kill such a magical creature.

"I fear Miles might be lost to us forever." She sniffled. "Unless we ask Cross to take over the thrall."

Mr. Hunter frowned. "It would just be another vampire controlling Miles."

"Except Cross would never control Miles," I said. "Just think of it as a Plan B worst-case scenario. The first step is finding Adriel."

Mrs. Hunter nodded.

"When was the last time you ate?" I asked.

They shook their heads as if not knowing.

"Slept?" I asked.

They shook their heads again.

"In bed. Both of you."

"There's so much more work," Mrs. Hunter began.

"You said you've exhausted your contacts and research. You need to sleep. Weren't you the one who lectured Vena and me about the correlation between the brain and lack of sleep? Something about lack of sleep would make us as dimwitted as trolls?"

She sighed and stood with a groan. "I might have. Very well. If you're going to start quoting me, I can hardly argue with myself."

Mrs. Hunter gave me a hug before falling into bed with her husband.

I closed the door and went to the dining hall. It was empty at this time of morning, which was exactly what I needed. Taking a seat, I checked my messages from Vena, which were pretty much telling me our house was beyond trashed. Knowing there was little I could do about that, I texted my mom, thanking her for the pictures and wishing them a good time for the remainder of their trip.

What would happen if their trip ended before this nightmare was over?

Restless, I stood. I needed to bake.

I found the kitchen was mostly empty as well. Lisa, the den mother, was in there with the lead cook, Cathy. They glanced at me with friendly smiles.

"You doing okay?" Lisa asked me.

"I need some baking therapy," I said with a hopeful smile and a plea in my voice.

They both chuckled.

"You can bake to your heart's content," Cathy said as she took off her apron. "You know where everything is. Just make sure there's room for lunch prep in an hour. We'll need at least one of the prep tables and the cook range today. Otherwise, the kitchen is yours."

"Thank you."

Taking an apron from the many that were hung on the wall, I decided to make a dessert that my grandma used to make for me. I needed that bit of nostalgia to get me through the uncertainty.

Time passed quickly as I lost myself in the methodical rhythm that baking provided. By the time I was pulling the grape pie out of the oven, the ladies were arriving to prep the next meal.

I let the dessert cool to the side and stood out of the way as the ladies took their positions and seamlessly began to work together. I was about to offer to help when I felt my phone buzz.

The message wasn't from any number I knew, which should have been enough to stop me from opening it, but I did. And I felt my heart drop.

Pivoting, I raced out of the kitchen, ignoring the ladies' questioning calls. The image of the little girl from across the street tied to one of the kitchen chairs in our trashed house was burned into my brain. So was the message that had gone with it.

Unknown: You have fifteen minutes. Come alone or the girl dies.

I was out the front doors and in my SUV before some semblance of reasoning kicked in. As I started the engine, I sent a text to the group chat I had with Shepard and Cross.

Me: They have the little girl from across the street at my house. I'm headed there now. They said alone. It's daylight, so I should be safe enough until one of you gets there. I can't ignore this. I'm sorry.

My phone started ringing a second later. I didn't answer. I was too focused on weaving in and out of traffic as I raced across town.

The minutes ticked by, and my phone quieted just as I pulled up in front of my house.

I was three minutes late.

Fumbling for the door handle, I spilled out of the SUV and raced for the front door.

The door to our house stood slightly ajar.

Without hesitating, I rushed in.

Harper sat on a single chair in the middle of our empty, graffitied living room. Her hair was in two cute pigtails, but she wasn't tied or bound.

She smiled at me and said, "No bleeding."

Pain exploded in the back of my head, and everything went dark.

CHAPTER TWENTY-THREE

THE STEADY THROB IN MY HEAD FORCED ME OUT OF unconsciousness.

With a groan, I tried to reach for the source of pain. My hands wouldn't move. No, that wasn't right. They were moving; I just couldn't lift them. They were stuck behind me.

Confused, I blinked my eyes open and tried to make sense of what they might be caught on. Turning my head made my stomach lurch. Nausea rose, and I closed my eyes and took a few calming breaths before trying to look again. The room swam in and out of focus for a few seconds.

I waited for my sight to clear. As it did, so did my thoughts.

No bleeding.

I'd gone to the house to save Harper, and someone had hit the back of my head.

Lifting my gaze, I looked around the unfamiliar space. A strip of twinkly lights strung overhead cast more shadows than light. But it was enough to see my elderly neighbor and his grand-daughter kneeling not far away from me, near a ratty bed.

I took in their vacant stares and the bite marks on Harper's grandpa's neck and knew they were thralled.

I am so screwed.

My gaze swept the space, looking for clues regarding where they'd taken me. Straight ahead, I saw a steel railing. Beyond that, nothing but darkness. The break in the railing was wide enough for a set of stairs. So a loft apartment?

I breathed in the faded scent of old oil, exhaust, and chemicals. A loft in a warehouse?

My gaze swept the space again, taking in the dilapidated, sparse furnishings then down at myself. They'd tied me to my own damn kitchen chair, and my necklace was gone. How in the hell had they gotten it off if it was anti-theft? I spotted it on a table not far from me. Beside it were two blood bags. Condensation had already beaded on the plastic, showing they'd been out for a while.

I glanced at the windows near the roofline, trying to gauge the time. The windows gave no light whatsoever. Was it because of the paper covering them or because the sun had already set?

Panic set in hard. This shouldn't have happened. Cross could move fast. Shepard could track me on the app. How did they not reach me in time? I'd called them. I looked for my phone and didn't see it. I'd left it in the car.

Internally yelling at myself for my stupidity, I tried to think of a way out of the trouble I'd landed in.

If they couldn't track me with the app, I needed to bleed. Cross always showed up when I bled. Fingernails in my palm? No, I might need my hands. Same with abrading my wrist with the rope.

That left one simple solution—I just needed to bite my tongue or cheek.

No problem. You can do this, Everly.

I sucked the side of my cheek between my molars and bit down. My eyes watered, and I felt a loose bit of skin, but there was no metallic tang of blood. A tear spilled over and tracked down my cheek as I tried again.

It hurt so damn bad, but I finally tasted blood.

The pair by the bed hadn't moved. Good.

Come on, Cross. Come and save me already.

While I thought that, I carefully turned my hands in their bindings, trying to find where they were tied. I was all for a good rescue, but I wasn't about to sit still and hope it would be in time. I had way too many close calls for that. My fingers found the end of a rope, and I traced it as I glanced at the windows again.

Just when I thought I'd found the knot, which I could barely touch with the tips of my fingers, something crashed below us. I was the only one who flinched. My gaze darted toward the opening in the railing that led to whatever was below us.

Please be Cross. Please be Cross.

I heard a faint scrape of noise. The room instantly brightened as three lamps turned on in the loft. I glanced away from the gap in the railing for less than a second. When I looked back, Vivian, Adriel's lover, stood there.

He wore the same black leather pants as the last time I saw him and a black t-shirt that accentuated the dark makeup around his eyes.

His lips curved as he inhaled deeply, and I watched the telltale black veins spread out from under his heavy makeup.

"What did you do?" he asked more calmly than I would have thought he possessed. "I smell your blood."

When I didn't answer, he blurred and was suddenly in front of me.

He had his tongue inside my mouth before I knew what was happening. But it was over as soon as it had started.

He grinned at me. "Calling Cross to save you? I didn't think you had it in you to hurt yourself on purpose. I thought I'd have to do the honors for you."

My mind slowly caught up to what he was saying.

"You *want* Cross here?"

"Not just him. Where Cross goes, a certain wolf will eventu-

ally follow. And they will pay dearly for nearly killing Master."
He went over to Harper and ran his fingers over her hair.

"Don't hurt her," I said.

His gaze whipped to mine, and he grinned right before he
blurred.

My wrists burned as he tore me from the chair and threw me
face-first into the mattress. He landed on my back, his hips
pinning mine as he straddled me.

"She's not the one who'll hurt," he growled in my ear. "They
tossed Master into a mass grave like garbage to be forgotten.
Master gifted them the same, only with their precious humans.
But I want more."

Vivian's hand fisted the back of my shirt and yanked hard, the
force of it pulling me up as the material tore. I tried to scrabble
away, but he shoved me back down. What was left of my shirt
disappeared.

"I had nothing to do with what happened at the alpha fight," I
said desperately.

My need for Shepard and Cross to save me warred with my
fear for them. Why did Vivian want them to come here? What
did he have planned?

Vivian grabbed my shorts, and I struggled in earnest to
dislodge his weight.

"This isn't about revenge," I shouted. "This is about getting the
rings for Orphia, you sick prick."

"I don't give a damn about the bitch. She might be my queen,
but she is not my master." He leaned down, his breath tickling my
neck over my frantic pulse. "Only Adriel gets that title."

My body jerked as he ripped my shorts free.

"Thanks to you, I'll have my revenge for what they did to my
true master. And I'll enjoy every second of it, too."

His palm rubbed over my exposed butt cheek before he
slapped it hard. Panic slammed through me, making him laugh.

"You smell delicious when you're scared."

A crash sounded downstairs half a second before Vivian flew from me.

I scurried off the bed to crouch against the wall as two blurs slammed together.

They were too fast to see, but the fallout wasn't. The table broke. A lamp fell over, the bulb shattering. The mattress flipped off the bed.

I was so busy watching the carnage that I didn't notice a third blur until Adriel stood by the railing, holding Harper over the abyss below by an ankle.

Cross came to an abrupt stop, holding Vivian by the neck. Blood poured from Vivian's multiple wounds, and his head dropped forward as he clutched Cross' arm.

"Stop," Cross ordered.

"An exchange. Pet for the girl."

"And the others."

Adriel snarled but agreed. "On the count of three."

"One—" Adriel dropped the girl.

He and Cross blurred at the same time. Cross streaked down the stairs while Adriel whisked Vivian over the edge.

I dashed to the railing and saw Cross catch Harper. Vivian and Adriel were nowhere in sight.

My body wilted to the floor in relief.

Cross reappeared in the loft and told the grandfather and Harper to sleep. Then he swept me off the ground and held me close as he sat on the bed.

"Did he bite you?"

I could feel my need to answer him truthfully and knew Cross had compelled me.

"He didn't bite me; I did so that you would come. I was scared you wouldn't get here in time. I'm sorry I left."

He smoothed his hand over my hair and kissed my forehead. Then he kissed my lips. I melted into his touch and felt his tongue swipe over my cheek, even though it had already been healed by Vivian's disgusting tongue. He withdrew and hugged me again.

Tears started to fall in earnest. He rubbed my back and rocked us as he held me. But my breakdown wasn't just about this moment. It was about all of them combined. It was the fear that this would never end. That people would forever try to use me to hurt Cross and Shepard.

When my tears slowed, he scooted me from his lap and stripped off his t-shirt. He helped put it on me then gathered me close again.

A few moments later, Shepard called for us from below.

I didn't lift my head from where it was buried in Cross' very damp shoulder.

"We're up here," Cross called over the sounds of my hitched breathing.

I heard several sets of feet pounding up the stairs.

"Is she all right?" Shepard asked softly.

"She's fine. Vivian and Adriel were here a few moments ago."

"We're on it," I heard Tank say. This time, only a whisper of sound marked their departure.

The bed moved as Shepard sat beside us and ran his hand over my hair. Neither spoke as they tried to comfort me. It sort of made me want to cry more—out of guilt—but I forced myself to focus on deep, calming breaths until the tears stopped.

"I shouldn't have gone without you," I managed to say.

"It doesn't matter," Shepard said. "You're safe now. That's all that matters."

A fresh wash of tears made me sniffle against Cross. Sure, I was safe, but it'd been so close. Again.

"Are you hurt anywhere?" Shepard asked.

I was. My wrists burned fiercely, and my armpits hurt where my shirt had caught before ripping. And I was pretty sure I had bruises from where Vivian had grabbed me. But I didn't say any of that.

"I'm fine. What about Harper and her grandpa?" I finally lifted my head to look for them and saw both resting peacefully on a tattered couch spattered with old blood stains. "Did Vivian and Adriel hurt her?"

Cross kissed my forehead. "I'll find out what happened."

He passed me to Shepard, who held me just as comfortingly as Cross had and approached the pair. He woke them up then started asking questions. When and how did they first meet Vivian? What were they told to do? Had either Vivian or Adriel done anything to them besides feeding?

I listened to the girl explain that they had been the ones to put the tracking device on my car and had been watching my movements. "Pet," which I knew was what Vivian preferred to be called, had only fed from them each visit. The most recent being today, just before dawn, when he'd told them how to capture me.

"He said it wasn't because of the rings," I said. "It was because of what happened to Adriel at the alpha challenge. He was angry you threw Adriel in a mass grave. That's why they've been dumping those bodies like that too. Revenge." I started to shake a little. "That's why he wanted me. He wanted you to pay for what you did to Adriel."

"Do you believe that?" Shepard asked Cross.

"I don't doubt it. Orphia isn't one to evoke any sense of loyalty. However, he and Adriel would willingly use Everly to get the rings. I'm just not certain whether they would hand them over to Orphia or keep them for themselves."

My shaking didn't stop, and I knew it was bothering Shepard when he kissed my temple and buried his head against my neck.

"This is killing me, Everly. I hate your fear."

"Me too," I said.

Cross asked the little girl if she knew where they were.

"This is my master's home," she said.

"You may both sleep now."

After they fell back onto the couch again, Cross picked up my necklace and gently clasped it onto my neck.

"I don't understand how they took it off," I said.

"Vivian ensured Harper's intent wasn't to hurt you," he said. "And she had no interest in robbing you. Using an innocent girl was sadly brilliant." He kissed my forehead while Shepard was still holding me then crossed to the room to check the fridge.

"It does appear that this was their primary home. I wonder where they were, though, if neither was here when you woke." He inhaled deeply. "The only scents under the reek of exhaust and oil are Vivian's and Adriel's."

Tank came up the steps again. His gaze swept over me, and I saw nothing but concern as it shifted to Shepard.

"We found the trail and followed it to a sewer cap. Do you want us to follow?"

"No," Shepard said. "It's harder to pick up any distinct scents down there, and I don't need anyone else going missing."

"Missing?" I lifted my head. "What do you mean?"

"One of the patrols I sent out last night still hasn't come back," Shepard said.

I could see his worry and returned my head to his shoulder.

"I'm so sorry I left, Shepard. I didn't mean to add to your stress."

"You wouldn't be the person I love if you stopped caring about other people, Everly. I know you left to save the girl, and you let me know where you were going." He exhaled heavily. "Maybe next time you could pick up after sending something like that though."

I turned my head to meet his gaze. "I knew you would tell me not to go."

He nodded and kissed my forehead.

"What about these two?" Tank asked.

"We'll take them to the house with us," Shepard said. "Even with Miles and Sierra, we still have room."

He stood and set me on my feet, straightening the shirt I wore so it mostly covered me.

It was dark outside when we finally left. I looked back at the old, rusty building and shuddered, knowing it'd take up residence in my nightmares until both Master and Pet were dead.

Cross opened the passenger door to Shepard's SUV and helped me inside, even going so far as to buckle my seatbelt for me. It made me feel ridiculous that I was such a mess that they were treating me with kid gloves, but at the same time, it was exactly what I needed.

I murmured my thanks after he hopped in the backseat.

As Shepard drove, he assured me and Cross that Doc had already picked up the company car and it would be at the pack house.

"I don't care about that," Cross said. "We need to meet with Effora. All of us. The longer we wait, the more situations like this will occur."

"Before Everly texted us, Hugh was able to pin down Effora."

"What time is the meeting?" Cross asked.

"Noon tomorrow. Hugh will tell us where."

Tomorrow. Noon. The idea of either of them leaving my side made my stomach churn.

"Can I go, too? I don't want to be alone."

Both agreed.

CHAPTER TWENTY-FOUR

At the pack house, Cross said goodbye and told Shepard he would keep looking for Vivian and Adriel.

Shepard walked me to the door, his arm around my shoulders. The men we passed on the way in gave me funny looks, and I wondered if it was because I only wore a shirt or because I reeked of vampire from my time in Adriel and Vivian's love-slash-murder nest.

I shivered, and Shepard hurried me to his suite. He steered me right into the master bathroom where he programmed the shower, eased me out of the shirt, and helped me under the warm spray.

His eyes darkened as he scanned my bruise-riddled body, and I saw guilt.

"It's not your fault," I said. "It's mine. Let's both let go of the guilt and just appreciate the fact that everyone is safe for now. And for at least the next twenty-four hours, you'll get that clinginess you craved."

With a small nod, he gently washed me, taking care not to press too hard on my skin.

Afterward, he pulled a soft t-shirt from his dresser, slipped it on me, and helped me into bed. I snuggled against him, creating as many contact points as possible. Finally feeling safe, I let myself sleep.

THE NEXT MORNING, I found myself comfortably sandwiched between Cross and Shepard. Shepard was spooning me from behind with an arm looped around my waist as if he was ensuring I couldn't wander away in his sleep.

Cross opened his eyes to watch me as I quietly yawned.

"What time is it?" I asked softly.

"Just after ten," he returned just as quietly.

I knew I needed to get up but didn't want to wake up Shepard.

"Your phone's been making noise for the past thirty minutes," Cross said.

I made a face, and he kissed my nose.

We both heard the outer door to Shepard's suite open. Cross' eyes flashed black for half a second before he closed them. The bedroom door banged open a second later, startling me.

I looked up and caught Vena's angry scowl shift to surprise then delight.

"Shhh. Shepard's still sleeping," I said.

"Not anymore," he said from behind me.

"Girl, I told you to be the cream in their otherworld sandwich, but I didn't think you'd actually go for it."

"We were just sleeping, Vena."

"Sure." She wiggled her eyebrows at me.

"Is there a reason you barged in here?"

"Oh, yeah. I *was* mad at you. First, you left without me. Then you got kidnapped and didn't even tell me."

"You're upset Everly was kidnapped without you?" Cross asked,

"And…" Vena said loudly as if speaking over Cross, even though he was already done. "Apparently, getting kidnapped isn't the only secret you're keeping. You've been enjoying this sleep sandwich often, haven't you? You're not even blushing or telling me to get out, which means this isn't your first time."

"Get out, Vena," I said without rancor.

"It's too late to try to hide the truth. It's out. Anything else out under those covers?"

I knew my friend well enough to understand why Vena broke in as she had and why she wasn't ranting at me. She was worried.

"I'm okay, Vena. If I was hurt, do you think they'd just be sleeping next to me?"

"If you were fine, they wouldn't be just sleeping next to you. You'd really be sandwiched. I mean, with the way Shepard's positioned, you could—"

"Vena, don't," I said, fighting not to flush as I imagined what she was imagining.

"Fine. But no more 'Vena does this while Everly does that' bullshit. We stick together."

"You're not getting into this bed," Shepard said, his voice still rough with sleep. "It's already too crowded."

Cross chuckled as Shepard drew me closer to him and away from Cross.

"I'm not interested in joining your bed sport," Vena said. "I want in on the meeting today."

"Will it get you to leave the room faster?" Shepard asked.

"Yep."

"Be at the front door by eleven-thirty."

"You got it, Alpha. Tap that hard, Everly."

I listened to the sound of the door closing and shook my head.

Cross winked at me. "Neither of us would mind any tapping."

"Ha. Not happening. My wrists are still sore from yesterday."

I held them up to look at them but found myself stolen from

Shepard—he didn't protest—and carried to the bathroom where Cross put some ointment on the marks and wrapped them.

After, he left me alone to wash up and dress. I had some bruises on my arms and legs where Vivian had grabbed me, but nothing more serious than that. It could have been much worse and just added to the bruises left over from the car accident.

At the appointed time, Vena and Anchor met us at Shepard's SUV.

It didn't take us long to reach the location that Hugh had selected. It was the same restaurant Cross had taken me to a few days ago. It looked a little different today, though. Rather than tuxedoed men waiting to open the doors for us, two men in all-black gear guarded the entrance and nodded to Shepard as our group of five approached.

Inside, another set of men waited. They didn't talk to us as they stood sentinel outside the only open door in the hallway. The room was larger than the previous private dining room we'd used.

We were the first to arrive, and Hugh greeted Shepard warmly.

"Welcome, Alpha. Your guard may sit on the chairs against the walls. Help yourself to the appetizers on the table, and order whatever beverage you would like as we wait."

He turned to Cross and extended his hand. "Brodier Cross, it is a pleasure to meet you. I've learned much about you in the last twenty-four hours."

"Just Cross," he said, shaking the man's hand, then eyeing the table that had name cards already set out. "We'll need another chair at the table."

"Oh?" Hugh asked.

"Everly sits with us," Shepard said, placing an arm around my shoulders.

"I can sit off to the side with Vena and Anchor."

"No," both Cross and Shepard said at the same time.

Hugh smiled. "Consider it done."

With a gentle wave of his hand, two attendants helped move a chair and added a setting, putting me in between Shepard and Cross.

King Curran and Princess Indri entered with Tryn, the head of His Majesty's personal guards, before they finished. Tryn scanned the room and moved off to the side by Vena and Anchor.

"It is good to see you both again," Hugh said. He shook the king's hand but brought the princess' hand to his mouth in a mock kiss gesture that made her weary expression turn lighter.

Curran turned to Cross and Shepard, offering his hand in greeting. Although he was polite, I could feel his impatience.

"I've heard the death toll is climbing, Alpha, and the vampires are as skillful at evading your efforts to find them as Adriel is at evading mine. What do you plan to do next?"

"Queen Effora should arrive soon," Hugh said. "I would prefer we wait to begin our discussion until then."

Curran grumbled under his breath. "This problem won't solve itself while we stand around the table." But he took his seat.

We followed his lead.

I nibbled on a few appetizers at Cross' encouragement and made small talk with the princess in an attempt to distract the king from his impatience. However, once the appetizers were gone, Curran began getting antsy and checked the time often. Irritation turned to anger when it was a few minutes past the appointed time and still no sign of the fae queen.

Cross reached under the table and gave my hand a gentle squeeze. At the same time, Shepard looked at the door.

One of the prettiest women I'd ever seen entered the room. Her silky blonde hair was woven with strands of diamonds that sparkled in the light. Her eyes were the lightest shade of blue, and her dress showed off all her attributes to the fullest.

Her expression lit as soon as her gaze landed on Shepard. She veered over to him, standing next to his chair. He stiffened when she rested her hand on his shoulder.

"You are looking as delectable as ever," she said, drawing a line with her long fingernail down from his shoulder to his chest. "After this meeting, I think you and I should have a private one."

Poor Shepard, always the gentleman, looked flustered at how to handle her without causing offense or making a scene in front of the others. I had no such problem when he fisted his hands under the table. I reached over with my free hand, set it over his, and leaned forward to claim Effora's attention.

"Queen Effora, I presume," I said.

Her gaze lifted from Shepard and swept over me. "You must be Everly. I can see the attraction." Her gaze shifted back to Shepard. "You should bring her with. Our time together would be positively delicious."

Shepard moved to dislodge Effora's hand from his shoulder, but she caught his hand and turned it toward her, laying it on her hip so she could inch closer. One step more and she'd be straddling him.

"Queen Effora," I said, drawing her attention to me again. I couldn't keep quiet any longer. What she needed was Vena's spray bottle, but I knew I couldn't pull a stunt like that without repercussions.

This wasn't the time or place for her feeding needs, and Shepard had already expressed his desire for me, not her. I had to set boundaries now.

"Shepard is too much of a gentleman to tell you that you're making him uncomfortable, but you are. Please release him and take a seat so we can focus on why we're really here. King Curran and Princess Indri have a long drive home."

Effora narrowed her eyes at me, but Hugh said, "You promised your cooperation in this meeting."

With the barest eye roll, she left Shepard's side and sat at her chair opposite of him.

"All right. I'm seated. Now what?"

"Now we discuss the problem at hand," Hugh said. "The discovery of the mass graves does not only affect humans.

"The vampire population is out of control and needs immediate mitigation. And the werewolf efforts alone are no longer enough. All the races need to cooperate in the resolution of this problem."

"And how do you expect my people to help?" the queen asked. "We are not the fighters the werewolves are. And we neither have the strength or fortitude of the dwarves."

Curran's face grew progressively redder with each word she spoke.

"Are you suggesting that the fae race is useless?" I asked, angry that she still took a passive stance when there had been so many deaths. "I'm not sure your people would agree."

She shot me a disdainful look. "Not at all. We definitely have our uses."

Vena snorted. "Not the use anyone here is interested in."

"You wish to speak, human?" Effora asked, a small smile tugging at her mouth as she looked at Vena.

"I do." My best friend stood and approached the table to set her scrying crystal on it. "This is the kind of help we need."

The queen picked up the crystal and arched a brow at it. "A crystal to find cats? No wonder you have a vampire problem."

She tossed the crystal to the table again.

"*We* have a problem," Shepard said to Effora. "Unless you suddenly live in a different city."

Her gaze was like a caress as it skimmed over Shepard. The woman seriously needed a cold shower.

Vena snatched her crystal and shook her head at the queen. "Stupid isn't a good look on you, so stop pretending. This crystal isn't just for black cats but for Adriel, the only vampire some fae gifted with the ability to shift. Wonder who that fae could be?"

The queen's gaze turned truly cold as it shifted to Vena. "Take care how you speak to me, human. You have no place at this table."

"Vena might not be at the table, but you invited her to speak, and she's not wrong," I said. "We know that a powerful fae granted Adriel's ability to shift. And because of his ability, Adriel snuck into the mountain to kill Prince Hakon. Doesn't that mean that the fae are then partially to blame for what also happened?"

Effora's gaze lingered on me as Curran's fist slammed down on the table, making the china rattle.

"We are owed answers," he said. The princess put her hand on his arm, trying to calm him.

"Much is owed at this table," Hugh said. "Humans were promised safety in return for welcoming otherworlders here, and now, many have died. Things have progressed too far for those who I represent to remain quiet. Any who do not wish to contribute to correcting this situation will no longer be welcomed by my kind.

"Now, how do each of you propose to contribute to the removal of the vampires?"

Effora opened her mouth to respond, but the door opened again, cutting her off.

A woman almost as pretty as the queen walked in and smiled as her gaze swept the room. In the hallway behind her, I glimpsed the two guards kissing passionately. It was so shocking it took a few seconds for me to understand what was happening.

The woman was a fae who'd bespelled the guards to win her way into the room.

Tryn, King Curran's guard, moved to stop the woman, but she calmly held up a hand to stop him.

"I'm here to attend this meeting of the greater races."

The queen lazily looked over at the woman. "And what right do you have to be here?"

"My name is Xiana, and I am here on behalf of my queen."

Effora laughed. "I am here on my own behalf."

"I am here on behalf of Orphia, Queen and rightful representative of the vampires." As the woman spoke, her gaze shifted to Cross.

"Your queen misses you, Cross."

CHAPTER TWENTY-FIVE

I GLANCED AT CROSS AND CAUGHT HIS BORED LOOK AS HE LEANED back in his chair.

"We both know it's not me Orphia misses," he said.

"It's interesting that she wishes to be represented here when her kind is the problem we're discussing," Hugh said.

I bristled at Hugh's comment, offended on Cross' behalf because it wasn't *all* vampires who were the problem.

"Vampires are not the problem," Xiana said. "I can tell you firsthand which group is responsible for most of the city's problems. But I'm not here to point fingers. I'm here because you have held this meeting at a time when my queen cannot defend herself. Does she not deserve representation?"

"This isn't a trial," Hugh said. "But if you must speak on her behalf, make it brief."

"Are you serious?" Curran demanded. "What rights do the vampires have to speak when they are killing and stealing? They are nothing but monsters."

"Not all vampires are monsters, King Curran," I said, unable to keep quiet.

Cross gently squeezed my leg under the table. In gratitude or warning, though?

"Precisely," Xiana said. "Vampires live and breathe and have a pulse like the rest of you. On what basis do the fae, dwarves, and werewolves have the right to exist, but we do not? This is persecution, and on behalf of the vampire race, I object and demand equal rights."

Shepard leaned back and crossed his arms. "Equal rights? To who? Humans? Vampires are not equal to humans. They're stronger and faster and can take over a human's mind with a gaze or a bite. There's no equality between vampires and humans, only hunter and prey.

"And vampires have left body piles to prove exactly how they view humans. So stop trying to play a game you've already lost and just tell us your angle. Orphia is up to something. I want to know what it is."

"Yes, I'm curious as well," Cross said. He gazed intently at the woman. "What is Orphia's motivation in sending you here?"

The woman laughed. "Think again, Cross. Your compelling tricks don't work on me. I'm half fae and half is vampire, like you."

I felt the shock of that kernel of knowledge right down to my toes and glanced at Vena. I hadn't known that vampire and fae babies were possible. From her identical surprised expression reaction, she didn't either.

Hugh cleared his throat, gaining Xiana's attention. "While I realize equality between the races is a touchy situation, you can't cry persecution on behalf of all vampires. The other supernaturals are not killing humans. Only vampires are doing that."

"If this is about the bodies you've discovered, they aren't what you think they are," Xiana said. "Those were failed conversions. We have signed waivers indemnifying their chosen mentors from all wrongdoing. If you provide the appropriate contact information, we can forward all the related paperwork to you immediately."

I sat back, stunned at what she was saying.

Conversions? Waivers? Mentors? No way all those people were willing.

However, I felt a thread of doubt. Who wanted to die? No one. Yet, were people really willing to risk their mortal lives for the chance at an immortal one?

Vena snorted. "What about Master?"

"Orphia is my master. She has done no harm."

"Adriel," Vena said impatiently. "We already know he's a killer. He's proven time and again that he will kill."

"As Everly said, not all vampires are monsters. One bad vampire should not condemn an entire race, but rather the individual."

No one had introduced me or said my name. Panic wormed its way into my chest as she met my gaze and slowly smiled before turning to Hugh.

"And you know the other races aren't as innocent as they appear.

"The dwarves are destroying the planet with their mining and paying the humans to look the other way. The werewolves are indiscriminate killers, ending the lives of vampires who haven't even fed from a human. And not every fae's food source lives long once they're released."

I watched Effora's gaze narrow on Xiana. When she caught my gaze, her expression smoothed out to indifference again.

"I have never killed anyone," Xiana continued. "Yet, because I have vampire blood, does that mean I deserve to die?"

Curran made a disgruntled noise. Shepard looked angry, but Cross looked thoughtful.

"You do make a valid point," Cross said. "And it's one that's already been recognized by the members at this table, or I wouldn't be comfortably sitting here, would I? So rather than waste our time with pointless propaganda, why don't you get to the point and prove you're really here on behalf of all vampires and not simply here on behalf of Orphia."

"Can't I be here for both?" she asked. "Perhaps you should speak directly to Orphia."

She walked to the head of the table and pulled a tablet out of her purse. Propping it on the table so we could all see it, she said, "Since my words hold no weight, perhaps hers will."

She turned on the screen, and a woman who looked to be in her late twenties or early thirties appeared. She had dark hair and arching eyebrows. The dark makeup she wore was stark against her pale skin. Her thin smile never reached her cold gaze, which swept over the people seated at the table.

My gaze did the same. Curran and Indri looked like they weren't sure what was going on. A slow flush was creeping up Effora's neck. Hugh wore his passive mask like Cross did. Shepard looked thoughtful.

"Hello, everyone," Orphia said. "I've been listening to the conversation so far and fear you have misunderstood our intention. I would like a chance to speak with you all in person and arrange for another meeting at a time when I can attend."

Had it been from anyone else, her request might have seemed reasonable. But even hearing her hollow voice gave me the chills. An in-person meeting with her was a hard pass for me.

"You're here now," Shepard said. "Why waste time? Unless there's another reason you'd like to meet us in person?"

A real smile curved her lips, completely changing her appearance. She actually looked approachable and pretty like that, and I could see why Cross had briefly liked her.

"I must say I never thought I would see the day the alpha would sit at a table with a vampire. It is a sight I would dearly love to see in person." Her gaze shifted to Cross. "It would also be a good chance for me to renew very old acquaintanceships. I've missed you, Cross."

He chuckled and shook his head. "I haven't missed you, Orphia. And we both know you only ever sought my company because of my jewelry. There is nothing for us to renew."

Some of her humor faded, and she looked at me.

"Everly Anne Reid, twenty-three-year-old daughter of Nadeen and Terry Reid. A modest 64 inches tall, afraid of fairies, and deeply bonded with Vena Bree Hunter."

I knew a threat when I heard one and felt my blood turn cold with each fact she listed. I refused to be cowed, though.

"I'm surprised someone as old as you knows how to use the internet," I said.

Orphia's smile turned positively vicious before she looked at Cross.

"I can see why you like her. You always did have a thing for the sweet-and-sassy combination, didn't you?" She looked at Shepard. "You surprised me, though. Willing to share with a vampire? What*ever* will your people think?"

Curran slammed his hand down again, knocking the tablet over.

"Enough of this. The uninvited should leave."

Instead of listening, Xiana straightened the tablet so Orphia's amused smile was in full view again.

"I think you'll want to take the time to listen to me, Curran. I can give you what no one else can...*if* we meet in person."

I watched Curran's anger fade. "You have my son's killer?"

"No. However, he is one of my people, and I can easily find and detain him for you."

"The only promises you know to give are broken ones," Cross said.

"Ah, but not to get what I want," Orphia said. Her gaze and tone turned hard. "If you refuse to discuss the inequality of the races, you will suffer the consequences as we have.

"Werewolves prosper because of their anonymity. I wonder how loving the public will be if a list of werewolf names and locations is released. I doubt your efforts to paint yourselves as human-loving creatures will hold long when the public understands the reason for your very existence is to kill."

"Kill vampires," Shepard said.

"Considering the number of people who willingly gave their lives for a chance to become immortal, I don't believe that will endear you to anyone."

Orphia's gaze moved to the fae queen.

"Effora, likewise, I believe your precious humans would have a completely different view of your kind if they knew how many you've purchased over the decades. These before and after pictures are truly something to behold."

Pictures of people replaced Orphia's face. Each one showed a healthy, happy person and then an emaciated version of that person. I thought back to every fae who had ever hit on me at Blur and felt a surge of revulsion.

"I believe I've given you all enough reason to meet with me, have I not?" Orphia said. "Vampires want the same as all the other races: freedom to live and feed openly without persecution. You have twenty-four hours to set a time and place before I release everything I've promised. And during the fallout, my people will show the world the kind of killers you've painted us to be."

The screen went black, and Orphia's representative placed the tablet back into her purse.

"It would be wise to meet with my queen to give her what she wants. If you comply, she will ensure your lives don't change. Defy her, and my queen will ensure your lives fall apart."

Xiana swept out of the room as quickly as she'd entered and spoke to the guards who were still making out in the hallway. They jerked apart and wiped at their mouths as they glared after her.

"Close the door, please," Hugh said calmly.

Once they did, he looked at Curran, Effora, Shepard, and Cross. "I believe she seeks to sway the unfavorable opinion of her people's existence as a distraction to obtain all of the rings, which we cannot allow."

"Agreed," Shepard said.

"I agree as well," Effora said as she stood. "I wish you all well in your quest."

"Does that mean you no longer want to be welcomed by humankind?" I asked. My gaze shifted from her to Hugh. "I believe you said, 'Any who do not wish to contribute to correcting this situation will no longer be welcomed by my kind.' Right?"

Effora eyed me. "Know your place, human."

A low growl came from Shepard, which only amused Effora.

"Such a virile beast," she said and aimed a sly grin at him.

"Everly is right, Effora," Cross said. "We need your help."

Vena held out the crystal scry to Effora. "Maybe you can't hunt like a werewolf or kick ass like a dwarf, but you can do magic. So help us by putting a better spell on this thing. It finds every black cat, but not Adriel."

Effora looked at it with a frown. "You get what you pay for. And sadly, this is a cheap toy." From the depths of her cleavage, she pulled out a crystal on a silver chain necklace and held it in her palm. I could clearly see the difference in quality between her stone and Vena's.

I felt the surge of electric energy in the room as Effora silently cast her spell. After, she handed it to Vena.

"It will locate clusters of vampires. Happy hunting."

"I want Adriel, not a bunch of vampires," Vena complained. "Redo the spell."

"I will not. This is your best chance at finding the one you seek. Beyond the low quality of your scry, why do you think it located all black cats and not the single one you want? Scrying can be a useful tool, but they are not all-seeing. The bigger the nest of vampires, the better the scry will work."

Vena slipped the necklace on with a grumbled thanks.

"One more thing about the scry," Effora said as an afterthought. "Only a human should wield it since it focuses on otherworlders' blood."

Effora glanced at Shepard. "If you care for my company, you know where to find me."

Shepard stood abruptly. "Effora, I appreciate your help with the scry, but your people need to take an active role in this search as well. The vampires are killing humans."

She arched a delicate brow. "That's why my ancestors made your kind, darling. To keep the vampires in check because we were unable to. Nothing has changed during the centuries that followed."

"Then your ancestors shouldn't have made vampires in the first place," I said. "Stop passing the responsibility for your people's mistakes onto others. Fix the problem you made, or that problem will turn around and bite you in the ass."

"Are you encouraging my appetite or my assistance?" Effora asked with a smirk. "It's difficult to tell with the promises you're making."

Anchor set a hand on Vena's shoulder to stop her from saying or doing whatever was brewing behind her stormy gaze.

"So the pictures Orphia showed us don't bother you?" I asked. "When it comes to light that you've been buying humans from vampires, that's going to turn public opinion big time. Everything Orphia said about how humans will react is true."

I looked at the liaison. "How many body piles do you think it'll take before it can't be hidden anymore?"

Hugh considered me then looked at Effora. "Your *active* participation is required. If you refuse, you are breaking the oath you made to live peacefully with all the races."

Effora's expression completely shut down as her gaze shifted between the liaison, me, and Shepard, who rubbed his forehead.

"I'm not asking you to send your people to fight with vampires directly," Shepard said. "We've been cleaning out nests for weeks. I think what we're looking for, based on the number of bodies we found, isn't here. So, I need the fae and dwarves to agree to cover the city while we go to wherever the scrying stone says the vampire clusters are." He looked from Effora to Curran. "Today."

Curran nodded right away. Effora's cold expression turned calculating, and I didn't like the way she glanced at me. "I suppose you'll need to leave your mated women behind at your pack house, won't you? It would be our honor to guard what's most precious to you and your people."

"Does she think they're dumb?" Vena asked, not so under her breath.

"Everly and Vena will be with my pack," Shepard said. "Curran and Effora, I will let you both work out how to protect the city in our absence. I'll need you to relay your plan to both me and Hugh before the end of the day. And remember to stay in contact."

When all had agreed, Hugh ended the meeting.

"I'll be in touch within the hour," Effora said to Curran before she swept from the room.

CHAPTER TWENTY-SIX

W HEN WE RETURNED TO THE COMPLEX, THE YARD SWARMED WITH men I didn't recognize.

"What's going on?" I asked. "Who are all these people?"

"Help from other packs," Shepard said as he parked. "I sent a message to Doc to have everyone meet here. Orphia gave us twenty-four hours, not that I believe she'll keep her word. So, we don't have any time to spare. We need to find and exterminate the big nests so Orphia doesn't have the numbers to do whatever she has planned. We must stop the situation before this escalates any further.

"Everyone, stay here."

He opened the door, and I saw he already had everyone's attention in the yard.

"Open the window so I can hear," Vena said from behind me. She was sandwiched in the back seat with Anchor and Cross.

Rolling down the window, we heard Shepard greet the masses. "Thank you all for gathering quickly. We have a serious vampire infestation on our hands. Give me a few minutes to coordinate our search efforts and put together groups. I'll get you out of here and hunting in a bit.

"Also, the rumors about me working with a vampire are true."

A collective growl rose, and I glanced back at Cross who winked at me before resuming his study of the men outside.

"He has been an invaluable resource, gaining information we couldn't have found on our own," Shepard continued. "Although it goes against everything we were made to do, I'm humbly asking you to refrain from attacking him as he helps us hunt down his own kind."

I glanced back at Cross again. "Refrain?"

He grinned at me, and Vena waved for me to hush, which was very unlike her. However, I saw that every eye in the yard was now on me. At least, Shepard's gaze was amused in the sea of distaste-filled stares. He motioned for us to join him.

The low rumble of growls increased at Cross' appearance, but no one made any move to attack him as we joined the group.

"Grab something from the kitchen," Shepard said. "Eat. Drink. Use the next hour wisely, and be ready to head out when we return."

I glanced back at Cross, who was walking between Vena and Anchor. Vena briefly saluted me before resuming her scowl at the men who were eyeing Cross, and I loved her even more for her unconditional support.

Shepard led us inside to his suite where Doc, Buzz, Detroit, Tank, Army, and Boulder waited with a map of the greater D.C. area. Vena lit up when she saw it.

"Vena, if you'd do the honors, please," Shepard said, motioning to the map.

Her excitement fell as her gaze bounced between the map, the guys present, and Shepard.

"You're going to use me to find the locations, and Everly and I will get stuck sitting in a city devoid of shifters while you go hunting."

Shepard sighed. "You were in the room when Effora offered to watch over you, and as you mentioned, I'm not stupid. The only safe place for you and Everly is with us. You have my word you won't be left behind."

Her suspicion vanished. "Okay. I'll scry."

She removed her crystal and dangled it over the map, moving it in a slow circle that grew bigger with each pass. The crystal suddenly stopped over a spot to the northeast of the city.

"That's not far from one of the dump sites," Doc said.

She repeated the process until the crystal had covered every inch of the map and found five more locations, each within ten miles of the dump sites that had already been discovered.

Detroit removed that map and unfolded another one. I watched Vena's crystal slowly circle over the entire East Coast, one state map at a time, until Shepard had a good idea of where all the nests were located.

"I felt a subtle vibration in the crystal's chain when it was over the locations closest to D.C.," Vena said. "It didn't vibrate as much over the other ones, except this one in northern New York." She pointed to the spot on the map. "I think the vibration means more vampires and not nearness."

"Agreed," Shepard said. "It would take more than six hours for our people to get there, so I doubt that nest would be part of Orphia's plan. But I'll notify New York's Alpha and have him put eyes on that location. For now, we'll deal with the larger nests closest to D.C."

Shepard assigned locations to Buzz, Detroit, Tank, Army, and Boulder and said he would take the one west of D.C. himself.

"Cross and Anchor, you're with me. Anchor, your only job is to stay with Everly and Vena. Doc, you stay here as our main point of contact."

"You got it."

"Everyone checks in with Doc before they go in and immediately after clean-up.

"We've got six hours of daylight left. Let's get in and out of these locations before sunset to minimize the risk."

"No fewer than twenty-five wolves in each group. Find your volunteers outside. If the vampire presence in your assigned location is bigger than your group can successfully take on, wait. Call for backup. No risks. Do you understand?"

Everyone agreed, and the others left to coordinate their volunteers as Shepard's phone rang. As he answered it, Cross took my hand and led me to a chair where he pulled me onto his lap.

"Will you be all right?" he asked.

I knew what he meant and nodded. "Vivian put a lot of effort into tracking me. I'd rather be with you than left behind where he's probably lurking, waiting for another opportunity to grab me."

"Our thoughts, too," Cross said, looking at Shepard.

I did the same and caught Shepard's scowl.

"It's Effora testing his patience again," Cross said softly. "She's cooperating, though, so we should be able to leave soon."

Shepard hung up the phone and looked at us.

"Ready?"

Cross helped me to my feet as I checked the time and saw it was just after three in the afternoon.

"Got somewhere to be?" Shepard asked with a smile.

"Yeah, safely home in bed before dark. Are you sure six hours will be enough time?"

He kissed my cheek. "It will be. I promise."

Outside, Tank, Army, Detroit, Buzz, and Boulder already had their groups set. Shepard wished them all good hunting, reminded them not to take risks, and watched them leave. Once they were gone, he signaled to the remaining twenty-seven men.

"Let's head out." They divided up between the seven vehicles while we went to Shepard's SUV.

Cross drove so Shepard could answer any messages, and Anchor, Vena, and I sat in the back. Vena used the drive to sharpen the knives she kept in a leather roll, and the scrape of metal against stone slowly drove me crazy.

When I couldn't stand the sound anymore, I elbowed her.

"What?" she asked. "I have to be ready."

"Weren't they already sharp."

She shook her head. "Not sharp enough for what I have planned."

"Which is nothing," Shepard said. "Right?"

Shepard waited for Vena's defeated nod before once again reminding Anchor he was responsible for keeping us in the vehicle.

"It's coming up," Shepard said. "Let's drive through first and get a feel for where they might be. If we need to, we can split up and do a grid search to cover every street. The town doesn't look that big according to the map."

I leaned toward Vena to get a view of the town around Shepard. The century-old brick buildings were beautiful and mostly businesses. A few cars were parked on the main street, but I didn't see any people. The businesses were all dark and had the signs turned to closed. Just after four on a Sunday? Maybe.

We turned down a more residential street and found the same thing. Cars in driveways or on the street, but no people. It was a beautiful day.

"Where are the kids?" I asked.

"This is eerie," Vena said. "It's like the start of a zombie apocalypse movie. Where are all the people?"

Shepard rolled to a stop. "I'll have our group search one building at a time. I don't know how long it will take. This town isn't big, but even a small town with a group our size sweeping it might take more time than what we have. Move fast, but stay alert."

"Wait," I said before he could get out of the SUV. "Remember what Hugh said. If Orphia's been taking people and turning them, not all of them were willing. Don't assume every vampire is bad."

Cross looked back at me. "He doesn't. But right now, we don't have the luxury to question each one. Newly turned vampires are hungry, Everly. Whether they want to or not, the majority would kill you on sight. And that's not a risk we can afford."

"Then watch for the ones who don't want to fight. They deserve a chance to be on our side, right?"

I knew it was a long shot to ask, but it didn't seem right to blindly kill either. What if I had been turned into a vampire? What if we never gave Cross a chance?

I couldn't imagine life without him now.

"We'll try," Cross said.

Shepard and Cross both shot Anchor a weighted glance before slipping out of the SUV. They met with the other wolves and divided into smaller groups.

I watched Shepard motion to one end of the street and then the other. Cross nodded and led half the men toward the end of our caravan while Shepard's group went in the opposite direction.

"Is it smart to split up like that?" I asked Anchor softly.

"Yeah. While the sun's up, the vamps will be slower and easier to kill. And"–he tapped his nose–"we'll know where and how many there are. Don't worry, everyone here, except for Cross, has a lot of experience with cleaning out nests. They'll be careful."

Vena and I watched Shepard's group disappear into a distant house.

She sat back and tucked the knife she'd been sharpening into its place in the leather roll. I heard her mutter under her breath about wolves having all the fun as she took out another knife to sharpen.

After a few minutes, Shepard's group came out of the first home. They were splattered in blood but didn't look like they were in a panic as they quickly moved to the next house.

"Are some partly shifted?" she asked.

"It happens during hunting, especially to the younger wolves who can't control their shifting as well," Anchor said.

The sun was sinking lower to the horizon as the groups went from home to home, working their way toward the middle. When they cleared the street, a few of the guys ran back to the vehicles to move them to the next street.

Anchor drove Shepard's SUV, which was a good thing, considering the amount of red on Shepard.

Everything progressed quietly for the next several streets since most of those homes were empty.

"Not as big of a nest as Shepard hoped," Anchor said from the front seat as we drove to the next street over.

Shepard and Cross' groups had just reached the opposite ends of the street and disappeared into the houses when Vena suddenly tossed the knife she'd been working on to the seat between us and reached into her pocket.

The crystal she withdrew danced in the palm of her open hand.

"What the heck?"

"Um, that can't be good," I said.

We both looked up as a man ran out of the home Shepard's group had entered. He immediately burst into flames in the sunlight and let out an unholy scream.

I covered my ears.

"Lock the doors," Anchor said.

The SUV rocked as Anchor sprinted out faster than I could see. I clamped my eyes closed when his blur reached the flaming vampire.

"Holy crap," Vena said. "I think we're in trouble."

I opened my eyes, and she showed me the crystal was no longer vibrating but wildly spinning.

Vampires suddenly poured out of buildings all around us. Some ignited instantly in flames. Some had wrapped themselves in blankets or tarps and were running toward the parked cars.

"Lock the doors!" I said, already slamming mine down.

Vena nimbly stretched forward to hit the main lock.

"It's okay," she said. "We'll be okay."

I didn't believe her.

A vampire ran past our car and paused, only momentarily, but it was enough to show they could smell us. Something crashed behind us, and I swiveled to see one of the escaping cars had backed into one of ours.

Fully shifted wolves sprinted from the house Shepard's group had invaded, joining the growing chaos outside the car. They fought furiously with Anchor, killing the vampires as they tried to escape.

However, a few vampires still managed to run for the woods at the end of the street.

And more just kept pouring out of the buildings. Hundreds, easily.

"That's him," Vena breathed, drawing my attention.

I looked and saw a man dressed in all black emerge from a home. He was completely covered with a hat and veil thing that made it impossible to see his face. However, the black leather pants and the way he moved struck a chord in me.

Vivian.

Fear shivered through me.

The black cat at his feet surveyed the mayhem.

"You're not getting away this time, fleabag," Vena said under her breath.

The cat's head turned toward our vehicle, and it hissed before running and jumping onto the hood of our SUV. Then, it sat, lifted a leg, and started licking itself.

Vena exploded. "Mother fucker, you're mine."

She had the door open before I could stop her.

"Vena, no!" I slid across the seat to grab her, but she was too fast.

She bolted for the front of the car as I clasped the open door. From the corner of my eye, I saw Vivian's veiled head turn toward me.

It felt like the world dropped out from under me. Everything slowed.

Vivian blurred. I heaved back on the door. Then, he was there, in the opening, his hand holding the edge of the door. A red glow emanated from under his veil.

I couldn't see his face, but his low laughter sent a shiver through me as he easily opened the door again. I heard him inhale deeply, and what he'd said the last time played in my mind.

You smell delicious when you're scared.

Twisting, I tried scrambling across the seat. His hands closed over my calves, and he jerked me backward.

My belly slid along the seat, and I scrabbled for anything to hold onto. My fingers caught on something hard as he shifted his hold to my waist and plucked me free of the vehicle. I held onto the object as panic and fear flooded me.

He flipped me to face him, and I lashed out without thought while screaming my terror.

Vivian screamed and dropped me, clawing at his veil and the shiny handled knife sticking from it. Vena's knife.

I screamed again and tried crawling back to my seat...to safety. I didn't get far. The sound of Vena's yelling and a cat's screeching barely registered over Vivian's cursing and the feel of his hand closing over my ankle.

His grip vanished suddenly, and I was left panting and shaking on the seat. I didn't linger there. Bolting upright, I twisted around to grab for the door. Instead, I saw the back of Cross' very bloodied shirt filling the opening.

He jerked a few times then disappeared.

Eyes wide, I stared at the spot where he'd been. The harsh sounds of my gasps filled the interior of the car.

Where did he go?

I wanted to look but couldn't tear my gaze from where he'd been...from where Vivian had been.

"Everly!" The sound of Cross' voice snapped me out of my daze. I blinked and saw him in front of me.

He carefully removed the bloodied shirt, leaving his clean chiseled torso bare to my gaze. After mopping off his arms and hands with the shirt before tossing it to the side, he stretched a hand out toward me, and a tormented cry ripped from me as I threw myself into his arms. I pressed my face to his chest as I closed my eyes.

"Are you hurt?" he asked, smoothing a hand over the back of my head.

"No." The word warbled. "Is he gone?"

"Vivian is gone. He ran."

A shaky exhale escaped me, and I leaned back to look at Cross.

"Thank you for stopping him."

He tilted his head and looked at me.

"I didn't stop him. You and Vena did."

"What do you mean?"

"When you stabbed Vivian with the knife, it was the distraction Vena needed to end her fight with Adriel. His death cry distracted Vivian."

He nodded toward the front of the car. I followed his gaze and saw Anchor holding a crying Vena with one arm and a limp cat out to the side with the other.

CHAPTER TWENTY-SEVEN

It took several seconds for my brain to catch up to what my eyes saw.

"Adriel's dead? As in, dead for good?"

"Doubtful. He didn't turn back to his original form yet."

A bloody man approached us.

"We need your help."

Cross kissed my forehead and guided me so I could sit in the back seat again.

"Stay here, okay?"

I nodded and moved so I was fully inside. He locked the door then closed it before following the man toward the back of our caravan, where two shrouded people waited.

A glance at Vena showed her still crying in Anchor's arms. Another of Shepard's men had taken Adriel from him so he could hold her. The rest were walking in and out of buildings.

I twisted in my seat to watch Cross. He was talking, but I couldn't hear what he was saying. One of the shrouded people nodded. The other one kept wiping at its face under the blanket it wore. Cross opened a car door and helped the vampires get in.

A long, mournful howl rang out.

Everyone looked toward the other end of the street where Shepard and three other men carried bodies out of one of the houses. They all wore grief-stricken expressions as they proceeded past our car and placed them in the bed of the truck in our caravan.

I didn't know what was happening and knew I would never learn if I stayed locked away in the backseat. So, after a glance at the ash-strewn yards, I opened the door and joined Vena and Anchor.

Vena had finally stopped crying as she patted Anchor.

"What happened?" I asked.

"We found our missing men," Anchor said. "They're dead."

My gaze sought out Shepard, and my heart hurt for him as he pulled out his phone to make a call.

Cross left the car and came over to us.

"Shepard will want to leave as soon as possible. May I?" He took the cat from the man beside Anchor and started walking away.

Vena grabbed my hand. We, along with Anchor and at least a dozen of Shepard's men, followed Cross to the shade of a building. He tossed Adriel to the ground and pulled the knife from his chest.

I watched the cat morph into the man, naked and wounded. His body was already beginning to heal.

"Fuck, that hurt," Adriel groaned.

"Where is the dwarven ring?" Cross asked.

Adriel blinked his eyes open and weakly grinned. "Out of your reach."

Cross grabbed him by the throat and lifted him off the ground.

"It will be out of your reach, too. Answer or die."

Adriel actually laughed.

"I'm a dead man anyway. Whether by your hand or another's.

I never wanted the rings. All I ever wanted was Pet. He is the only reason I was obedient.

"But I'm tired of these games. Tired of always being a pawn." He held Cross' gaze. "This life is so long, isn't it? A torturous hell that has no end. I heard you escaped her by hiding in a cave, but I'll never escape. I'm forever bound."

With a tear streaking down his cheek, he tipped his head back and yelled, "In this life and the next, I am yours, Pet. Always."

Adriel blurred out of Cross' hold, but he didn't get far.

As soon as he left the shade of the building, he burst into flames and turned to ash. He was gone.

An anguished cry echoed from the trees, and I knew it was Vivian.

A chill stole through me.

Vena stepped over to Adriel's ash and kicked it, raising a cloud. "He's gone? My brother is free?" she asked, looking at Cross.

"He's gone. For good this time," Cross said.

His gaze shifted to the woods at the end of the street where Vivian's cry had come from.

Vena called her parents. "Mom, check Miles. Is he normal?"

While she waited, Shepard joined us.

"I know you have more calls to make," Cross said. "Go. I'll stay with Everly."

"I'll find something clean for you to wear," Shepard said, stepping away.

Cross, still shirtless, wrapped me in a hug I'd needed more than I'd realized.

"Really?" I heard Vena ask.

My friend bowed her head and huffed out a laugh. "Yeah. Tell him I watched the bastard turn to ash myself. Cross says there's no coming back from that. M'kay. Love you too. Bye."

She hung up and looked at Anchor. "Miles really is free."

Anchor wrapped her in a hug and started speaking softly to her.

Cross turned us away from them to give them privacy, and I happened to see the car he'd put the two vampires in was still surrounded by wolves.

"What's the story with those two?" I asked.

"They didn't fight us and begged to be saved. They went to a meeting with friends who wanted to be vampires. They had to sign NDAs to attend the meeting. What happened after was so fast that they never got a chance to say no."

"So it wasn't like Xiana had claimed."

"Not for some, at least."

"Do you think it was like this in all the other locations?" I asked.

"I don't know. I hope not," Cross said, his gaze taking in all of the ash piles.

I understood what he meant. The number of vampires here had been terrifying. If the other locations were as bad or even worse, I feared for those groups. Yet, I also felt incredibly sad for the lives that had been lost. I refused to believe every vampire here had been evil like Vivian and Adriel. That meant innocent people had been killed today.

"What do you think Orphia will do if all of her followers are wiped out like this?" I asked.

"She'll try again."

"So she won't stop until she gets what she wants, then," I said, hating the woman even more.

"No, she won't."

I leaned my head against Cross' bare shoulder, and he ran his fingers through my hair, likely trying to comfort me. Instead, he touched a spot on the back of my head that felt a little tender, and I winced.

"Are you okay?" he asked.

"Yeah. I think I hit my head on the car when Vivian pulled me out of it."

I stood beside him, watching the shadows from the setting sun grow as Shepard's men took turns using the homes to wash up and change.

When Shepard finally emerged from one of the houses, barely any light remained. Freshly showered, he carried a shirt for Cross while speaking on the phone.

"Let me know if anyone else reports in. I'll reach out to Hugh with the news. We need to be ready for any backlash from this. Yeah. We'll leave soon."

He hung up and tossed the shirt to Cross, who caught it with ease.

"Detroit, Tank, and Army have already checked in with Doc. Their locations were like this one. Towns empty of humans. They've already left to check on Boulder and Buzz. Once Anchor and Vena are done cleaning up, we can head out."

"Has it been quiet back home?" Cross asked.

"Yeah, which either means we took them by surprise with this move, or these nests are just the tip of the iceberg. We might need to expand our scrying."

Cross let go of me to put the shirt on, which gave Shepard the opening he needed to steal a hug from me.

"She hit her head," Cross said. "She's got a headache that's getting worse."

I frowned at him, not sure how he knew, but he wasn't wrong.

"I'm fine," I said to Shepard. "Why do you need to call Hugh?"

"He needs to know we haven't found Orphia or the ring."

Shepard kissed my head when Anchor and Vena appeared then moved away to tell everyone we were leaving in five minutes.

Once we were ready, Anchor got in behind the wheel, and Vena took the copilot seat, leaving me to sit between Cross and Shepard.

Cross toyed with the ends of my hair while Shepard called Hugh. His half of the conversation was brief, summarizing an estimate of vampires killed in each location, that he was waiting to hear back from the last few groups, and that he had doubts they would find the ring or Orphia based on what Adriel had said before he died.

"Make sure Effora knows this isn't over and that her cooperation is still needed." Shepard paused and sighed. "I know. We'll do our best."

Shepard ended the call and reached down to rest a hand on my leg. He looked tired. I took his hand in mine and smiled at him.

"Do alphas take vacations?" I asked.

"Occasionally," he said. "You're welcome to plan ours."

"I'd like to go somewhere tropical," Cross said. "I haven't seen a palm tree yet."

"You're not invited," Shepard said without rancor.

I shook my head, which made my stomach lurch a little. However, I made sure my grin stayed firmly in place.

"I've always wanted to go to Hawaii," I said. "Maybe when all of this is over, we can go."

"I'd like that," Cross said.

"Still not invited," Shepard said as his phone rang.

"He forgets I don't need an invitation."

"Curran," he said when he answered. "I was just about to call you. Yes, you heard right. Adriel is dead. He killed himself, or I would have brought him to you." He paused to listen, and I heard the deep, rumbling voice of the dwarven king, though I couldn't make out what he said.

"Adriel said he didn't have the ring," Shepard continued. "You have my word we'll keep searching for it, but I can't guarantee we'll find it." Shepard nodded even though Curran couldn't see it. "That's my belief as well. We'll find Orphia. We have to."

As soon as Shepard ended the call, his phone rang again.

He groaned when he looked at the display. I peeked and saw that it said, "Caution" for the name.

"Effora," he explained.

"Ah. Maybe she's just calling for an update," I said.

Cross laughed, and Shepard shot him a dark look.

"Go ahead, lover," Cross teased. "Put it on speaker. Let's see what kind of update Effora has for you."

Shepard answered on speaker.

"Effora," he said curtly in greeting. "Do you have an update?"

"I have two bottles of wine on ice and am lying in your bed without a stitch on. When are you coming home?"

If I wasn't already queasy, the thought of her on his bed where I had just been would do it. Shepard looked like he was getting queasy too.

"We'll be home in about five minutes, Effora," I said on his behalf. "And Shepard would very much like you to strip the bed, not yourself. You'll probably want to burn that bedding too."

"Oh?" she said with less warmth as Vena swiveled in her seat to smirk at me. "And why would I do that?"

"Because they remind Shepard of everything he did with me in that bed."

Shepard's fingers threaded through mine, and Cross covered his mouth to keep from laughing.

"I wish I would have met you first, Everly," Effora said. "I think we could have been lovely friends."

"Is there anything else, Effora?" Shepard asked.

"Your home and your people are safe. You can thank me at another time."

She hung up without another word.

"Did I go too far?" I asked, looking at Shepard.

He smiled and shook his head. Then his smile vanished, and he leaned forward suddenly to look into my eyes.

"Look at Cross for a second," he said.

Confused, I did as he asked.

"Notice anything?" Shepard asked.

"Yes, before we started driving. I didn't want to distract you, though. I'll take her to the hospital after we reach your place."

I frowned at both of them and looked at Vena, who was still turned around, staring at me.

"Looks like you have a concussion, Ev. Means you'll get the princess treatment for a few days." She patted my hand. "I'm sorry you got hurt, but I'm really proud of you for stabbing Vivian like you did. It was the perfect distraction. Without it, I would have never been able to kill Adriel."

My stomach did a three-sixty flip that had me gagging hard.

"Look at me, Everly," Cross said.

When I did, my stomach felt instantly calm, and the fact that I was in the car faded away. All I could feel was his fingers playing with the ends of my hair and a sense of calm.

Then, suddenly, he was lifting me out of the car at the complex in a yard full of people, including the Hunters.

I patted Cross to put me down as they hurried toward us.

"How is Miles?" Vena asked.

Her mom hugged her. "Himself again. He remembers everything and is wracked with guilt. So we want to take him home where he can process everything in familiar surroundings."

"Is it safe?" Vena asked. "Some of the vampires escaped. And there are more we haven't found yet."

"If you give me an hour, I can provide security," Shepard said.

"We'll gladly wait for your kind offer," Mr. Hunter said. "It will give us time to pack. Thank you so much for your hospitality these last few days...and for freeing Miles. I don't know what we would have done without your help."

"You're welcome," Shepard said.

"Do you want to come home with us, Vena?" Mr. Hunter asked.

She glanced at Anchor. "Um. No. But I do want to talk to Miles and offer a hug or two."

"He could use it, but don't be upset if he says he doesn't want one."

Mrs. Hunter glanced at me. "You look a little pale, Everly."

"I'm about to take her to a hospital," Cross said. "We think she has a mild concussion."

"Give Miles an extra hug from me," I said.

Mrs. Hunter nodded, and they moved toward the main entrance with Vena and Anchor. Shepard lingered beside me for a moment, even though several of the people in the yard were trying to call his attention.

"Go," I said. "I'm in good hands, and I know that Cross will keep you updated. I'll see you soon."

He kissed my forehead and looked at Cross.

"I'll keep her safe and distracted until you're free," Cross said.

"Thank you."

I watched Shepard walk away and looked up at Cross, slightly in awe of how their relationship had changed over the last week.

Cross grinned at me and kissed the same spot Shepard had.

"Let's get your precious head checked then see what kind of progress has been made on our place."

I nodded and let him help me into the car.

JUST AFTER MIDNIGHT, we pulled into the parking lot of the construction site. I had orders from the doctor to avoid electronics, which I never spent much time on anyway, and to do nothing strenuous. Cross had a list of things I should and shouldn't do, which pretty much boiled down to the princess treatment for a few days as Vena had said. And I didn't hate the idea of it.

The lights were on inside the building, and men were walking in and out of the newly-installed front door.

Cross helped me out of the business SUV, shielding my head from the frame with his hand so I wouldn't hit myself again.

Then he led me inside where I was stunned by the transformation.

The entry was finished—glass doors, tiles, and paint. Inside, the main ordering area was tiled. Beyond that, the wood flooring was already installed and covered with protective paper. The men moving around were carrying equipment and shelving.

"Come on," Cross said when my pace slowed. "I want to make sure there's a place for you to lie down."

He led me toward the stairs. A thick steel door at the top of them was wide open.

"How?" I said, turning a slow circle when we reached the top.

The second floor's construction was finished—the rooms, the painting, the floors, the appliances—everything.

A plastic-wrapped sectional sofa took up a large portion of the main space, and a pair of wrapped chairs sat off to the side.

"I had the designer pick out some basic furnishings. If there's something you don't like, it'll be easy for us to change it. Now, I promise I'll take you on a real tour tomorrow. Let's check the bedroom first."

As we were headed back there, someone walked out, carrying an armful of plastic.

He saw Cross and nodded.

"I got your message," he said. "It's all set up. Let us know how the soundproofing is."

Cross nodded and continued leading me down a long hallway from the kitchen.

The master suite was jaw-dropping, painted in stunning deep hues that were calming and cozy, even with only a bed to furnish the space. It seemed unfair to use the term "only," though, when looking at the mammoth piece of furniture. It was solid and looked like it belonged in the Hunters' estate rather than a newly remodeled urban building.

I ran my hand over the tall bedpost that helped make the towering twelve-foot ceiling look less lofty.

"Do you like it?" he asked.

"I do. It's really pretty. The best part is that it's already made up."

He smiled and pulled back the covers even as he indicated another door.

"Do you want to shower first or go straight to bed?"

I wandered over to the bathroom and shook my head in awe.

"If Vena saw this, she'd want to move in."

"If you came as part of the deal, I agree," Cross said, wrapping his arms around me from behind.

I smiled and leaned back into his hold.

Sure, his crazy ex was still out there with her world-ending agenda, but here, wrapped in Cross' arms, it didn't matter.

Everything was finally peaceful again, and we'd worry about Orphia later.

Much later. After a shower and definitely after at least a week of being pampered like a princess.

I couldn't wait to check out the kitchen when I woke up.

EPILOGUE

VIVIAN (A.K.A. PET)

LONG AFTER THE human police left, I knelt beside my Master's ashes and wept.

"In this life and the next, I am yours, Master. I vow to make them all pay, especially her."

I removed my phone from my clothes and wiped my face before sending a text.

> **Me: The west D.C. nest was wiped out by Cross and Shepard.**
> **Queen Bitch: I'm already aware. You should have reported in hours ago. Send Adriel to his Master. It's time to show them who truly holds the power.**
> **Me: Adriel is dead. You'll have to find another pawn.**
> **Queen Bitch: That's why I have you. Go to his Master and tell her Shepard and Cross took her favorite pet from her. Her hunger will be their downfall.**

I pocketed my phone and touched the necklace Adriel had given me after our fight with Cross. Protection against all spells. A gift from the current fae queen to her favorite pet, Adriel.

He'd spent centuries serving her and arranging humans to satiate her hunger. She'd cared for him more than the Queen Bitch ever had. Yet, to the fae he'd still been a pawn.

"They will all pay, my love. Blood will be my gift to you in this life and the next."

****

Thank you for reading Death and Donuts! The series will conclude with *Magic and Muffins*, book 4 in the Ruin of Relics series.

AUTHOR'S NOTE

Thank you for continuing the Ruins of Relics series. Death and Donuts was a labor of love that took nearly a year to write and was accompanied by a slew of swear words and many emotional support pastries.

Melissa did her best to corral Nicole to outline and yet the story still got away from them. Everly, Vena, Shepard, and Cross were misbehaving, and not in the good way. *Wink, wink.* Although, we do hope you enjoyed the steamier scenes! You can thank Melissa for those. Nicole has been banned from writing them because Everly nearly lost an eye with a loaded shot. *Wink, wink* again. That scene was sadly deleted.

Our efforts finally solidified (yay!) and we are thrilled with the outcome (although Nicole is still in mourning over Master). We hope you enjoyed it too!

We can't wait for the next book, *Magic and Muffins*! In fact, we are going on a work-cation to write it. If you want to see some pictures from the trip, join our Facebook group, Melissa Nicole Fan Group, where we will post a few fun ones. *If you're from the future, head back to the posts from December 2024.

If you're interested in making some Fairy Trash treats for yourself, check out the bonus content on our website melissani coleauthor.com/bonus-content. While you're there, be sure to sign up for our newsletter for any other tasty updates.

Your ~~half~~ fully cocked authors,

Melissa and Nicole

MORE BOOKS BY MELISSA NICOLE

THE SHADOW TRADE WORLD

Ruin of Relics

(Sexy shifters and a hottie vampire!)

Blood and BonBons

Fangs and Fudge

Death and Donuts

Magic and Muffins

Connect with the author

Website: melissanicoleauthor.com

Newsletter: melissanicoleauthor.com/subscribe

MORE BOOKS BY MELISSA HAAG

Did you know that Melissa Nicole is a co-authored pen name? Check out these amazing books by the "Melissa" part of Melissa Nicole!

JUDGEMENT OF THE SIX SERIES (AND COMPANION BOOKS) IN ORDER:

(more shifters to make you "grr")

Hope(less)

Clay's Hope*

(Mis)fortune

Emmitt's Treasure*

(Un)wise

Luke's Dream*

(Un)bidden

Thomas' Heart*

(Dis)content

Carlos' Peace*

(Sur)real**

*optional companion book

**written in dual point of view

Connect with the author

Website: melissahaag.com

Newsletter: melissahaag.com/subscribe

MORE BOOKS BY NICOLETTE PIERCE

Check out these amazing books by the "Nicole" part of Melissa Nicole!

Black Moon Novels

(Paranormal romance mystery series)

Whiskers & Warrants

Kittens & Kidnappers

Jade Sommer Novels

(Contemporary romance mystery series)

Mostaccioli Murder

Penne Pyro

Fettuccini Fiasco

Rigatoni Ruin

Lasagna Larceny

Bucatini Bomber

Connect with the author

Website: nicolettepierce.com

Newsletter: nicolettepierce.com/newsletter/